No Strings

USA TODAY BESTSELLING AUTHOR

NIKKI ASH

We could never be stringless.

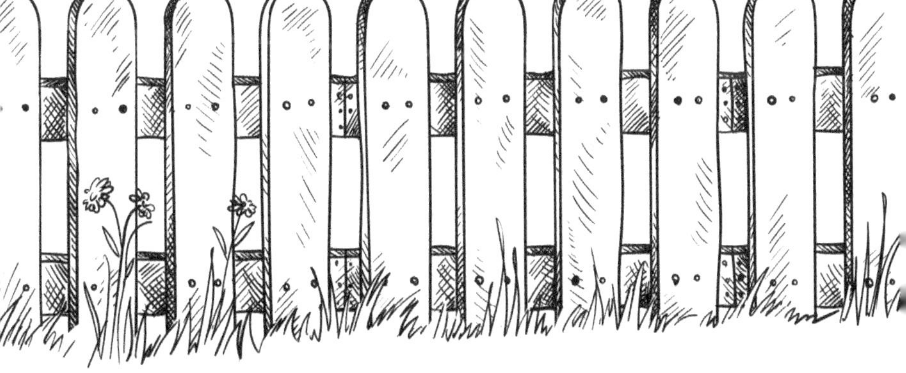

Playlist

Starving- Hailee Steinfeld & Grey feat. Zedd

Please Don't Go- Joel Adams

Let You Love Me- Rita Ora

I'm a Mess- Bebe Rexha

History- Olivia Holt

Sorry Not Sorry- Demi Lovato

Intentions- Justin Bieber feat. Quavo

Slow Dance- AJ Mitchell feat. Ava Max

Nobody's Love- Maroon 5

Monster- Shawn Mendes & Justin Bieber

Love You Like That- Parker McCollum

Be Kind- Marshmello & Halsey

Savage Love- Jawsh 685 x Jason Derulo

Anyone- Justin Bieber

Prologue

Benjamin

can't do this anymore."

"Can't do what? Parent?"

The mother of my son glares my way, but I'm unfazed. I've been on the receiving end of her wrath for the past fifteen years.

"You've been traveling since he was born. It's easy to play dad from afar, but you haven't actually *been here*. He's been getting into fights and failing his classes. Now he's been expelled." Her tear-filled eyes lock with mine, pleading. "He needs his father."

Her words hit me like a punch to the gut. I didn't ask to

become a father and never wanted to become one. I watched what having kids did to our parents. Listened to their constant arguing over finances and parenting until our mom, someone who was supposed to love and protect us, had finally had enough and did the unthinkable, leaving us all to drown in our guilt and grief.

I never wanted that for myself or my kids. I didn't want the responsibility that came with parenting, and I didn't want my kids to ever be put in the position my sister and I were in, which is why I made it clear to Paola I didn't want to have any. She promised she understood and swore she was on birth control. But she lied. She went behind my back and got pregnant, thinking that I'd magically change my tune. The only thing that changed when she told me she was pregnant was our relationship status. I walked away that day, losing any trust and respect I had for her.

It took some time for me to come around, but I went to the hospital when Paola called me the day Brody was born, planning to give up my rights. This wasn't an accident. She did this on purpose. But the second I looked at my son, my heart swelled with a kind of love I had never felt, and despite my disdain for his mother, I became a father that day and promised Brody I would do whatever it took to be there for him.

"You're not around," she adds. "And I can't do this on my own anymore."

Her accusation knocks me out of my thoughts.

"Yeah, I've been busy working. You know, to pay your child support and the private school our son *was* attending. I had no idea he was getting into trouble because you never said anything." She could've called, texted, emailed. I spent part of Christmas break with Brody, and neither of them said anything. Yeah, he seemed moodier than usual, but I figured it was just a part of him being a teenager.

"It's only gotten worse as of lately. It's like one minute, he was a sweet little boy, and the next, he's skipping school and getting into fights. Please, Benjamin. I need you to take him. I... I can't do this." Tears leak from her eyelids, sliding down her cheeks, and I'm reminded of my mother. Of the last time I saw her alive...

"I want to watch the TV!" my sister, Amalia, yells.

"It's my turn!" I shout back, snatching the controller from her.

"Both of you shut up!" Mom screams, tears streaming down her

cheeks. "I can't handle all the fighting. Get in your rooms now!"

We both groan but do as she says, not wanting to upset her more.

A few hours later, I'm playing my PlayStation when Amalia comes running into my room. "Hey! Get out!"

"Benjamin," she sobs. "Mom..." She drops in front of me, covered in... is that blood?

"What's wrong?" I jump up and run over to her. "What happened?"

"Mom's bleeding everywhere. I think she's... I think she's dead."

"Benjamin," Paola says, bringing me back to the present. Her eyes are rimmed red, and her nose is running from crying. Her cheeks are splotchy and tearstained. A part of the reason I stayed away from Paola was so what happened between my parents would never happen to us. If I wasn't around, we couldn't fight. Yet somehow, here we are...

"Okay." I walk over to her and wrap her in my arms. "I'll take him." I might've been too young to save my mom from ending her life, too young to understand she needed help, despite my dad thinking he could fix her himself, but I'm older now, and I can make sure Paola is never in the same position as my mom.

"Thank you."

As she sobs into my chest, I catch a bit of movement out

of the corner of my eye. Brody. He's home. He must've come in through the garage. He's listening and watching from around the corner. Our gazes clash, and the sad as fuck look in his eyes tells me he's been listening.

"Brody, come out here, please," I tell him, stepping away from Paola.

He stumbles from around the corner. "Hey, Dad," he mumbles, completely ignoring his mom.

"What do you say to your mom?" I'll be damned if he's going to disrespect her anymore.

"Hi, Mom," he mutters without looking at her.

"How would you feel about moving in with me?" I ask.

His hazel eyes, identical to mine, remain devoid of all emotion as he shrugs.

"Hey." I step toward him and tip his chin up, locking eyes with him. "I asked you a question." It's then I notice his eyes are bloodshot. I inhale and smell it—weed. He's high. Jesus Christ, when did he get old enough to smoke?

"Does it really matter what I want?" he retorts.

"Of course it matters," Paola cries, fresh tears sliding down her cheeks. "But you fight with Ted every day, and I don't know what else to do."

Brody glances up at his mom with a sadness in his eyes that breaks my heart. "Does Ted make you happy?" His question comes out of left field, shocking me. I'm not sure what her happiness has to do with anything.

"O-Of course he does," she stammers, sounding as confused as I am at the turn of this conversation.

Brody nods once, looking almost... resigned, then looks at me. "Yeah, I'll go live with you. I hate this city anyway."

"Oh, well, then you better start liking it because I'm moving home."

Paola gasps, and Brody's eyes widen at my words. Since Paola told me she was pregnant, and I walked out the door, I've never lived in a place longer than a few years. Only long enough to open another nightclub and then move on. It's not until at this moment, as I stand in front of my son—who's almost as tall as me and is as high as a kite and sad as fuck—and his mother—who's in tears, looking exhausted and confused—that I realize I've messed up.

"Home?" she breathes.

"Yeah, I'm back for good." I look at Brody. "Go pack

whatever you need, and don't even think about bringing any drugs with you."

After he walks out of the room, I turn my attention back to Paola. "I'm sorry. I should've paid more attention and come home sooner." I was so caught up in running from my own demons, pissed at Paola for her betrayal while trying to make a name for myself—when she told me I'd never amount to anything after I dropped out of college—that I lost track of the important shit, like my son. I told myself quality was more important than quantity, but I was wrong. My son needs us both. But right now, it's clear he needs *me*. He's hurting and lashing out, and opening a new club sure as hell isn't more important than taking care of him.

Paola sniffles. "For how long?"

"I meant what I said. I'm back for good."

Savannah

"I'M SORRY. WE DIDN'T MEAN FOR IT TO HAPPEN," LOIS SAYS, ATTEMPTING and failing to sound sincere. Too bad I know her well enough to know that the way the corner of her lip is quirking up just slightly, along with the brightness in her shitty brown eyes, means she's anything but sorry, and she most definitely meant for it to happen.

Like me, Lois spent most of her childhood in foster care. It's where we met. We would talk for hours at night from our beds in our crappy, loveless foster home about how we would find love when we got older. We might not have had a loving home growing up, but we would create our own once we were old enough. The men of our dreams would sweep us off our feet and love us and take care of us. They would buy us the biggest houses with the whitest picket fences, and then we would have the most beautiful babies. And we would love them and cherish them. We wouldn't take what we have for granted because we know what it's like to be on the other side of that fence.

When we graduated from high school, Lois stayed behind, working at the local gas station because she didn't have the grades or ambition to go to college, while I went off to the University of Tennessee on a full academic scholarship. While there, I met Neil when I interned at his father's company, Everton Construction. He wasn't the white knight I imagined, and he didn't sweep me off my feet, but he offered me everything I dreamed of on a silver platter, so I went all in. Beggars can't be choosers after all.

He proposed after I graduated, and three months later, we were married and living in his home. It didn't actually have a white picket fence because he said they were ugly and preferred wrought iron. Maybe that should've been my first clue he wasn't really the one. Lois came to visit for the wedding and fell in love with the city. Since she had no money or means to move and live on her own, I offered to let her stay with us. Until Neil, she was the closest thing to a family I've ever had.

"How long has this been going on?" I ask, glancing at the two of them while keeping my tone under control so I don't show just how much my heart hurts. It's not over the fact that my husband cheated on me with another woman—our relationship has been over for a while since I came home from work and smelled the woman's perfume on him—but because it was with my best friend. The irony that she was my maid of honor isn't lost on me. Or that she told me dozens of times how lucky I was and how she hoped to find a man like Neil one day.

"For a little while," Lois says softly.

I nod and stand, ready to leave and get as far away from my ex-husband and ex-best friend as possible. *Too bad I have nowhere to go.* "Him, I understand. He has zero respect for women, including his wife. But you... you were supposed to be my best friend."

"I really am sorry," Lois cries, crocodile tears skating down her cheeks. "We didn't mean to fall in love. It just happened."

Yes, she did. Like me, she has been so desperate for love and attention for years. I have no doubt the second Neil paid the slightest bit of attention to her, she soaked it up—just like I did.

Looking over at Neil, whose features are devoid of any emotion, I wonder what I ever saw in him. How I could be so desperate to find love that I would allow myself to fall for a man like him.

I pluck my keys from my back pocket and hand them to Lois. "I guess these are yours now."

"Where are you going to go?" she asks. "If you need to stay here..."

I bark out a humorless laugh at my ex-best friend's offer to stay in my ex-home with her and my ex-husband. The same home I opened up to her, where she and my husband proceeded to have an affair behind my back.

At first, when I called him out on his cheating and told him I wanted out, he begged for forgiveness. Promised he was just stressed. I didn't accept that as an excuse and made it clear I wanted a divorce. For several days afterward, he pleaded with me to change my mind, offered to go to counseling, and came home with gifts galore, thinking I would forgive him.

Then, one day, something in him changed. I came home from work and was served divorce papers. And because he's rich and I'm not, I lost everything. Because everything of mine was because of him. I gave him all of me, and now I'm left with nothing. I'll never make that mistake again.

I spend the next hour packing up my clothes and putting them into boxes in the back of my SUV while Neil and Lois make themselves scarce. Technically, Neil didn't kick me out, but there's no way I'm staying under the same roof as them. I still have an iota of my dignity intact.

Once I've gotten everything that's mine from the house—which isn't much—I get in my vehicle, refusing to let the tears fall. But the second I turn on the ignition, it hits me. Aside from a little bit of money I've saved and the car Neil gave me as a wedding gift that's in my name, I literally have nothing. No home, no place to go. I have my clothes in my trunk and nowhere to take them.

Because Neil's father holds a lot of weight in this town, our divorce was expedited. I couldn't afford a lawyer, and I didn't want to fight, so I let him handle it. It only took seven weeks to finalize the divorce and leave me homeless.

I knew Neil was having an affair, but I didn't know it was with Lois. I knew I would need to move out, but I thought I would have some time. It all just happened so quickly. In the blink of an eye, I lost everything. Then again, maybe I never really had anything to begin with.

My phone rings over the Bluetooth, startling me out of my thoughts. I glance at the caller ID and see it's Brianne. It's like she knew I needed her. "Hey."

"Oh my fucking God! That trifling, no-good, husband-stealing skank! Did you see her post? Did you know?"

I bark out a watery laugh, loving that my friend has my back. "I'm assuming you're referring to Lois and Neil."

"Yes! That bitch. I knew I never liked her."

It's the truth. I met Brianne in college, and we immediately clicked. She was my dormmate for two years, and then we shared an apartment off campus for another two. Every time Lois would come to visit, Brianne would tell me something about her felt off. *Guess I should've listened...*

"You can't steal someone's husband. He obviously wanted to be with her. Besides, we're no longer married. Our divorce was finalized today, and I moved my stuff out."

"And you really let him get away scot-free?" When I told her I would agree to whatever Neil wanted, she offered to hire a lawyer to fight him. Since he cheated, she thought I'd have a shot at walking away with some money and maybe even the house.

"I don't want anything from him. None of it was ever really mine." It might've been my dream—the doting husband, the loving home, the kids, the dream job—but it wasn't my reality, and fighting with him over stupid, materialistic possessions wasn't going to change anything. Our relationship was over several months ago when he turned to another woman instead of his wife.

"You're a better person than I am. What are you going to

do now?"

My stomach sinks at her question. "I don't know. Start over... For tonight, I plan to just check into a motel."

"A motel? No way! Move here."

"What?" She can't be serious. She lives in New York, almost a thousand miles away.

"Our CFO retired unexpectedly, and Lucas and my dad have been interviewing people to replace him. It's perfect timing! You've spent the past four years working for a construction company. You're more qualified than anyone they're interviewing."

"Brianne, you're crazy! A CFO? Me?"

"Yes, you! You're a freaking math genius! You could move here and start fresh. Plus, you know how much I miss you. And you would love living in New York."

She's lost her mind. That has to be it. I can't possibly pick up and move my entire life to the East Coast. At the same time, is it really such a crazy idea? Not to work for her family's architecture and construction company because there's no way they would actually hire me, but to move to New York. I've only been there twice, but she's right. I did love it.

"I'm a licensed CPA in Tennessee," I point out.

"So, you'll transfer it to New York." She's quiet for a moment before she says, "I texted Lucas, and he said he can interview you tomorrow."

"I can't fly out there tomorrow!"

Brianne laughs. "Through video chat, silly. Although I hate the idea of you staying at a motel and am tempted to get you on a flight out tonight. I'm not sure if the company jet is in use..."

"One, I'm fine staying at a motel." I've lived in worse. "Two, are you serious? He's willing to interview me? This isn't a pity offer, is it?"

"Savy, you're practically the smartest person I know, and when it comes to math, you might as well be an alien. You can do math in your head quicker than I can with a calculator. You got your degree *and* MBA in the time it took me to get my single design degree. Sharp Architecture and Construction would be lucky to have you. This is not a pity offer. This is a smart business decision with the bonus of having one of my best friends living in the same zip code as me."

I can't be considering this. It's insane. Absurd. Senseless.

Yet…

"I would have to find a place to live." New York isn't cheap, and it'll take time to save—

"Shut up! You'd live with me, of course! I have the extra room, and my father owns the building, so if you want to live on your own once a place opens up, you can. He would rent to you for cheap since you work for the company. And before you argue, he does it for all of our employees. There's also a garage where you can park your vehicle. Though I would recommend you sell it since having a car here is kind of pointless. It would give you some extra cash in the bank."

"Bri." She has this all figured out, and I can't think of a single reason to say no. I might not have the marriage, or the family, or the love, but at least I could have a career, which would allow me to create my own future without depending on anyone but myself. Maybe I set my expectations too high. Instead of looking for love, I should've been working for security. Love got me a broken heart, but a career will give me stability, which is more important.

"Eeek!" she shrieks when I don't come up with a new argument. "It's totally happening. You're moving here!"

"You don't even know if your brother and father will hire me." She might be a part of the company, but her brother and father own the other two-thirds. Brianne focuses on what she loves—design—and leaves them to make the business decisions.

"Oh, I know they will. The interview is just a formality. What do you say?"

"I don't know. Let me think about it. I'll interview with your brother tomorrow and let you know."

"Fine." She sighs. "I want to beg, but I know this has to be your decision. If you need anything, call me. I'll just be over here pricking my Lois and Neil voodoo dolls with needles."

I laugh as we hang up, totally imagining her doing just that, and then once it's quiet, I stare at my phone for a moment. Could I really do it? Move to New York? Tennessee is all I've ever known. It's where I've lived my entire life... but at the same time, what life have I actually lived?

My screen flashes with a notification I missed while I was on the phone. I click on it, and it takes me to a post. It must be the one Brianne was talking about. It's a picture of Lois's ring finger with a big rock on it, and in the caption, it reads: It's official! Neil and I are engaged! #longtimecoming

I exit out of the post and shoot a text to Brianne.

Me: If your brother thinks I'll be a good fit, I'm in.

Then I pull my ring off my finger. *Wonder how much I can pawn this for?*

One

Benjamin

ON MOST MORNINGS, MY EYES OPEN BEFORE THE ALARM GOES OFF. I LOOK over at my phone and see it's 5:59 a.m. Before it changes to six o'clock, I quickly switch off my alarm, preventing me from being forced to listen to the ridiculous loud buzzing sound. I'm not even sure why I set it since my brain and body know I wake up every morning at six.

Getting out of bed, I head to the bathroom to begin my daily routine. After I take a quick piss and brush my teeth, I wake Brody to get ready for his first day of school. Once I know he's half-awake, I throw on my workout clothes and head down to the gym located on the basement level of the building where I live.

I enter the gym and grab a towel from the rack to wipe down the treadmill. Then I click on the television to watch the morning news on the big screen in front of me as I start my warm-up. Before I step it up to a run, I check my emails. How is it possible I already have forty-six new emails? I checked them before I went to bed not even three hours ago. Exhaustion sets in when I think about my lack of sleep. I always say I'm going to go to bed earlier, but then insomnia keeps me awake. Before I know it, it's after three in the morning, and I'm prying my eyes from my laptop and forcing myself to get a few hours of shut-eye.

Scrolling through the emails, I see one from my sister with Valentine's Day on the subject line. I click it open and quickly skim through it, noting it's about the upcoming event happening at Lush—the restaurants/nightclubs I own. Next month is Valentine's Day, and since Amalia oversees all the events for my clubs, she's planning a big event to celebrate the holiday. I notice my on-site managers are copied in the email, so I ignore it, clicking on the next one. It's from Moti, the assistant manager at the Las Vegas location, asking about the food and beverage report. Some numbers aren't adding up, and he'd like to seek clarification. He's emailed my dad, who is the accounting manager, but hasn't heard back... *Weird.* My dad's always on top of his shit. I forward the email to my dad, then put my phone back into my pocket. I'll deal with the rest later.

The biggest hurdle I've had to overcome in the past fifteen years since I bought my first club is delegating and trusting that they'll do their job right. I'm a firm believer that if you want something done right, you do it your damn self, so letting go of the reins has been challenging. While I'm justified in my need to manage everything myself—the mother of my son *handling* the birth control herself, only to lie and get pregnant, as just one example—I also understand the other side of it. When you own a half dozen nightclubs and restaurants, it's impossible to control every detail. I can't be everywhere at once, especially not now.

Increasing the speed on the treadmill, I bring myself to a steady pace of nine miles per hour while I get lost in the news, trying to block out the shit running through my mind. I have a meeting with Lucas, my best friend and architect, this morning before he takes off on a business trip to discuss the property I recently acquired as a gift to my sister and her new husband. Gerald is a fabulous chef and hopes to open a French restaurant. Only it'll have a twist. Since my sister loves art, she wants to attach a gallery to it and call it Artfully Delicious. I think the concept is brilliant and will do well here, so I'm meeting with everyone to go over the plans.

I also have a conference this afternoon with Brody's guidance counselor to go over the expectations for the remainder of the year. Since he was expelled from his private school, I enrolled him in the local public school, and he's behind on credits since he failed so many classes. Paola damn near lost her shit when she found out our son is attending a public school, but I don't care—and I told her as much. My sister and I both went to a public school, and we turned out just fine.

I'm about ten minutes into my run when the door opens, and a woman I've never seen before walks in. Instinctually, my eyes roam over her, taking her in. Caramel hair with various shades of blond highlights are pulled up into a loose ponytail. Tanned, toned legs are barely covered with yellow cotton shorts—if you can even call them that. I'd bet all my money, if she turned around, I'd see a hint of her ass cheeks peeking out. I chuckle at the shoes on her feet. Instead of wearing tennis shoes, she's sporting light pink fluffy boots. Her face is free of makeup, and her tits look real—perky but not in the so-perky-they-hit-her-chin sort of way.

It's not often I see a naturally beautiful woman free of plastic surgery and makeup. Especially living in the places where I've lived. You want a fake woman? They're a dime a dozen. I've learned the hard way women are good for one thing, to sink into and find release with. It doesn't matter if their tits are real or fake. As long as they can handle their own in the bedroom and understand what the term *no strings* means, we're good to go.

Realizing I'm still staring at her, I drag my eyes back to the television, but when she comes over and steps onto the treadmill next to me, I can't help but check out her backside. I was right. Her ass is firm, just like the rest of her body, and her shorts are so tiny, the bottom swells of her cheeks are popping out. She has this thickness to her that I can imagine grabbing ahold of in bed. This woman is either new to this building or has changed her workout time because I damn sure would've remembered seeing her here before. Then again, I haven't been around much for the past several years, so it's possible we just haven't crossed paths.

When I force my gaze to move from her ass back up to her face, I notice she's staring at the treadmill screen with the most adorable look. Her nose is scrunched up in confusion... or maybe frustration. Either way, she's staring at the gym equipment like it's from another planet. Based on her furry boots, I'm going to assume she's new to working out.

"Need some help?"

She turns her attention to me and hits me with the bluest eyes I've ever seen. It's like getting lost in an ocean of warmth. I'm in such shock by how beautiful she is, I almost trip over my feet. In fear of face-planting, I grab the emergency stopper and yank it out, bringing the machine to a sudden halt. Not realizing how quickly it would stop, my feet keep running, and my stomach hits the front of the machine, causing me to release a loud grunt.

She smiles wide at the scene in front of her and giggles. *Fucking giggles.* I almost ended up facedown on a potentially deadly machine, and she's laughing at me.

"I think I should be asking you that question." Her words are wrapped in a cute Southern twang. It's not strong, but enough to tell me she's not from here. When I look at her pink shirt, I notice it reads *Southern girls do it better* across her chest. I would *definitely* like to find out what it is exactly they do better.

I clear my throat and force my attention back up to her face, *again*. Her eyes dance with mirth, telling me she caught me checking out her assets.

"I was reading your shirt," I say dumbly as a way of explanation.

"Uh-huh," she says with humor in her voice. She goes back to looking at the treadmill, except now with what looks like determination in her eyes. *Is she willing it to turn on?*

"You just pick a program, enter the info, and hit start," I explain, pointing at the program button.

She lets out a sigh and presses the button, then begins to enter all the necessary info:

Sex: female—damn right she is.

Age: 24—ten years my junior...a bit young for me, but I'm an equal opportunist. Age is just a number, after all.

Weight...

She looks at me and gives me a mock glare. "You already know my age. At least let my weight remain a mystery."

I bark out a laugh and press the start button on my treadmill. She hits start on hers as well and begins to walk. Her machine makes a faint screeching sound my machine doesn't make, like it's scratching against the bottom. *Screech, screech, screech, screech, screech, screech.* Holy shit, it's annoying.

She picks up the pace a little, and the sound gets louder. Thank God I never use that machine. How is it not bothering her? Then I notice at some point while I was once again ogling her, she put earbuds in. I can faintly hear the sound of country music playing from them.

After several minutes of this annoying noise, I look to see how long she set her workout for. She catches me staring and takes one earbud out. "Whew! This machine is gonna work me hard."

Is she serious? She's walking at an unhurried pace. The people on the streets of New York walk quicker on their way to work.

"How long are you planning to walk for?" I ask while I slow

my run down to a brisk jog.

"I'm not really sure. I guess until I get tired."

Great. At that speed, she'll be here all day, which means I'm stuck listening to that screeching noise for the rest of my run so this woman can go for a leisurely stroll.

"Have you worked out before?"

"Nope. A part of the new me is to become healthier, and because there's no way I'm giving up my fried chicken or ice cream, I figured my best bet is to work out. It just so happens my new living situation means I have this gym at my disposal, so I thought, what the heck."

Would it be piggish of me to tell her that her body looks just fine and there's no reason to waste her time on that treadmill—driving me nuts with that screeching noise while I'm trying to listen to the news and enjoy my workout in peace? If she wants a workout, I can *gladly* accommodate her, and I guarantee she'll work up more of a sweat than she's doing right now. The thin material of my shorts stretches against my growing erection. It's been a while since I've gotten laid. Between finishing up the club in LA and moving back here with my teenage son, who hates his parents and the world, I've been a little preoccupied.

A few minutes go by and then she presses stop on the machine.

"You're done?" She's only burned thirty calories.

"Yeah. Don't want to overdo it on the first day. Figure I'll work my way up slowly."

I stifle my laugh at how ridiculous this woman is, but I'm also pleased that horrid machine is now quiet.

"Have a good day," she says, waving as she walks out of the gym. "Maybe I'll see you around."

You bet your fine ass you will.

Two

Savannah

"IS THAT WHAT YOU WORE TO THE GYM?" BRIANNE LAUGHS, HANDING ME A steaming mug of coffee. "Your UGGs and pajama shorts?"

"I don't own any workout clothes. And anyway, I only lasted like ten minutes before I got winded."

We both crack up laughing.

"Are you going tomorrow?"

"Sure. Why not? New city, new me, right?" Plus, aside from my appointment on Friday to fill out paperwork and get a tour of the office, I have the remainder of the week with nothing to do but get acquainted with my new living arrangements.

Monday will be my first official day of work.

Brianne smiles sadly. "There's nothing wrong with the *old* you. You're perfect."

I want to believe her, I do. But it's hard to believe you're perfect when nobody in your life has ever wanted you enough to keep you... to put you first. To show you that you're their everything. Not my parents, not my foster parents, not my best friend, not even my husband.

Cue pity party for one.

"I guess I just want to figure out who I am."

"You will. And when I get back, I'll help you." She winks playfully. "This city is filled with wealthy, yummy men. Trust me."

"You aren't lying," I agree, remembering that sexy man jogging on the treadmill.

When Brianne quirks a brow, silently asking me to elaborate, I do. "I ran into some hot guy at the gym. I didn't plan to get a workout *and* a show, but hey, I'm not complaining. If I have to suffer through a grueling workout, a bit of eye candy makes it worth it."

She shakes her head and giggles. "There you go! Did you ask

him for his number?"

"No! My divorce was finalized like five seconds ago."

Brianne's answer to getting over Neil is to get back out there, but I don't agree. I put myself out there once, gave Neil my all, and ended up husbandless, best-friendless, and homeless. This time around, I'm going to do things differently, starting with focusing on myself.

Brianne takes her cup to the sink, rinses it out, and then comes back with her luggage.

"I hate that I'm leaving you when you just arrived. You sure you don't want to come? The resort we're staying at has a ski lodge. You can sit by the fire and drink hot cocoa."

She and her brother, Lucas, scheduled a trip to Wintergreen to meet with a huge investor to discuss remodeling a ski resort. Since it was planned before I knew I would be moving here, they couldn't reschedule—and there's no reason for them to. I'm a big girl and can handle being in the city by myself. Besides, their dad is meeting me Monday morning to walk me through my responsibilities.

"No, I appreciate it, but I'm going to spend this time getting settled... working out." Maybe, if I'm lucky, that guy will be down there working out again tomorrow.

Brianne laughs. "Yeah, okay. Just don't overdo it. Wouldn't want you laid up in bed before you start working." She rolls her luggage to the front door. "There's food in the fridge, or you can order from any of the takeout places listed on the board. Those are the good ones. On Friday, take a cab, not the subway. It's quicker from where we're located." Her green eyes scan the area, trying to think of anything else, but before she can convince herself to cancel her trip, I walk over and hug her.

"I'll be fine. I promise."

"If you need anything, I'm only a phone call away. I have a meeting this morning, but my flight isn't scheduled until after lunch."

"Got it, but I'll be okay."

I spend the morning putting my clothes away and organizing everything in my new room and en suite bathroom. Since Brianne used it as a guest room, it was already furnished with beautiful white wood furniture that easily holds my clothes. And what doesn't fit in the drawers, I hang up in the walk-in closet. I set out the few picture frames I have left that don't include Neil or Lois and then line up my paperbacks on the bookshelf. I don't have a whole lot, but they're all my favorites.

By lunch, I'm going stir-crazy, so instead of making something to eat, I grab a jacket and venture out. The elevator dings, bringing me to the lobby, and I step out, taking in my surroundings. When I arrived yesterday, I was so overwhelmed that I didn't pay attention to the area, so I have no clue where I am, but I do know this building is high-class. Between the gorgeous fountain, the marble floors, and the sleek front desk with someone behind it twenty-four hours a day, the lobby alone looks like it belongs in an architectural magazine. It's no wonder Sharp is one of the most sought-after architectural and construction firms.

"Good morning, Miss Cartwright. Can I assist you with anything this morning?" My eyes go wide at the elderly, gray-haired gentleman who apparently knows my name. "I'm Fred, the concierge," he says with a light chuckle. "I work Monday through Friday, seven a.m. to three thirty p.m. If you need anything during that time, I'm your man."

I smile, remembering Brianne telling me about Fred, who is like an uncle to her. He came from the previous building they lived in and has worked here for several years.

"Nice to meet you. You can call me Savy. I'm just going to go for a walk to find some food."

"Very well. Enjoy your hunt." He winks, making me laugh.

As I'm exiting the building, tightening my hold on my jacket since it's chilly outside, I run smack into another person. "Oh, I'm so sorry."

When our eyes connect, he glares before a sly smirk graces his lips as his eyes descend over my body. He has a cigarette between his fingers, yet he's clearly too young to be smoking.

"Damn, you're hot," he says with crass only a teenager could pull off.

"One, you don't tell a woman she's *hot*. You tell her she's beautiful. Two, smoking kills, and women don't think it's sexy. It makes you smell and taste like an ashtray, and *nobody* thinks that's sexy." I pluck the cancer stick from his fingers and toss it into the ashtray part of the garbage can. "Now, if you'll excuse me..." I let out a huff and head down the street in search of somewhere to eat.

A few seconds later, I hear him yell out for me to wait. "Sorry," he says, looking at me sheepishly, "for saying you're hot. It worked on a show I was watching."

"Apology accepted." I stop in my place to give him my attention. "How old are you?"

"Uh…" He clears his throat. "Eighteen."

"Try again," I say with a laugh.

He sighs and runs his fingers through his shortish yet floppy brown hair. "Fourteen."

"Shouldn't you be in school?"

"Yeah, so?" He smirks, and the way his hazel eyes catch with mine, I have no doubt that one day, when he's older, *much older*, he'll be a heartbreaker, but right now, he's just a teenage wannabe bad boy. I grew up with dozens of them in foster care.

"Like smoking, dropping out of school isn't a turn-on either. Women like men who are educated, so you might want to get your butt back in school and get an education… That's if you ever want to meet a woman."

He scoffs. "Doubtful. My dad has women falling all over him, and he dropped out of college."

Little shit…

Before I can think of a comeback, he points behind him at the building. "Do you live there?"

"Yeah, I just moved in. I'm new to New York."

"I live there too. Just moved in, but I've lived in New York my entire life." Like a gentleman, he extends his hand. "I'm Brody."

"Savy." I shake his hand. "Do you still have time to get to school?"

"Nah, school gets out soon. It's a half-day. My dad's totally going to kill me for skipping." He says it like it's a fact—one he's not at all worried about, reminding me of the foster kids I'd lived with growing up, who'd do things like skip school to get a rise out of the people taking care of them. I don't know this kid, but based on his comments, the smoking, and the truancy, I'd bet he's seeking attention.

"Well, I need to find somewhere to eat. How about you show me somewhere good, and I'll buy you your last meal?" I wink playfully, making him chuckle.

"I know just the place."

We end up a few blocks down at a little hole-in-the-wall deli that, according to Brody, serves the best sandwiches. Brody tells me how he's recently moved in with his dad and was supposed to start school today.

"So, what happened?"

Brody shrugs, averting his gaze.

"You get scared?"

"Pfft," he huffs. "I'm a man. We don't get scared."

I raise a brow. "Even *men* get scared."

He sighs and takes a bite of his sandwich. When he's done chewing, he swallows it down with a gulp of his lemonade and is about to speak when his cell phone rings.

"Shit, it's my dad."

"Shoot," I correct, feeling a bit of sympathy for his dad. "And you better answer it. He's probably worried sick." I know I would be if my son were wandering around the streets of this vast city on his own.

Brody rolls his eyes as he hits answer. "Hello?"

I can't hear what his dad is saying, but I can hear him yelling.

Brody huffs, then says, "Whatever... I'm sorry." His tone doesn't match the last two words. He's not sorry. His eyes meet mine as he tells his dad where he's at. "Fine... I'll be back soon." He hangs up and groans. "I forgot he was meeting with my guidance counselor today to go over my credit-retrieval schedule. He's at my school now."

"And you're not."

He nods.

"What's credit retrieval?" I ask curiously before taking another bite of my delicious sandwich.

"I failed a few classes last semester, so I have to take them online to get credit."

"What are you, a freshman?"

"Yeah." He shoves the final bite of his food into his mouth, chews, then swallows, sucking down his drink to wash it down.

"That's a bad way to start high school. You planning to go to college?"

"Nah, I'm going to work for my dad. He has the best job there is." His eyes light up, making it clear, despite his act of rebellion, that he loves his dad very much.

"What does he do?"

"He owns a bunch of nightclubs. His job is literally to party."

I cough out a laugh. "I think there's more than that to owning nightclubs. I doubt he makes money by partying."

Brody shrugs. "I don't know." His phone rings, and he curses under his breath. "It's my dad again."

"You should probably get going."

"Or we could have cake for dessert. This place makes the best éclair cake. It is my last meal after all."

"Nice try." I reach over and tousle his hair. "You made your choice, and now you have to face the consequences."

Three

Benjamin

MY ALARM GOES OFF, AND I GROAN, EXHAUSTED. YESTERDAY FELT LIKE THE never-ending day from hell. After a shitty meeting, where I learned we've hit some red tape on acquiring the permits to get started with Artfully Delicious, I headed to Brody's school to meet with the counselor. When I got there and learned he wasn't there, I nearly lost my shit. Apparently, my damn kid thought school was optional.

After a long talk about our roles and responsibilities— where I did all the talking, and he grunted and rolled his eyes—I took his phone away. He stormed out pissed and stayed in his room for the remainder of the day, refusing to come out for dinner. Hopefully, today goes a bit smoother.

After getting dressed in my workout clothes, I wake Brody up so he can start getting ready. To ensure he makes it through the doors of his school today, I'm going to have to deviate from my routine and drop his ass off myself.

When I enter the gym, I'm taken aback by the woman already on the treadmill. Caramel hair up in a ponytail, tiny cotton shorts that show off her thick thighs and plump ass, fluffy boots—beige today—and instead of a T-shirt, she's sporting a tank top. She's walking once again at a leisurely pace. Only, unlike yesterday, today her treadmill isn't squeaking... because she's on mine.

I stalk over to her and cut around the front so I can look her in the eyes, and when I do, I'm stunned silent. The woman is eating a goddamned bag of Doritos while walking on the treadmill. Is she fucking for real? My gaze slides from her mouth to her ample cleavage peeking out of the confines of her top. The saying on the front reads *Mind your own biscuits & life will be gravy.*

"Oh, hey," she says with a bright smile, pulling one earbud

out of her ear. "Fancy seeing you here again."

"You're on my treadmill," I deadpan, ignoring the way her smile and accent fuck with my head.

She glances around, confused. "Really? Do we sign up somewhere to reserve certain equipment?"

"No, but I use that treadmill every day at this time." I've been using it for years at this time—since I bought a place in this building to use as my home base—and not once has anyone else ever joined me to work out... until now.

"Oh." She pops an orange chip into her mouth. "Well, good thing there're two." She plucks another chip from the bag and drops it into her mouth, then wraps her lips around the tip of her finger, sucking the orange residue off. My thoughts go to her using those same lips and tongue to suck my dick... Fuck, I need to get laid.

She puts her earbud back in and hits something on her treadmill. Frustrated in more ways than one, I walk around to get on the screechy machine next to hers and see she has a tablet resting on the front of her treadmill. What. The. Hell. She's... reading a book. This woman is barely walking while eating a bag of Doritos and listening to a goddamned audiobook.

I jump on the treadmill and hit the quick start, pushing the speed up to my usual nine miles per hour. The screeching begins immediately, and the faster the speed, the louder it gets. This can't be happening. I'm never going to make it for an hour. I pound my feet onto the belt of the machine, trying to rid myself of the anxiety and frustration I'm feeling. One minute, I was building nightclubs, partying it up and getting laid in LA, and the next, I'm trying to raise a teenager—one who's failing out of school, almost burned my apartment down a few days ago when he was trying to smoke in his bathroom, and refuses to speak to me unless I force him to.

My schedule is fucked, and my routine is shot. I don't even know which way is up, and this goddamn woman is messing with my morning workout.

After several minutes of the obnoxious noise, I give up. Getting off the machine, I instead focus on my upper body. When I glance over, I find her stepping off the machine. I still have a good thirty minutes, so after she smiles and waves, dumping her empty chip bag in the garbage on her way out, I jump on the machine to get a few miles in.

Tomorrow, I'm getting here early, getting my damn

treadmill, and unplugging that screechy-ass other one. If she wants to go for a stroll, she can take a walk through Central Park.

After I shower and get dressed, I take Brody to school, stopping at a deli for breakfast along the way. I need to order food so we can start eating at home. I just haven't found the time.

"Have a good day at school," I tell him once we reach the front of the school.

He nods, looking bored. "Yeah, okay."

"Come home right after school, and I'll pick up dinner."

"'Kay," he says, walking through the gates.

I wait until he's all the way in and then start to walk away, only I get a weird feeling, so I turn around and go back. And sure enough, there he is, walking out of the damn school.

"Are you kidding me?" I bark, making him jump.

"Shit, I mean shoot." He blanches.

"Get your ass in school!"

"All right, all right." He raises his hands in a placating manner, then turns around and goes in.

This time, I wait until I hear the bell ring before I walk

away. This kid is going to be the death of me.

"BENJAMIN, HOW ARE YOU?" MY DAD ASKS WHEN I WALK INTO THE DELI TO meet him and my sister for lunch. "How's Brody?"

"He skipped school yesterday, so I'm hoping he actually stays put today."

"He'll be okay," Dad says. "At his age, you were doing the same thing."

"Yeah, because my mom killed herself, we were living in our car, and I was lashing out," I point out. "What does he have to act out about? He has a damn good life."

Dad flinches. "Sometimes people are going through things we don't know about. Maybe cut him some slack."

I'm about to ask what he means by that when the waitress walks over, interrupting our conversation to ask what we would like to drink.

"Water, please." I don't drink during the business day.

"Same for me," Dad says.

"Make it three," I tell her. "We have someone on their way."

"Sorry I'm late," Amalia says, rushing over. "With Valentine's Day coming up, we're slammed with the upcoming events." She leans over and kisses our dad's cheek, then mine before she sits down. "I can't believe Valentine's Day is—"

Her words are cut off by the sound of my phone ringing. "Give me a second. It's the office." I raise a single finger, halting our conversation. "Benjamin Fields."

"Mr. Fields, it's Owen Ross...from accounting."

"Yes, I know who you are. Is everything okay?" While all my employees have my cell phone number, very rarely does anyone use it since, up until recently, I'm usually out of town, and they have a person of contact in the office. For Owen, it's my dad.

"I've been trying to get ahold of your dad, but I can't seem to track him down. There's an issue with—"

"Benjamin," Dad cuts in. "Everything okay?"

"Owen's been trying to get ahold of you."

His brow furrows, and he extends his hand, silently asking for the phone. "Owen, I'm going to put my dad on." I hand him the phone.

"Owen, I'll be in this afternoon." He pauses to listen to whatever Owen is saying. "Okay, I'll handle it when I get back."

He hangs up and hands me back my phone. "Sorry about that. I was out of town for a few days."

"Where'd you go?" I didn't even realize he was gone. But then again, I've been so busy with Brody I don't even know what day it is.

"It was just a quick business trip. I'll get everything sorted this afternoon."

"Thanks, Dad." I pat him on his shoulder, thankful to have him on my team. For a long time, I was worried about him, afraid he would regress and go back down the dark path he spent too much time on after Mom's death, but he's stayed on the straight and narrow, and I'm damn proud of him.

The waitress sets our drinks down and then takes our orders.

"How'd the meeting go with the city this morning?" Amalia asks once the waitress leaves.

"Good. We got the green light to move forward."

She squeals. "I can't believe it's really happening. Gerald and I owe you so much."

"You don't owe me anything. It's a damn good investment. Between your love and knowledge of art and his culinary skills, it's going to be a huge success. Besides, everything else is running smoothly, and with me here for the foreseeable future, it's the perfect time."

It's taken close to fifteen years, but I'm finally at a point where it feels like all my business ventures are running like well-oiled machines. I'll have to travel occasionally to check on them, but I'll be able to handle everything from here for the most part. Which is good since my son needs me to be as hands-on as possible. Paola texted me last night that Ted is going out of town for business, and since Brody is with me, she's decided to go.

"Maybe it's time to finally settle down," Amalia says for the millionth time.

"I already told you—" My phone rings again, and when I glance at the screen, I groan, recognizing the number. "Hello."

"Good afternoon, I'm looking for the parent or guardian of Brody Fields."

"This is his father, Benjamin Fields."

"Hello, this is Dean Thomas. Your son was in a fight and has been suspended. We're going to need you to come down so we can discuss this in person, and you can pick him up."

"I'm on my way." I stand, and Dad and Amalia both look at me curiously.

"Brody was in a fight and got suspended... So much for him staying at school."

"RISE AND SHINE." I SNAG BRODY'S BLANKET AND PULL IT OFF HIS BODY.

"What the hell?" he rasps. "What time is it?"

"Quit cursing. You're fourteen, not thirty. And it's five thirty. Time to get up."

"What? Why?" he whines.

"Because you're suspended, and I don't trust you to stay home alone." His eyes pop open. "You're coming to work with me. I'm going downstairs to work out. Be dressed and ready to go by seven thirty."

He groans, grabbing a pillow and placing it over his face. I snag it and toss it onto the floor.

"I'm not kidding. Get up."

I enter the gym with a bounce in my step, knowing that I'm early and will get my treadmill. But when I turn the corner and find *her* walking on my treadmill, I growl under my breath.

"Hey!" She waves with a cheerful smile. "You're here early."

"So are you."

"Yeah." She nods, taking a sip of her Starbucks coffee before setting it back down. "I couldn't sleep, so I figured I would start my day early. Got coffee and then came here."

My gaze slides down to her shirt of the day: *If you love Southern women, raise your glass. If not, raise your standards.*

"How many of those shirts do you own?"

She looks down and laughs. "A lot. There was a gift shop in the quad of the college I attended, and every time my friend would see a new shirt, she would buy it for me as a joke because, as you can tell from my accent, I'm a little Southern." When she winks, I can't help but smile, despite my workout being ruined yet again. Something about her is sexy, and it's not just her looks. Maybe it's her carefree attitude.

"Where did you go to school?" I find myself asking.

"Tennessee."

Wait a second...

"What's your name?"

"Savy."

"Short for Savannah?"

"Yep."

Well, shit, either it's a small world or a coincidence. Lucas told me about her before he left. Said she was a friend of Brianne's from college, and he hired her as his new CFO. Apparently, she's some sort of math genius. I skim over her once more, a bit confused. It's got to be a coincidence.

"What's your name?" she asks.

"Benjamin."

She grins, showing off her perfectly straight white teeth. "Benjamin, huh? Mind if I call you Benji?"

"It's Benjamin," I repeat. No respectable businessman would agree to being called *Benji*.

She snorts. "How about Ben?"

"Benjamin."

This time, it's a giggle that shouldn't shoot straight to my dick but does. "Benjamin is so long and formal. How about...?"

"Benjamin," I repeat.

At the same time, she says, "Benny?"

"Benjamin," I deadpan. "Ben-ja-min."

"We'll see," she says, stopping her treadmill. "You can have it. I'm done for today." She takes one last sip of her coffee, then chucks it into the bin on her way out, leaving me standing here speechless.

"BRODY, LET'S GO!" I YELL, CHECKING THE TIME. IT'S SEVEN THIRTY, AND we need to get going. I scheduled an early meeting, and it looks bad when the boss is late.

"I'm coming," he groans, stepping around the corner. He's wearing a beanie on his head, a hoodie with a skateboard across the front, also covering the top of his head, and jeans with more holes than material. He looks more grunge than professional, and if I had time, I'd make him change. How did I not notice the way he dresses until now? Maybe because his private school required a uniform.

"What?" He glances down when he catches me staring.

"You look like the homeless guys under the bridge. Your mom lets you dress like that?"

He rolls his eyes. "It's a vibe, Dad. You don't get it."

"I make enough money for your *vibe* to be a bit more

polished than that. Appearances speak volumes, and yours says you don't care."

"Because I don't," he says as he walks past me and out the door.

I grab my briefcase and lock up behind me. Once we're downstairs, I nod toward Fred, so he can hail us a car. As I'm opening the door and sliding in after Brody, I hear a woman yell, "Hold, please!"

I glance out from inside and see Savannah running out the door and straight for our car. Oh no… This won't do. I have a schedule to keep and can't be sharing a car. There are a million cars in the city. She can't grab one of those?

But before I can tell her this, she stumbles in, knocking me into Brody, and slams the door shut. "Whew, thank you! I'm running late."

"Must've been that *long* workout," I mutter sarcastically, annoyed that now I'm going to have to be a gentleman and allow for her to be dropped off first. This is going to set my entire morning back.

Savannah laughs, the sound melodic and carefree. "Probably. I might need to get up even earlier if I'm going to make working out part of my routine once I start working."

Well, at least if she does that, she'll be out of the gym before I arrive since she doesn't seem to walk more than ten minutes.

"Hey, Savy," Brody says, sounding more chipper than I've heard him the past several days.

Savannah looks around me. "Hey, you. I didn't see you there."

"You two know each other?" I dart my eyes from her to him.

"Brody showed me a delicious restaurant to have lunch at the other day."

When the hell would he... and then it clicks. "You were eating with her when you were skipping school?"

"Where to?" the driver asks impatiently before Brody can answer.

I glance at Savannah.

"Oh! Umm..." She pulls her phone out and taps away at it. "Fields Tower? I can't find the address."

Well shit, I guess she *is* the friend Lucas hired. At least I don't have to worry about being late since we're going to the same place.

"Yep! Fields Tower," she repeats. "Have you heard of it?"

"Yeah... my office is there as well."

Brody snorts, and I elbow him, making him chuckle.

"Really?" Savannah asks. "Do you work for Sharp Architecture and Construction?"

"No, but Uncle Lucas is Dad's best friend and my godfather," Brody announces.

Savannah's bright blue eyes go wide. "Oh, wow, what a small world." She smiles at my son, who smiles back. The kid hasn't done anything more than grimace and occasionally grunt since he's moved in, and now, he's over there grinning like a damn fool.

Brody spends the car ride telling Savannah about other restaurants he likes, and she makes note of them in her phone so she can check them out. Once the driver stops in front of the building, I quickly swipe my card as Savannah opens the door and scoots out, and I follow while Brody gets out on the other side.

As she steps onto the sidewalk, sliding her coat on since it's a bit chilly outside this morning, I take in her attire from behind. She's dressed differently than what she's been wearing to the gym, more professional, which makes sense since she's going to work. Her black pencil skirt is tight in all the right places, hugging her ass. It's just long enough to be deemed professional and short enough to show off those toned legs of hers, which are unfortunately covered in black pantyhose. She's sporting come-fuck-me heels that have me imagining what they would feel like digging into my back as I fuck her on my office desk.

"Benny," Savannah says, knocking me out of my thoughts.

"Benny?" Brody laughs, knowing I hate nicknames. "Can I call you Benny too?"

"You can call me Dad." I glare at him. "The building is right there." I point at the twelve-story building in front of us that reads Fields Tower in mirrored letters across the front.

"Thanks." She tips her head upward. "It's big." When she doesn't make any move to walk in, Brody and I stay standing by her. He gives me an odd look, and I shrug.

"You okay?" I ask.

Her eyes dart over to me. "Yeah, just nervous, I guess." Her Southern accent comes out heavy. "It's intimidating. New city, new job. I guess it's all just hitting me." She glances around. "I was hoping to get breakfast, maybe coffee, before my meeting."

She looks at her watch. "I have some time. I wasn't sure how long it would take to get here. Do you know of anywhere? Maybe a bit of food and caffeine will help."

Her azure eyes meet mine, and it feels as though my breath has been knocked out of me. With her hair down in waves and a bit of makeup on her face, she's gorgeous. But it's the way she looks at me, with vulnerability in her eyes, that has my attention. It feels as though she's cracked open the vault to her soul and is giving me a glimpse. She's so open, like what you see is what you get, and I'm not used to that. In my world, people put up a wall and hide behind it, only showing what they want others to see. But with one look, it's as if Savannah's bared herself to the world.

"You can come with us," Brody says first. "Dad's house has no food, so he has to feed me anyway."

Savannah looks at him and laughs. It's carefree and melodic, and I know I'm fucked.

"I know of a place," I tell her, extending my hand. She takes it, and I lead her and Brody to a deli that serves breakfast and coffee.

After we order our drinks and food, we find a small table

near the window to sit at while we wait. When our number is called, Brody surprisingly offers to grab it all. He passes out everyone's food and drinks when he gets back.

"Thank you," Savannah says to him, handing him a napkin. "This smells delicious."

"So, how did you two meet?" I ask them, taking a sip of my coffee.

Brody averts his gaze while Savannah shrugs. "He told me I'm hot."

"What?" I glance at my son, who has the decency to look sheepishly at me.

"And I explained women are beautiful, not hot." She laughs softly. "I also told him women prefer men who are educated, so he should stop skipping school."

Brody smirks and looks at me. "And I told her my dad dropped out of college and still gets plenty of women."

I internally groan. "I graduated high school, and I did attend college. It's where I met your mom."

"Yeah, but then you dropped out and bought a strip club," he argues, making me choke on my coffee. Shit, I never realized how much kids pay attention.

"Brody," I warn, ready to strangle him. It's not that I'm embarrassed. I don't own them anymore, but at the time, it was a damn good investment. After I renovated and sold them, my return on investment was fifty percent. I used that money to open Lush after paying Lucas back in full with interest.

"What?" he asks, oblivious to the problem with his word vomit. "I don't see why it's a big deal. My friends think it's awesome."

"You don't go around telling people your dad owns strip clubs. Besides, I don't even own them anymore." I look at Savannah, who's hiding her grin behind her cup of coffee, obviously amused at the direction the conversation has taken. "I own several nightclubs called Lush."

"Oh! I've heard of that place. Bri mentioned it when we would talk. I've never been to a nightclub before, but the pictures she showed me were gorgeous."

Before I can think about what I'm doing, I say, "We should go some time."

Savannah's eyes lock with mine. "That would be fun. Bri and Lucas will be back next week. We can all go."

My phone rings, reminding me of my morning meeting

that I'm late for. "We need to get going. I'll walk you to where you need to go."

"Is your school over here?" she asks Brody.

"Um, no." He shakes his head, actually looking ashamed. "I got into a fight and got suspended."

She frowns at him in concern. "You're on quite a roll, huh?"

"I guess," he mutters with a shrug.

"Hopefully, he's not going to make this a habit," I add in, glaring at my son, who makes it a point to avoid my gaze.

After we leave Savannah in the reception area of Sharp, Brody and I take the elevator upstairs to where my company's offices are housed. I set him up at my desk to do the schoolwork he needs to have finished before returning next week and then head into my meeting.

Four

Savannah

"THIS WILL BE YOUR OFFICE," DAVID SAYS, STEPPING INTO THE SPACIOUS

room. To the left is a large window that overlooks the city, and

in the center is a beautiful mahogany desk. There's a comfy yet

elegant-looking couch in the corner with a coffee table and

several rows of bookshelves lining the walls. Near the window

is a small round table with four chairs, and behind it is a little

nook with a Keurig machine and a mini fridge.

"This is mine?" I splutter in shock, taking it all in. When

I finished filling out my paperwork, I ran into David Sharp,

Brianne's dad. He said since I was here and he wasn't busy, he would show me around himself. After only two minutes into the tour, I quickly realized how different Sharp is from the company Neil and his dad run. For starters, Sharp is warm and inviting. The people actually seem happy to be here, and instead of shitty cubicles, everyone has their own little—or in my case, big—space.

"Of course," David says with a genuine smile. The entire time he's been giving me a tour, I keep looking for a hint of calculation or fakeness, but I've yet to see any. "You're a vital part of this company and will be treated as such. This floor houses the finance and accounting department. We'll hold a meeting on Monday so you can meet everyone and get brought up to speed."

"Thank you. I can't wait." I step farther inside and run my fingers along the smooth top of the desk, excited to make the space my own. While I was in college, I dreamed of having my own office one day, but when I went to work for Neil, he stuck me in a small cubicle. Not only did he claim he didn't want to play favorites, but it was also pointless because I wouldn't be there long. Once I got pregnant, I was expected to quit and stay home with the baby. It turns out, he was right. I wasn't there long... but it wasn't to stay home with a baby.

After letting me know he'll be around if I need anything, David excuses himself. I walk around the desk and slide into the comfy plush leather chair. This is mine, all mine. All those years of my parents, and then later my foster parents, telling me I'd never amount to anything only made me want to succeed and work that much harder, and it paid off. I did it. I really freaking did it. I'm a CFO.

I can't help the squeal that escapes my lips as I spin in my chair, fist-pumping the air. When the chair swivels back to the front, I find Brody standing in the doorway with a grin splayed across his face.

"I could hear you screaming from the lobby." He steps into my office and plops into a guest chair on the other side of my desk

"Oops." I cover my mouth. "I guess I couldn't contain my excitement."

"Over getting a job?" He laughs.

"Yeah." I nod. "I worked hard in school, and it feels good to see it finally paying off. I graduated at the top of my class and passed the CPA certification on the first try. I'm excited to work."

Brody's face sobers. "My dad loves working too." He doesn't say it, but I can hear it in his tone—his dad works a lot.

"Speaking of which, what are you doing here?" The last I heard, he was supposed to spend the day in his dad's office doing schoolwork since he's suspended.

"Dad got caught up in his meetings and forgot about lunch." He shrugs, acting like it's no big deal. "I ordered a shitload of food, so I came to see if you wanted to join me." My heart aches for the sadness in Brody's words. He's lonely, craving attention, and his dad doesn't see it. I only do because I can relate. Before my mom took off and my dad lost custody of me, all I ever craved was their attention, but the only thing *they* craved was the drugs they were addicted to. Ben isn't addicted to drugs, but it's clear, based on what Brody's just said, he might be addicted to his work.

"I'd love to." I don't have any plans for the rest of the day anyway.

Brody grants me a small smile. "Cool."

I say goodbye to Doris, who works in HR, on my way out and follow Brody to the elevator. When we get off on the top floor, the large sign in the expansive, opulent lobby reads: Fields Enterprises.

"Your dad works here?" The company owns the entire building, and from what Doris said, it's worth millions.

"My dad is Benjamin Fields. He owns the company and this building."

Well, Christ on a cracker. Who knew Mr. Uptight was some big shot business owner? He mentioned owning some clubs… Guess this explains why he's a workaholic.

When my features display my shock, Brody chuckles. "One day, I'm going to work here too." The pride in his voice makes me wonder if Ben knows how much his son looks up to him.

Brody shows me back to Ben's office, which makes mine look like a cubicle. The entire eastern wall is glass, showing off the beauty of Central Park, and in the far corner is a table and chairs that seat eight people. A couch and loveseat are set up in another area with a massive oak desk. I swear this office is bigger than most people's apartments.

"The food should be here soon," Brody says. "I'll go grab us some drinks. What do you drink?"

"Any chance you have sweet tea?"

"We should."

"Can you point me in the direction of the bathroom?" It's been a long morning, and I need to use the bathroom and freshen up.

"Yeah, umm… it's straight down the hall. Make a right, and then it's on the left, I think. My dad has a bathroom in here…" He points at the closed door. "But he forgot to unlock it."

"Thanks." I find the bathroom quickly, and after relieving myself and washing my hands, I head back. Somewhere along the way, though, I must make a wrong turn because the next thing I know, I'm walking into a conference room where a meeting is being held by none other than Benjamin Fields. Everyone is quiet as he speaks, his tone brooking no room for argument. It's clear he's not reprimanding anyone, but he means business. He isn't rude in any way, but he's authoritative. Every word demands respect. His employees are all typing away on their laptops, I'm sure taking notes.

My thoughts go back to the past few mornings at the gym. How serious he was about his precious treadmill and workout. When the other one made a horrible screeching noise that sounded like a poor cat on his death bed, he almost lost it. It was so much fun to see him all riled up. I planned to return anyway, but seeing the look on his face when he arrived early, and I was already there... Priceless.

Oh! And when I asked if I could call him Benji or Benny... The way he corrected me all deadpan and broody like the idea of his name being shortened was going to give him an anxiety attack.

Before I can stop myself, I let out an extremely unladylike snort, capturing everyone in the room's attention, including Ben—yeah, I refuse to call him Benjamin. Our eyes meet, and the wolfish look in his gaze has the V between my legs tightening.

"Can I help you?" His question comes out more like a demand. His voice is deep and throaty, dripping with sexy confidence. I briefly wonder if he's this way in *all* aspects of his life. I bet he fucks the way he runs his company—with complete and utter control.

Images of him tying me up and having his way with me flicker through my brain, heading straight to my lady parts. Would he let me ride him or demand to be on top? I bet his dick is big, too. Neil was extremely insecure, and he had a small dick. Ben, on the other hand, seems very, very sure of himself.

"Ms. Cartwright, can I help you?" he asks again, popping my fantasy bubble.

I clear my throat. "No... umm... Yes?" I squeak out.

He tilts his head to the side slightly. "Which is it? No or yes? In case you haven't noticed, I'm in the middle of conducting a meeting right now."

I don't know what comes over me, but when he raises a single brow in what looks like half-curiosity, half-impatience, the words just fly out. "Sorry to interrupt, *Benji*"—his team of employees gasp at the nickname—"Brody ordered lunch, and I was wondering when you'll be joining us." It's a simple question, but my tone conveys how I feel about him forgetting about his son.

Ben's jaw ticks, no doubt in anger and probably annoyance, but I can also spot a hint of regret. He glances down at his watch, then looks back at me. "It would seem I lost track of time." He turns his attention to his employees. "Everyone, go ahead and break for lunch. We'll reconvene in thirty minutes."

"Make it sixty," I say. "Thirty minutes is hardly enough time to eat lunch."

His eyes go wide, and a devilish smirk plays in the corner of his mouth as his employees' gazes volley between the two of us, waiting for their boss to confirm one way or the other. "Sixty minutes." He shakes his head slightly as if he can't believe he's agreeing to something so ludicrous.

Once everyone is gone, and it's only the two of us, Ben closes his laptop and stalks over to me, only stopping once he's cornered me against the wall with our faces mere inches apart. Up close, his hazel eyes are like nothing I've ever seen— different shades of greens and blues and browns all mixed in a beautiful, chaotic way. His chocolate brown hair is cut short on the sides and slightly longer on the top. My fingers itch to run through the strands to see if his hair is as soft as it looks. He's sporting several days of stubble, yet it's trimmed neatly. When his eyes sear into mine and his tongue darts out to wet his lips, I wonder what it would feel like to kiss him, like *really* kiss him. So deep his stubble would burn my face. And then my thoughts shift, as I imagine that same stubble burning between my legs as he licks his way—

"Nobody interrupts my meetings, ever," he says, knocking me out of my erotic fantasy. "They don't argue with me or question me, and they sure as hell don't call me *Benji*. Who the hell are you, and what are you doing to me?" His questions come out less accusatory and more in wonderment. They're clearly rhetorical, more or less aimed at himself.

I open my mouth to answer him—something sarcastic at the tip of my tongue—when Brody crashes into the room. "I thought you left," he says to me, hurt and relief woven in his features.

Ben backs up slightly, taking his eyes off me to look at his son.

"I was just telling your dad we were about to eat. He lost track of time, but once I snapped him out of it, he ended his meeting so he could have lunch with us."

Brody's lip quirks up enough to hint at a tiny smile. "Really? You ended your meeting?"

"I did," Ben tells him. "Is the food here?"

"Yeah. I ordered Italian. Your favorite."

Ben smiles. "That sounds good. I just need to have a quick word with Savannah, and then we'll meet you in my office."

Brody looks confused but shrugs. "All right, but hurry. It's going to get cold."

He leaves through the same door he came in, and once we're alone, I turn to Ben, trying to appear nonchalant when I'm anything but. Being this close to him has me feeling things I have no business feeling. "What's up?"

"I can't remember the last time I felt this way," he murmurs, scarily voicing my same thoughts. "First you take over my gym, messing with my morning workout, then somehow you win over my son... a kid who seems to hate everyone these days." He steps forward, encroaching on my personal space. "Then, you crash my meeting, undermining my authority with my employees..." He drags his eyes over my face. "Calling me a name you know I hate..."

I swallow thickly as he drags his tongue across the seam of his lips, looking at me like I'm a puzzle he can't figure out.

"I can't decide if I want to hate you or if I want to fuck you." There's a predatory gleam in his eye, one that says the desire to fuck me is winning over the want to hate me. And I get it because as much as he's pissing me off, I can't help but feel this attraction toward him... this pull...

A neon red sign flashes, as if saying, *"Not good, Savy. Not good. Back away and run. Men like him will chew you up and spit you out,"* snapping me back to reality. I can't afford to be under this man's spell. I've already lost everything: the idea of a loving home and a devoted husband, the possibility of creating a family. Ben is the type of man who'll take and take and take. And I have nothing left to give. And with that thought, I erect a wall ten feet high to protect myself.

"I don't particularly want you to hate me," I say, internally cringing at how breathy my words come out. "I think your kid is pretty damn cool, we live and work in the same building, and our best friends are related, which means we'll probably be seeing a lot of each other, but if it's between fucking me and hating me, you can consider me a foe because I just divorced a man like you: an uptight, control-driven, selfish asshole, and I have no desire to ever go back to anyone like that again. So, hate me or like me, I don't care. But you will *never* fuck me."

I turn on my heel and saunter out without looking back. He's hot on my heels, but he doesn't say a word until we're back in his office and seated with Brody, who's dishing out the food.

"How's your schoolwork coming along?" Ben asks Brody once our plates are full.

"Fine," Brody mumbles.

"Do you need help with anything?"

"Nope."

Ben nods, then tries again. "Did you ask about the football team at your school? Are they any good?"

This time, Brody just glares.

Ben sighs, clearly frustrated Brody isn't participating in the conversation. Poor guy is at least trying, and Brody isn't giving him an inch.

Feeling like maybe I should do something to thaw the ice a bit, I do what my grandpa used to do when I was little and things got awkward.

"What happened to the Indian who drank too much sweet tea?"

Both guys look at me like I've lost my mind.

"He slept in his teepee... Get it?" I cackle. "Tea... Pee?"

Brody is the first to crack a smile, then Ben follows.

"Tough crowd." I take a sip of my sweet tea—which is nothing like the sweet tea from where I'm from—and try again. "How do you organize a space party?" The guys' smiles grow. "You planet... Get it? You *plan* it..."

This time, they both grant me a full-megawatt grin, but

neither actually laughs.

"Really? That's it? That one was one of my best." I pout playfully.

"If you want us to laugh, you have to actually be funny," Brody smarts. "I've got a good one. What do you call it when Batman skips church?"

Ben snorts out a laugh. "Christian Bale."

They high five, both apparently thinking the joke was clever, while I'm left stumped.

"Get it?" Brody asks. "Christian Bale?"

When I shake my head, he looks at me like I have two heads. "Haven't you seen *Batman*?"

"No."

"What?" they both say in unison.

"How is that possible?" Ben asks. "Everyone's seen *Batman*."

"Not me." I shrug. "What's it about?"

For the rest of our meal, Brody and Ben explain to me all about *Batman*. Apparently, there are several movies, but the one with Christian Bale—who's an actor, in case you didn't know— is the best one. They're so animated as they talk, so I simply listen while they finish each other's sentences, recounting the entire movie. When they've finally replayed the entire movie for me, Brody says, "So, Savy, what's your favorite movie?"

"*Sweet Home Alabama.*"

They both raise their brows, obviously not having heard of it, and now it's my turn to tell them all about the best movie ever.

Lunch flies by, and before I know it, my plate is empty, and my belly is full. "That was some good food," I say, setting my fork and knife into my container and closing the lid. "Thank you for the invite."

I stand, ready to clean up, when Ben's hand lands on top of mine, making my heart skip a beat. A simple touch from him shouldn't affect me like that, but it does. "Leave it. My assistant will clean up."

"Okay, well, then I better get going." I remove my hand out from under his, breaking the connection. "Your lunch is about over." I shoot him a knowing wink, and he shakes his head.

"Can I go with you?" Brody asks. "It's boring as sh—" When I give him a pointed look, he stops in his tracks and changes his wording. "It's boring here."

"Brody—" Ben begins.

At the same time, I say, "I don't care if your dad doesn't mind."

Ben's eyes meet mine. "I'm sure you have better things to do than have a teenager tagging along."

"Not really. Plus, I enjoy Brody's company, and he knows the city. He can show me where the store is and carry my bags for me."

"Can I go?" Brody asks.

Ben groans. "Fine." He pulls something out from his desk and hands it to Brody—his phone. "You're still grounded. This is only to be used if I call you or you have an emergency." He looks at me. "I should be off around six. I'll come by and get him on my way up."

"Sounds good. Try not to work too hard, *Benji*." With a smirk that I know is sure to drive him nuts, I gather my purse and walk out of his office with Brody laughing as he follows.

I GRAB A CAN OF TOMATO SAUCE AND HAND IT TO BRODY. "WANNA INVITE your dad for dinner?"

"No."

"Why not?"

"Because I'm not speaking to him," he says, sounding very much like the surly teenager he is.

"You spoke to him during lunch."

He rolls his eyes. "That was about Batman. Besides, he'd say no anyway. He works twenty-four seven. He won't really be by to get me at six. More like nine or ten. I have a key, though, so I can go home any time. I don't need a babysitter."

"You sound like you hate his job, yet you told me you want to work there."

He glances at me and shrugs. "I figure if I'm there to help, he won't have to work so much. There'll be two people doing the work instead of one."

Oh boy, I'd bet Ben has no idea how his son feels.

Brody's phone rings from his pocket, but he ignores it, continuing to push the buggy down the aisle.

"I think your phone has rang a dozen times since we left your dad's office. It's not your dad calling, is it?" I grab some dough for the pizza we're going to make and drop it into the buggy.

"No. It's my mom."

"Ahh. So, I take it, you're not speaking to her either?" Until now, I haven't heard a single word about his mom.

Brody fidgets, suddenly looking uncomfortable. "We got into it…" His eyes drop to his feet. "I got in trouble at school… and I…" He clears his throat, still refusing to look at me. "I don't get along with Ted… He's a dick." He lifts his head, and something about the way he looks at me makes my chest tighten. "She had enough of my shit, so my dad moved home and moved me in with him."

I ignore his foul language. "Okay, that explains why you're not talking to her…" We'll get back to that later. There's obviously more to that situation. "But that doesn't explain why you're giving your dad a hard time." I toss a container of cherry tomatoes at him, and he sets it in the buggy.

"He only asked me to move in with him because my mom made him. Can we get mushrooms? I love mushrooms on pizza."

"Sure." I snag a container and hand it to him. "I don't think anyone can make your dad do anything he doesn't want to do." I've only known him for barely a minute, and I can already tell that about him.

"Maybe." He shrugs. "He doesn't even want to live here."

"Yet, he *is* living here... So why are you trying to push him away?"

"I'm not." He scoffs.

"Yes, you are." I stop in the middle of the produce section and look at Brody. "I was raised in a foster home, so I've seen it a million times. The smoking, the skipping, the attitude... You're pushing your dad to see if he'll stick or run."

"He never stays!" Brody barks. "He always leaves. Might as well get it over with now."

Ding. Ding. Ding.

"And then where will you go? Back to your mom's?"

He blanches, as if he hadn't thought of that.

"I'm not going back there. I'd rather live on the streets."

Whoa, okay then...

"You'd rather live on the streets than live with your mom?"

"Than live with Ted," he spits.

"Who's Ted? Your stepdad?"

"My mom's fiancé. I hate him."

"Okay, so you hate him, and you don't want to live with your mom. That leaves your dad. Do you *want* to live with your dad?"

"Yeah, but he's going to leave. I'm telling you... he always does."

"One thing I've learned from being in foster care is that we can't control others. We can only control ourselves. Maybe your dad's here for good..." He opens his mouth to argue, so I raise my hand to stop him. "Maybes he's not. But while he's here, maybe you should try to give him the benefit of the doubt... get to know him, let him see the good in you instead of trying to push him away. Maybe he'll prove you wrong and stick around."

"And what if he doesn't?"

"Then it's his loss. Because I've only just met you and I already know you're worth sticking around for." I grab a container of pineapple and toss it to him.

"Eww, pineapple?"

"Best pizza topping ever."

Five

Benjamin

I CAN'T THINK. CAN'T FOCUS. I'M TRYING LIKE HELL TO GET SOME WORK done, and my only thought is Savannah fucking Cartwright. She and her Southern accent and her goddamn sass are going to be the death of me. Between her messing with my workout routine, undermining me in my own office, and giving me attitude when I confronted her, she has my head spinning every which way.

Most women would've jumped at the chance to fuck me. But not her. She gave that shit right back and then walked away, shaking those delectable hips of hers. And of course my son likes her. If I'm honest, I'm a little jealous of the way they get along. As if they've known each other for years when they only met a few days ago. The kid is mad at the world, but not at her...

While we were eating lunch, she even got him to talk to me for a few minutes, something he hasn't done in a long time. When we were done discussing our favorite movies, the remainder of lunch was spent with the two of them talking about random shit, laughing and joking. Without him even realizing he was doing it, he opened up to her. Through their conversation, I learned more about my son than he's given me since he moved in. He hates going to a new school because he misses his friends and knows nobody there, which is hard for a freshman who's been going to school with the same kids his entire life. Their football team sucks, so he doesn't want to play. There's a girl he has a crush on, but he's not sure if she feels the same way. Of course, Savannah told him to go for it and gave him advice on how to go about it—in person and with her favorite flowers. The woman is obviously a romantic.

I put a call into his private school, and with a donation that could probably buy them a new damn wing, they've agreed to let Brody back in on academic probation. I'm planning to tell him tonight—and hopefully win some points.

When I eye the clock and see it's just after four, and I'm clearly not going to get anything else accomplished today, I shut everything down and head out early—something I don't think I've ever done before.

I stop by my dad's office to see him, but when I ask his secretary if he's available, she tells me he's in a meeting. I shoot him a text, letting him know I stopped by and that we should do lunch soon to discuss our upcoming projects. It seems like since I've been home, aside from the one lunch Amalia insisted on, I haven't seen much of him lately.

When I arrive at Savannah's place, I knock, but the sound of music coming through the walls must drown it out because nobody answers. I knock again, and when it goes unanswered, I turn the knob to see if it's unlocked. My kid is in there after all. The door opens easily, and I walk in—I'll have to mention to her later that even though our building is safe, she's still in New York and needs to keep her door locked.

When I step over the threshold, I'm shocked by what I see—although, at this point, nothing Savannah does should surprise me. With the music at a deafening volume and their backs to me, Savannah and Brody are standing in the kitchen, flipping what looks like pizza dough into the air. Brody's head is thrown back in laughter while Savannah shakes her ass to the beat of the music, singing the lyrics at the top of her lungs. The entire area looks like a flour bomb exploded. The white powder covers the counters, the floor, their faces and hands...

Flashbacks of my mom flipping out over messes in the house sneak up on me. Of her trying to bake cookies with us but getting upset when we got icing everywhere. Of Amalia begging for Play-doh and then getting spanked when it got stuck in the carpeting. Every memory, every holiday, every family moment was tainted. Eventually, we stopped trying to create new memories and did our best to avoid making Mom mad. But we were young and still did things to upset her until the day she had enough and ended her life.

Brody glances at Savannah, raising the pizza dough roller to his lips to join in the musical duet like they're on stage. His smile is spread across his entire face, and his laughter is so loud, I can hear it over the music.

As I watch them sing and dance and laugh, something in

me cracks. I don't know what it is. I can't explain it, but the sight of my son looking so fucking happy damn near brings me to my knees. Maybe it's because in the fourteen years he's been alive, I've never once heard him laugh so carefree. We've hung out, gone to dinner, spent holidays together. I've heard him laugh, seen him smile, but right now, at this moment, I realize I've never seen him like *this*.

And I know it's my fault. I was scared to be a parent, to fuck my kid up the way my mom fucked up my sister and me, and because of that, I've kept my son at arm's length over the years. I've been going through the motions, but I've never allowed myself to really be a part of his life. I told myself I was doing what was best for him, but I was lying to myself.

As if sensing my presence, they both turn around at the same time. Savannah grins, but Brody's face falls slightly, and my heart shatters. I've done this to him. I've pushed him away, and now I need to fix it. He deserves better, and I'm going to give him that. I have a second chance, and I'm going to make the most of it.

Savannah grabs the remote and turns the volume down. "You're home early." *Home...* The four-letter word lands in my gut like lead. I don't think I've been *home* in years—if ever.

"You guys making pizza?"

"Yeah," Brody says. "Can I stay for dinner? Mine is going to blow Savy's away."

Savannah hip checks him playfully. "Mine is going to be delicious."

"Pineapple doesn't belong on pizza ever," he volleys, making Savannah roll her eyes.

"We're about to put the toppings on and throw them into the oven. We have plenty if you want to stay."

"Dad can't. He makes calls until—"

"I'd love to," I say, cutting him off. "I'm done with work for the weekend."

Brody's brows fly up in shock. "Oh... okay. Well, you can have some of my pizza. Trust me, you don't want hers."

Savannah laughs. "Pineapple is good, and you promised you would try it."

Brody just shakes his head and rolls his eyes.

"I have beer and wine in the fridge," she offers. "We're almost ready to put the toppings on, and then it'll take about thirty minutes to bake..."

"No rush." I open the fridge and grab a beer, then walk over to where they're rolling out their dough on blocks of wood. "Can I help?"

"You can slice the veggies if you want," Savannah says with a soft smile.

We work in comfortable silence with the music playing in the background for a few minutes before I remember I need to tell Brody about his school situation. I'm hoping it'll be the first step in defrosting the ice between us. "I spoke to your principal today."

Brody groans.

"The one at Trinity."

This gets his attention.

"He's agreed to let you back in."

"Seriously?"

"Seriously. But you're on academic probation and will have to prove yourself. One slipup and it's over, and you know they'll be watching."

"Hell, yeah! Thanks, Dad!" He stops chopping and looks at me. "I swear I'll behave. No more fights, and I'll get my grades up."

My eyes lock with Savannah, and she nods once. I'm not sure why, but her nonverbal approval gives me hope that I can make things right between Brody and me.

"I can't believe you got me back in! I need to call Ishmael and Sam..."

"You're still grounded," I remind him. "Through the weekend. Monday, we start fresh, and you can use your phone again."

"Alright," Brody agrees easily. "Thanks."

Once we've piled the toppings on the pizzas, Savannah puts them in the oven. Brody goes out to the living room to mess with the TV and add some more songs to the queue while Savannah and I clean up the kitchen.

I'm washing the dishes when my phone rings. I dry off my hands and pull it out of my pocket, silently groaning when I see who it is.

"Paola."

"I received an email from Trinity. Brody's back in?"

"He is."

"Wow, that must've cost a fortune." When I stay silent, she says, "Thank you."

"I did it for him."

"Still, I appreciate it. How's he doing?"

I glance over at him and Savannah debating country versus R&B. Brody must win because a few seconds later, a song that's clearly not country starts to play.

"He's doing good," I tell her truthfully.

Paola sighs. "He hasn't always been like this. It's why I haven't said anything to you. I don't know when it happened or why, but suddenly everything was just spinning out of control."

"It's okay. That's why he has two parents. I'm sorry I haven't been here more, but that's changing now." It sounds like she's sniffling on the other end, but I don't ask her.

"I'm going to be back in town next week. I have an appointment I can't reschedule. I was thinking he could come spend the night. I hate how we left things."

"I'm sure we can figure something out. Do you want to talk to him?"

"I've called and texted him several times, but he hasn't responded."

"He's been grounded from his phone," I explain, even though I know he has it on him. "But he's here with me now."

"At your office?"

"No, we're at a friend of ours having dinner. Hold on, and I'll get him." I walk into the living room. "Brody, your mom wants to talk to you."

That easy smile he's been sporting disappears. "I'm grounded from the phone."

"Not from speaking to your mom." I extend my hand, but he doesn't take it.

"I don't want to talk to her."

Unsure of how to handle the situation, I look at Savannah since she seems to get through to him, but she just frowns, keeping her mouth shut.

"He's busy right now. Can I have him call you later?"

"You mean he doesn't want to talk to me. I could hear everything."

"Yeah... I'll speak to him."

We hang up, and I pocket my phone, letting it go for now. Dinner at Savannah's isn't the place to discuss our family shit— even though he'd probably open up to her before he would me.

While we wait for the pizzas to bake, we discuss everything Savannah wants to see in the city. She's planning to spend the weekend playing tourist before she starts work on Monday. She has her phone out and is taking notes on everything we mention.

"Dad, you know the city better than anyone," Brody says. "We should just show her around."

"Oh, I couldn't ask you guys to give up your weekend."

"We'd love to," I say, shocking the shit out of myself. I hate the city. Sure, it's where I live and grew up, but when you live here, you rarely go anywhere. The city is overpopulated and ridiculously busy.

Her face lights up. "Really?"

"Sure. We're not doing anything this weekend. It'll be fun."

"Cool. What time should we go? After the gym?" She shoots me a playful wink.

"Actually, I go jogging in Bryant Park on Saturdays. You're more than welcome to join."

Savannah cracks up laughing. "Jogging? I'd croak over and die. I think I'll pass. Saturdays are for sleeping in anyway."

"I DON'T KNOW ABOUT THIS." SAVANNAH EYES THE ICE AS BRODY TAKES OFF on his skates like a pro.

We've spent the weekend doing all the cliché touristy shit everyone does here in the city. We went for a walk through Central Park, visiting popular attractions like the Delacorte Theater and the Belvedere Castle. We ate dinner in Times Square and did a little shopping, and then, at Brody's request, we went back to our place to watch a movie—*Batman*, with Christian Bale, of course. Savannah fell asleep halfway through it, and once it was over, and Brody went to bed, I walked her back to her place.

Today has been just as busy. After we had breakfast, we explored several of the museums, shared our favorite bakeries with her, and went up to the observatory deck of the Empire State Building. Now we're in Bryant Park at the ice-skating rink.

If I'm honest, I was dreading playing tourist. When you live in New York, you avoid all the places we've visited. But from the moment we stepped out of the building and began our weekend of showing Savannah around, my tune changed. Savannah was so excited about every damn thing we showed her, I couldn't help but enjoy myself. Her upbeat personality is contagious. She's taken picture after picture everywhere we've stopped, insisting on taking pictures of Brody and me, of Brody and her, and of the three of us.

Of course when she posted a few on social media, tagging me, Lucas made it a point to message me, asking what the hell I was doing and warning me away from Savannah. *"I can't have you fucking my new CFO. My luck, you'll break her heart, and she'll hightail it back to Tennessee."* I messaged him back that it's not like that, but I don't think he believed me.

"I'm going to fall and break my body, and then I won't be able to start work on Monday, and I'll be fired," she whines, making me chuckle.

"I've got you." I step into the rink and turn around. "Take my hands."

She eyes me skeptically for a second before she reaches out and intertwines her glove-covered fingers with mine.

Brody skates by with a couple of his friends he ran into when we got here, yelling for Savannah to get out here and skate.

She forces a smile and nods, then looks back at me. "I'm

going to die... or break something and then die."

"You're not going to die." I tug her toward me. "C'mon."

She flies forward, her legs shaking like a baby deer. "How do you know how to skate?" she asks as I glide backward, pulling her along with me slowly.

"I played hockey growing up. Both Lucas and I did. It's how we became friends. We went to the same school but didn't really know each other until we were put on the same hockey team."

Her gloved hands tremble, and I close the space between us, sliding my hands down to her waist to hold her easier. She moves her hands up to my shoulders, latching on tightly in fear of falling.

"I have you," I murmur.

She nods, focusing on moving her feet while I focus on her—something I've caught myself doing several times this weekend. She's dressed for the cold weather in a fuzzy ivory sweater and tight dark blue jeans that show off her curves. Her hair, which is down and straight, is lighter today, the blond overpowering the brown. Her eyes have a bit of makeup around them, making her blue eyes pop bright like the sky. And her lips... fuck, her lips. Because of the cold weather, she keeps reapplying some lip-gloss shit that makes her mouth look all wet and kissable— and no less than a dozen times today, I've had to stop myself from doing just that.

We do a lap around the rink, and since Savannah has caught on, I turn around so I can skate forward.

"Don't let go," she breathes, grabbing my hand.

"I won't. I promise."

Our eyes meet, and I look away, uncomfortable as hell at the way she's got me feeling. I can't remember the last time I spent an entire day with a woman, let alone a weekend—and completely enjoyed myself.

"It's so cold." She shivers dramatically.

"After we're done skating, we can get some hot chocolate."

Her blue orbs light up at the idea.

As we're turning the bend, Brody decides to be funny and sneak up on us. "Boo!" he yells, doing a skate-by with his friends, who all laugh at his antics. Savannah jumps in shock, losing her balance, but before she can go down, I slip in behind her, wrapping my arms around her torso to steady her.

"Oh my God! You saved my life," she says, sighing into me

in relief. Her backside rubs against the front of me, and I stifle a groan, needing to get off this ice and away from her before I make a move on her—proving Lucas right. And as tempting as it is—and trust me, it is—she's the best thing to happen to my son in a while, and I can't risk it getting awkward if I fuck her.

"I think I'm ready for the hot chocolate now," she says, glancing back at me.

"Sounds good."

We skate to the side, and I help her out of the rink so we can take our skates off. Once we both have our shoes back on, she offers to return the skates while I grab us some drinks. On my way to the café, I spot the igloos, giving me an idea.

"What are you doing?" Savannah asks when she catches up to me. "It's sooo cold!"

"I'm ordering us an igloo."

Her adorable nose scrunches up in confusion. "A what?"

"C'mon. You'll see."

Six

Savannah

 simply let loose and had this much fun. With Neil, everything was about show. If we went out, it was done with a purpose—to meet with a client, to discuss business. Looking back, I can now see where Neil and I went wrong. I wanted a family, a partner, a home. He wanted a trophy wife on his arm to have his babies and make him look good. And as much as I would love to one day have a family, I want it with a man who actually desires that—and not because it will make him look good.

"All right, this way," Ben says, leading us toward an area

filled with... What are those?

"Oh my God, they're igloos!"

"I told you," he says with a chuckle.

He did, but I didn't understand what he meant.

We step into the see-through dome, and I glance around in shock. The area isn't huge, but it's big enough to house four comfy-looking chairs, a table, and a couple of ottomans. It's the coolest thing I've ever seen, and then I realize... "It's heated!" I turn around and look at Ben, who nods.

"It is. And our hot chocolate, apple cider, and dinner have been ordered." He sits in the two-person chair, patting the seat next to him for me to join, so I do.

"Thank you for this weekend. I've had such a good time. The perfect weekend leading up to starting my new job." I never would've thought, after the first day I met him in the gym—all uptight and asshole-y—we'd be sitting here a few days later, in an igloo in Bryant Park, hanging out. But after spending the past few days with him, it's clear there's more to Benjamin Fields than meets the eye—more than he wants people on the outside to see. He's not just a stuffy, cold businessman in an expensive suit. He's a caring, thoughtful man, and despite the rocky start he and Brody had, he's a really good father. And surprisingly, I really enjoy his company.

"You're welcome. It's the least I could do after everything you've done for Brody and me."

"What have I done?" I ask, confused.

Ben laughs under his breath. "Of course you don't realize it..." He shakes his head. "These past few days are the happiest I've seen my son in a while. And the most pleasant. I even found his cigarettes in the garbage this morning. His cursing has decreased, and it's almost as if he doesn't hate the entire world."

"And you think I did that?"

"Yeah, I do," he says, his tone serious. "I don't know what's going on with him and his mom, but he's clearly taken to you during a time when he can use a friend, and I appreciate that."

"You don't have to thank me. He's a great kid. Just a little lost. I saw it many times over the years in foster care."

A gentleman steps inside and sets a carafe of hot chocolate on the table, along with a bowl of marshmallows and some peppermint sticks. Then he brings in a pitcher of apple cider and a plate of chicken tenders with fries and several dipping sauces.

"Thank you," Ben says, pulling out a bill to tip him. Once the gentleman exits, he returns his attention to me. "You grew up in foster care?"

"Yeah." I grab a mug and fill it with hot chocolate, then top it with some marshmallows and drop a peppermint stick inside. "Since my parents couldn't get their act together, choosing drugs over me, I was in and out, starting at seven years old."

"You didn't have any other family?"

"My grandpa on my mom's side tried to help, but he passed away when I was little, and my dad's parents refused to acknowledge us. I have one aunt, but she hated my mom so much, she wouldn't help, so that left me stuck in the system until I aged out at eighteen."

"I thought most get adopted..."

"Some do, but many don't. Kids like me, whose parents refuse to give up custody even though they shouldn't have had kids, nor do they want them, get stuck in foster care. It's like having one foot in and one out. And by the time their rights were revoked, I was no longer a cute kid people wanted to adopt."

Ben nods slowly as if contemplating what he wants to say. I hand him a steaming mug of hot chocolate, and he thanks me. After taking a sip, his eyes lock with mine. "I never wanted to be a dad. My mom always wanted to have kids. She and my dad were high school sweethearts and dated all through high school and college. They were together for almost twelve years before they decided to start a family. They had me and, shortly after, my sister. But after Mom had my sister, something in her changed. She would fight with my dad every day and yell at Amalia and me over everything. As the years went on, it got worse, but my dad refused to get her help. He was in love with her and kept saying things would get better."

I can see it in his face as he looks past me, stuck in his own head, that things didn't get better.

"When I was twelve, she committed suicide." His eyes meet mine. "My sister is the one who found her bleeding out on the floor in her bedroom, knowing we were home. My dad lost his shit and his grip on reality. He lost his job, our house. At one point, we were sleeping in the car. He finally somewhat got it together, got another job, and rented a shoebox-sized apartment. Watching my mom and dad..." He sighs. "I never wanted to have kids. Before she had us, she was perfect. Their relationship, their marriage, their life was perfect."

"You can't possibly blame yourself." It sounds like she might've had postpartum depression or some kind of chemical imbalance. I'm not a doctor, but in foster care, you see so many kids coming and going, all sharing their stories, that you learn about the various diseases that affect people, especially parents.

"I heard my dad say dozens of times she wasn't like that before she had kids." His elbows land on his knees, and he rubs his palms up and down his scruffy face. "I've never told anyone this before."

"You don't have to tell me."

"I need you to understand why my relationship with my son is so strained. Why I'm such a shitty dad."

"You're not a shitty dad."

"You compared his issues to those of kids in foster care." He chuckles self-deprecatingly. "I don't think I'll be winning any parent of the year awards."

"I didn't mean... I just meant I've seen kids lost like him." I try to backtrack, feeling bad for making it sound like Brody comes from the same type of home the other foster kids and I came from. "I wasn't implying that—"

"Stop." He smiles sadly. "I know you weren't trying to put me down or compare me to those other parents. But the fact you can even make the comparison is why I know I need to work on my relationship with my son." He sighs and shakes his head. "I just hope it's not too late."

"It's not... It's never too late." For years, I wished my parents would get their act together and come for me. Even when I was old enough to know better.

He nods and takes a sip of his drink. When he sets it down, he releases a harsh breath. "Paola and I started dating our freshman year of college. I told her from the get-go that I didn't want to have kids. I made it clear I had no intention of ever starting a family. I was up front because I knew, for most women, a man not wanting to have kids is a deal breaker. She told me she was okay with that, but apparently, she thought it was a phase I would grow out of. She swore she was on birth control, but she lied."

Holy shit.

"When Paola told me she was pregnant, I was scared shitless and pissed as fuck that she would deceive me. She showed me the ultrasound picture, and all I could see was our relationship turning into my parents'. The fighting, the name-calling, it turning physical. Her being driven to commit suicide. I couldn't do it. I couldn't put us in that position. I knew if I stayed, it wouldn't be good. I was filled with hate and resentment toward her, so I walked away. And I've been running ever since."

"But you're back now."

"Yeah, and I barely know my son. Fourteen years wasted."

"That's not true," I tell him, remembering some of the stories Brody shared with me when we were talking the other night before his dad arrived. "He loves you and looks up to you. He wants to work with you, run your business together."

"He doesn't like me."

"He's scared you're going to leave."

Ben's gaze connects with mine. "I'm not going anywhere."

"Then tell him that." I take his hands in mine. "And show him."

"Hey!" Brody steps into the tent. "This is so cool. I never knew these existed." His eyes drop down to our hands, and he smirks. "Am I interrupting something?"

"No." I pull my hands away. "Your dad and I were just

talking."

"While holding hands?" He laughs. "I would ask if you're dating, but I know my dad doesn't date."

"Ha-ha, very funny, you little punk." Ben grabs Brody by the neck and ruffles his hair, which provokes Brody into reciprocating.

As I watch the guys roughhouse, glad to see them laughing and joking, I'm thankful for the reminder that Ben is off-limits.

Not that I was planning to pursue him or anything because I'm off-limits as well. Taking a break. Focusing on me. But hearing it is a good reminder that even if I were interested in Ben like that—which I'm not—he's not emotionally available.

Good thing I'm not interested in him that way.

"LET'S WATCH A MOVIE," BRODY SAYS WHEN WE STEP ONTO THE ELEVATOR.

"Not tonight. Savannah starts her first day at work tomorrow. I'm sure she wants a little time to decompress. Plus, you have school tomorrow."

"Fine." Brody pouts.

"We should have dinner tomorrow night," I suggest. "You can tell me how your first day back at school and seeing Sariah went." Sariah is his crush, who he's planning to ask out.

Brody perks up. "All right, cool."

The elevator dings on my floor, but before I get off, I look at Brody and Ben. "Thank you for this weekend."

Matching grins spread across their faces.

"You're welcome," Ben says. "Good luck tomorrow."

Seven

Savannah

"DID YOU SLEEP HERE LAST NIGHT?" A MASCULINE VOICE ASKS, FILLED with humor. I twist around and find Ben walking into the gym, dressed in a pair of gray sweatpants slung low on his hips and a white T-shirt stretched taut across his chest. The sleeves are short enough I'm able to get a peek at the ink on his biceps. It's weird seeing him like this, dressed down and looking all normal. Even when we were hanging out this weekend, he was dressed nice.

"I wish," I tell him as he walks around to the front of the treadmills until he's facing me. "That would imply I actually slept."

He chuckles. "Nervous about your first day?"

"I spent the entire night tossing and turning. When I'd finally fall back asleep, I would get trapped in this horrible nightmare where I was calculating numbers, but every time I got so far, I would lose track and have to start all over again. It was exhausting."

"Sounds like it."

"I finally gave up on sleep and settled on going for a walk."

"I can see that." His gaze descends, and a sexy smirk quirks up in the corner of his mouth. "You're on my treadmill."

"Should've gotten here earlier." I lift my bag of peppermint-and-chocolate-covered pretzels. "Want some?"

"No." Ben snorts out a laugh.

"Whatever. Your loss." I pop a delicious pretzel into my mouth.

"Nice shirt." He raises his brows to his forehead. "Is that a warning I should heed?"

My shirt reads, *Here in the South, we don't hide crazy. We parade it on the front porch & give it a lemonade.*

"I don't know. You planning to do something that brings

out my crazy?" I sass, stepping off the machine. Since I couldn't sleep, I've been walking for a good thirty minutes while drinking my coffee and eating my snack.

I stop at the trash can to throw my garbage away, and Ben joins me. "If you're not too full from your morning snack, want to go to breakfast before work? We can share a cab."

"Wow, you're offering to share a cab *and* buy me breakfast?" I make my eyes go dramatically wide. "Things are getting serious rather quickly. I'm not sure I'm comfortable with this. Will Brody be joining us as a chaperone?"

Ben's mouth stretches into a wide smile that turns my insides to mush. "Brody gets a ride to school since his private school is closer to where his mom lives, so you'll have to settle for just me. But don't worry," he murmurs, his hazel eyes shining with mirth. "I don't do serious, *ever*, so you're safe."

"Hmm..." I tap my lips with my pointer finger in mock contemplation. "I guess I could share a cab with you, and I'm sure in a couple of hours, I'll be hungry again."

Ben chuckles. "I'll pick you up on my way down."

"Sounds good."

When I'm back home, I take an extra-long hot shower, then

focus on doing my hair and makeup until they're both perfect. Afterward, I go through several outfits, finally deciding on a flowy white blouse and black dress pants paired with my favorite Louboutin heels. I'm not a name-brand snob, but Neil was, and he insisted his fiancée—and later wife—be dressed to impress. At the time, I felt bad for letting him purchase such expensive clothes for me, appalled at the ridiculous amounts people spent to clothe themselves, but now... well, at least I have nice clothes at his expense, which means I'll fit in at Sharp. How one looks shouldn't represent how they'll do their job, but maybe looking the part will give me the confidence to get through my first day. Because the truth is, I'm nervous. While I spent years interning at Neil's company and then working for him, this is my first real job, and I want to succeed.

I'm checking myself out in the mirror one last time when there's a knock on the door. Since Ben told me he'd pick me up on the way down, I grab my purse so he doesn't have to wait, but when I swing the door open, I find not one but two guys standing at my door.

On the left is Ben, dressed in his crisp expensive gray suit that looks like it was tailored for him, and to the right of him is Brody, dressed in a pair of navy-blue dress slacks and a white button-up shirt with a blue, white, and maroon vest, complete with a matching tie. And in his hands is a... "Why do you have a plant?"

Both guys laugh.

"It's for your office," Brody says, handing it to me. "For good luck."

I take the plant from him and hold it close to my chest as Ben takes over. "It's a money plant. The guy at the store said it's supposed to enhance the energy of wealth. And since you deal with money..."

"You bought me a plant?" I choke out, suddenly filled with raw emotion. "For good luck?"

They both nod in unison, looking at me like I'm borderline crazy.

"Nobody's ever bought me flowers... or a plant before," I explain. "Thank you." I pull Brody into a hug and then Ben. "This means a lot to me."

My eyes sting with unshed tears, but I keep them at bay, not wanting to scare the guys away. I've learned over the years that men hate women who cry.

"I hope you have a wonderful first day back at school," I tell Brody a few minutes later as he steps into the hired car.

"Thanks. See you tonight." He looks at his dad. "Thank you again for getting me back in."

Ben nods once. "Have a good day."

Once he's gone, Ben snags us a cab. We stop in at the deli to have breakfast and coffee and then head into the building.

"You look nervous," Ben says, handing me my plant. Being the gentleman he is, he held it for me while we were walking so I could finish my coffee.

"I am. I want to be great, and this is all I have left. If I'm not great at this, then..." My words trail off, and Ben lifts my chin with his thumb and forefinger.

"You're going to be great. But remember it's your first day, so you'll probably be a little overwhelmed, and if you're not great today, it's okay."

His words relax me slightly. "Thank you."

The moment I step off the elevator, I'm met by David, who greets me with a smile. We spend the first part of the morning going over my job in detail as well as the expectations, and the second half is spent in what he calls the Monday morning meeting. Apparently, once I get the hang of things, I'll be running it for the accounting department. Everyone is warm and welcoming, and the morning flies by. Before I know it, it's after noon, I'm in my office running numbers, and my stomach is rumbling.

I'm about to ask Florence, the accounting department's secretary, if she knows of anywhere good to eat when there's a knock on my open door.

I glance up and find Ben standing in the doorway with a brown bag dangling from his fingers. My stomach tightens, but I push the feeling away. "Figured you might be hungry," he says with a small smile. "I brought Greek."

"I was just about to attempt to find somewhere to eat," I tell him, standing to greet him.

"Whenever I get busy with work, I forget to eat." He walks over to the table and sets the food down. "How's it going?"

"Really good." I sit while he dishes out the food. It all smells delicious and has my belly growling in want. "I was a little worried because the company I used to work at was owned by my ex-father-in-law and ex-husband, and both of them were horrible, and then the other day when I ran into your meeting..."

He chuckles. "So, you were scared every company comes with an egotistical, cold-hearted asshole?"

I shrug. "If it's worth anything, you're different outside of your boardroom."

He nods. "I'm not always like that. I was having a bad moment. I bought my team breakfast this morning to apologize." He pops open a can of sweet tea and hands it to me. "So, you were married?"

"Yeah. Stupid decision on my part. We're divorced now. It's the reason I moved here. For a fresh start."

"Savannah, I'm going to grab—" David pokes his head in, and when he sees Ben, he stops his train of thought and grins. "Oh, I'm sorry. I didn't realize you had a lunch date." He steps in, and Ben stands to shake David's hand, but he's pulled into a hug instead. "I heard you were back."

"I am. It's good to see you."

"You, too. How's your dad? I haven't seen him at the club lately, and he's missed the past few men's nights."

Benjamin frowns. "Really? He wasn't with you this weekend?"

David's brow furrows. "No... Did he say he was?"

"I must've misunderstood him," Ben mutters, but his tone conveys something is wrong.

"I'm leaving on a business trip tomorrow, but when I get back, we'll have to do dinner."

"Sounds good," Ben says. "I'm sure Brody will love to see you."

David laughs. "That's right. I heard from Lucas he's living with you. How's he doing?"

"He is." Ben's face lights up. "He's doing better. Was going through a rough patch, but I think we're getting through it." His eyes land on mine, and the corners of his lips spread into a sexy smile, making my heart beat faster.

"Good, good. I'm sure he's no worse than you and Lucas were at his age." David chuckles and glances at me. "It was a full-time job just to keep those boys out of trouble and in school." He clasps his hand on Ben's shoulder. "I'll let you two eat your lunch. I wanted to make sure Savannah was settling in okay and taking a break for lunch. But I can see she's in good hands." He turns his attention to me. "In case I don't see you before you leave today, Lucas and Brianne will be back in tomorrow, as I'm sure you know, so if you need anything while I'm gone, let them know."

"Thank you," I tell him. "Have a good trip."

Once he's gone, Benjamin and I continue our lunch, but he feels off, sort of distant. He's not rude, but his mind is clearly elsewhere. When his phone goes off with a text, he doesn't even notice until I point it out to him.

"It's Brody," he says. "The football coach invited him to join the team for practice after school, so he wants to know if he can stay."

"That's good. He said he wanted to play, and if I recall, participation requires good grades."

He nods absently, typing on his phone. "Yeah. I told him he could." He collects the trash and shoves it into the bag.

"Thank you again for lunch," I tell him as I walk him to the door.

"You're welcome. Enjoy the rest of your day."

He saunters out of the office with a confident swagger most couldn't pull off, and I can't help but notice all the women—and even some of the men—stare.

I spend the rest of the afternoon learning the ropes, and

when five o'clock comes, I shoot Ben a message asking if he wants to share a cab home. We exchanged numbers the day I took Brody with me in case of an emergency, but I haven't used it until now.

A few seconds later, a text comes through.

Ben: It'll be late before Brody gets home, so I'll probably stay and get some work in. Rain check?

Me: Sure. Have a good night.

When I get home, I rinse off and change into some comfy pajamas. I'm about to find a menu and order in when there's a knock on the door. Peeking through the peephole, I see Brody and Ben on the other side, and I can't help the butterflies that flutter in the pit of my belly as I swing open the door.

"What are you guys doing here?"

Brody steps in with Ben following. "Dad didn't realize practice only goes until five."

"We brought dinner," Ben adds. "Hope you're in the mood for tacos."

"Um, always."

"Perfect." Brody grins. "I can't wait to tell you about my day!"

We sit at the table, and Ben doles out tacos to each of us while Brody grabs us drinks.

"Did you see Sariah?" I ask, taking a bite of my delicious taco.

"I did." He beams, chomping on his food. "I asked her out, and she said yes."

Ben pats him on the shoulder. "That's awesome."

"Thanks." Brody glances at Ben and then me. "How was your guys' day?"

Ben goes first, telling us about his day, and my heart swells in my chest as it hits me that this is the first time I've experienced this—everyone coming together after a day of school and work to eat and talk and laugh. Neil and I never did this. He worked late, and I usually ate alone. My foster families had too many people, so we ate in shifts. My parents were too drugged up to even remember to feed me. But here with Ben and Brody, I imagine this is what a family does—

"Savannah, you okay?" Ben asks, shaking me from my thoughts. He and Brody are both looking at me with worry etched in their features, and it's then I realize, without meaning to, I've teared up.

"Yeah, sorry." I laugh softly, grabbing a napkin to dab at my eyes. "I'm just..." *I'm thankful to have met you, I enjoy spending time with you, your company makes me feel warm inside, and for the first time in my life, I don't feel alone.* "I just had a really good day."

Eight

Benjamin

Dad: Sorry. Headed out of town for a few days. Last-minute appointment.

I'M STARING AT THE MESSENGER APP ON MY COMPUTER, CONFUSED ABOUT what emergency Dad has that would justify canceling our bi-weekly meeting for the third time. When I got a notification the meeting was canceled, I checked with his secretary. She told me it's not on his calendar, which means it's not related to Fields Enterprises. Something feels off, and it's starting to grate on my nerves. My dad knows I don't do secrets and have zero tolerance for lying. He lied about how bad off Mom was for years, and she ended up taking her own life. I won't allow lies and secrets to worm their way into my business and destroy it from the inside out.

"Holy shit, I thought for sure when I returned, you'd be gone."

I glance up from my dad's cryptic message and lazily raise a hand to flip off Lucas. "I told you I'm back for good." I click out of the messenger app. *I'll deal with my dad when he returns.*

Lucas undoes the buttons of his suit jacket and drops into the seat on the other side of my desk, lacing his fingers together behind his head. "Yeah, but after almost fifteen years of you being gone, you can't blame me for being skeptical." He smirks, showing off his annoying two-dimpled grin that he swears is half the reason the ladies can't deny him. The other reason, according to him, is his big dick. I can't confirm whether it's true, nor do I have any desire to.

"I fucked up, but I'm fixing it."

"Good." Lucas nods, sitting up. "It's Tuesday... Poker night at my place, if you want to join."

"Hell yeah, I'm in." I always join whenever I'm in town. The weekly tradition started in high school. Our dads are good poker players and taught us how to play when we were younger. We were looking to make some extra cash—for me—and saw on a movie where some guys hosted a poker night and charged an entry fee. We took everyone for what they were worth, and so the tradition began. Every week, we would all play in Lucas's pool house with a hundred-dollar minimum buy-in. During the years my dad was checked out, it was how I got the money to buy us food—that and Lucas would raid his pantry and fridge for anything his dad wouldn't notice was missing. We continued to play during college until I dropped out, Paola got pregnant, and then I ran. But Lucas continued the tradition over the years. Only now, the stakes are higher since we're all rich as fuck and have nothing better to blow our money on.

"I saw the city gave you the green light."

"Yeah, about damn time." I lean back in my chair. "I also looked at the revised plans you sent over. I have a few minor changes I want to discuss, but aside from that, it all looks good."

"Sounds good." I expect him to excuse himself to go back to his own office since it's his first day back and he's as much of a workaholic as I am, so when a small grin spreads across his face, I know he came here for another reason that has nothing to do with poker or architecture.

"What?"

"Nothing." He shrugs.

"Sharp, get to whatever point you came here for. I have shit to do."

Lucas chuckles. "How was your weekend playing tourist with a certain blonde?"

"Fine."

"Despite my warning, you guys seemed pretty damn close."

"Are we gossiping like teenage girls now?"

Lucas laughs. "Does that mean there's something to gossip about?"

"No. We're friends. No need for a second warning," I say dryly.

Another laugh. "Friends? Since when do *you* have friends who are girls?"

I don't bother to argue because I wouldn't have a case. I don't have friends who are girls because I don't trust women. More often than not, they tend to have ulterior motives. They expect you to read their minds and then get pissed when you can't. They play games, aren't up front and honest about what they want, and I don't have time or the inclination for that nonsense, which is why I have no desire to settle down. I have a business to run and now a son who needs me.

But Savannah... She's different, but I don't know why. I can't quite put my finger on it. Maybe it's the way she is with Brody. The way she's connected with him. We spent the entire weekend together, and I should've been ready to walk away from her. She should've done something, said something to piss me off, but instead, yesterday morning, I was dragging my son out to buy her a goddamn plant, then making plans for dinner. Hell, this morning when I ran into her at the gym, I asked her to come over for dinner again, offering to feed her since she's been feeding us.

"She's different." When Lucas's brow hits the top of his forehead, I immediately wish I could take my words back. "She's been really good to Brody," I explain, trying to backpedal. I ramble on for several minutes about the shit Brody gave his mom and me, how he's taken to Savannah, and how, in such a short time, he's done a complete one-eighty, all while hoping Lucas will buy what I'm saying and not ask questions. Because if I'm honest, I don't have the answers. I don't do serious, but I can't get Savannah off my mind. And it's not just her gorgeous body or beautiful smile, or her sexy Southern accent, or the way she always seems to say what's on her mind, calling me out on my shit. It's more... Fuck, I'm screwed.

"So, you're really just friends," he says once I'm done speaking.

"Yep, just friends."

I can see the wheels turning in my best friend's head, but thankfully, before he can argue or ask questions, there's a knock on my door.

"Come in!" I call out, assuming it's my assistant.

The door opens, and *not my assistant* saunters in wearing a long-sleeved dress—the top half black and white polka-dotted, and the bottom half straight black with a belt that sits just below her tits—that covers the majority of her upper body, yet shows off every delicious curve. My gaze drags down her tanned thighs and lands on her tall heels that make her legs look long and toned. When I rode to work with her this morning, she was wrapped up in a black overcoat, hiding what was underneath.

She's carrying a bag in one hand, drinks in another, and

wears a bright smile. But when she realizes I'm not alone, she stops in her place, her lips curving into a soft frown. "I'm sorry. I didn't realize you were in a meeting. Your assistant said you were free…"

At her words, Lucas swivels around. "Savy?"

"Lucas," she says with a sincere smile.

Lucas stands and approaches her. "It's nice to finally meet you." *They've never met?*

"You too." She sets the drinks on the table so she can properly shake his hand while I get up and head over to them, taking the bag from her and setting it on the table.

"What are you doing here?" Lucas's tone is casual even though he's digging.

As if suddenly remembering he's her boss, her blue eyes widen slightly. "Oh, umm…" She darts her gaze back and forth between us before settling on him. "I'm on my lunch break. I wrote down the time like we're supposed to, and I'll be back in—"

"Whoa, whoa, it's okay," he says, cutting her off. "I wasn't questioning you. I was just asking what you were doing *here*."

"Oh." She sighs in relief. "I'm having lunch with Ben."

"*Ben*," he repeats, humor in his tone.

"Savannah doesn't know anyone," I explain, "so I stopped by yesterday with lunch, and she insisted on returning the favor today."

"That's very *friendly* of him." Lucas stretches out the word friendly like the asshole he is.

"There's plenty if you want to join us," she offers, her voice cracking a bit.

"Thank you, but I have to head into the office and play catch-up, and then I'm meeting Laura for a late lunch. I was just stopping by to welcome *Ben* home." Laura is his girlfriend of two years.

Savannah nods. "Is Bri back too? I haven't heard from her today."

"She is, but she's in a meeting. We wrapped up sooner than planned and took an earlier flight, so she rescheduled an appointment. I'm sure she'll be by to see you later. She's excited to have you here. Wouldn't stop talking about it all week."

Savannah laughs softly. "I'm very happy to be here. It hasn't even been two days, but I love it at Sharp. Everyone is extremely helpful and friendly."

Good," he says. "Enjoy your lunch. We'll talk later."

He turns on his heel and walks over to me. *"Friend, my ass,"* he mouths as his hand lands on my shoulder. "See you tonight," he says out loud.

Once he's gone, Savannah releases a loud sigh. "That was..." She trails off, trying to figure out what to say.

"Lucas," I finish.

"Huh?" She raises a single brow.

"That was typical Lucas." I open the bag and take out the cartons of food. "He thinks because we hung out and you posted some pics on social media, something is going on between us."

I keep my eyes trained on her face to gauge her reaction, but she doesn't give shit away as she says, "I'm sorry. I should've asked you if it was okay to post pictures. I didn't even—"

"Stop." I wave her off. "It's all good. Lucas has recently gotten serious with his on-again, off-again girlfriend, so now he thinks he has the right to play matchmaker. He wants everyone to be as happy as he is." I roll my eyes. "Between him and my sister, they're determined to make me join the Hitched Club. He saw those pictures of us and tried to make something out of nothing." I wait to see what her response is—if she'll hint that she wouldn't mind making something out of nothing—not that I would... But at least if she tries to wrangle me in somehow, I can cut the strings before she attempts to tie a knot.

Savannah opens the boxes and pushes one toward me, the smell of chicken lo mein filling my senses. "Oh, I know all about *that* club. I terminated my membership and have zero desire to reinstate it." Either she's a damn good liar, or she really doesn't see me like that because she genuinely sounds like she means it.

She twists the top of her sweet tea and gulps down a large sip before she continues. "Besides, I've only been around you for like a week, and even I know you're not the *getting hitched* type."

Her statement should make me happy. It's exactly what I wanted to hear. She knows the score and accepts it. We're friends and nothing more.

Then why the hell do her words make me want to defend myself?

"You know my reasons," I say instead. "But what are yours? What has you running from commitment when most women are running full speed toward it?"

"Been there, done that." She takes a bite of her food and swallows it down with a sip of her sweet tea. "Met my now ex-husband while I was in college. I was interning at the company his father owns. We dated for a short time, and then he proposed. We were married right after I graduated."

She exhales a deep breath, mentally preparing herself for whatever she's about to say next. "I was blinded by my desire to have that whole happily ever after and didn't see how selfish he was. That he didn't love *me* but loved the *idea* of having a trophy wife on his arm. He thought a woman's place was barefoot and pregnant, supporting her husband."

She smiles sadly. "When I couldn't be what he needed, he found someone who could. And the worst part? It was my best friend."

What an asshole. I've only known Savannah for a short time, but even I can see the amazing person she is. She's someone you dote on and cherish. If she were mine, I'd—

Fuck, nope, not going there. She's not mine, nor will she ever be.

"Just because he was a piece of shit doesn't mean every other guy is."

"True, but growing up, I had the worst home life. I would dream of that elusive family. The husband and kids and career and home… I think I need a break from those dreams. I have a fresh start, a career that most would dream of. I live in a beautiful apartment and have friends like Bri…"

"And Brody and me," I add.

"Yes." She smiles her first sincere smile since she started telling me about her ex-husband. "I have a lot to be thankful for, and maybe it's not the way I dreamed it, but it's mine. So I just want to focus on those things for a while. Maybe one day…" She clears her throat, and it seems like there's more she wants to say but doesn't. "Enough about me." She changes the subject. "Tell me, what are you cooking for me tonight?"

"Do you ever stop eating?" I joke. "You're eating and asking what I'm going to feed you next."

She shrugs. "It's all those workouts. They burn a lot of calories."

I chuckle. "Must be… Who said I'm cooking? Maybe I'm planning to order in."

"Oh, no… You said, and I quote, 'It's our turn to make you dinner.'" She points her finger at me. "There better be homemade food there."

Nine

Savannah

wrap her slender arms around me. "You're still here!"

"Of course I'm still here."

"I was so scared you would be here alone and second-guess your decision, and then I'd come home, and you'd be gone."

"You're crazy," I say through a laugh. "I'm not going anywhere." Besides, where the hell else would I go?

Brianne releases me, taking my hand and guiding me over to the couch. "Okay, spill. I let you get away with your vagueness while I was gone because I couldn't corner you over the phone, but now I'm back, and I want all the deets."

"About what?" I ask dumbly, knowing she's referring to my time spent with Brody and Ben. When Brianne gives me a look that says, *you know what*, I sigh. "We're just friends, so please don't make this more than it is. I enjoy their company, and if everyone tries to push us together, I'm afraid Ben'll push me away."

"Fine." She rolls her eyes. "Any plans tonight? The guys are playing poker, and Marcus will be there. Will you be my wingwoman, pleeaasssse?"

Marcus is Lucas's friend and Brianne's secret crush, but he doesn't even so much as look at her, let alone return her feelings.

"I'm having dinner with Ben and Brody."

She smirks saucily. "After... Lucas said Ben will be there."

"Oh." He never mentioned it. "Well, I guess..."

"Great!" She claps her hands together. "How's it going?" She glances around the office. "Need anything?"

"Nope. It's going great. Sharp uses the same program as Everton, so the transition so far has been smooth. Your dad is so sweet, and I met your brother in person today while I was having lunch with Ben. He told me he'd be by to check on me."

The two times I visited New York, Lucas was out of town, and when Brianne and I graduated, we walked at separate times because our majors were different. She invited me to dinner with her family to celebrate, but Neil insisted we go to dinner with his family instead. So, while I've met Lucas plenty of times through video chat while he and Brianne were chatting, and once during the interview, I hadn't met him in person.

"Good." She nods. "But if you need anything, I'm here." She leans over and hugs me tight. "I'm so glad you're here."

"WOW, THIS IS DELICIOUS!" I TAKE A BITE OF THE SPAGHETTI AND MEATBALLS Ben and Brody made. Ben texted me that he had to leave early for an appointment and to come over at six o'clock for dinner, so when I showed up after work, I thought for sure they would have ordered in. So I was delightfully shocked when I found the table set with salad and garlic bread to start, along with a bottle of wine.

Both guys nod as they shovel food into their mouths and

refuse to meet my eyes... weird. We eat for a few minutes in silence until Ben's phone rings. He glances at it and groans. It stops and then starts again.

"She won't stop until I answer." He sets his fork down and picks it up. "Paola..." He's quiet for a moment before he looks at Brody, who doesn't look back at him. "Okay, we're having dinner right now... Yes, dinner... Let me ask, and I'll call you after." He hangs up and goes back to eating, not saying another word.

"How was your day?" I ask Brody to make conversation.

"Good. Football practice about killed me, but Coach says I'm a natural, and if I keep playing the way I am, I'll be starting."

I don't know much about football, but starting sounds promising. "What position do you play?" Not that I would know what he did if he told me.

"QB." He shovels a forkful of food into his mouth.

"Quarterback," Ben clarifies. "He throws the ball, and another guy catches it."

"Thank you," I say with a laugh. "I was trying to pretend I had a clue, but I don't think I've ever even seen a game."

"What?" Brody asks. "Didn't you go to UT? Their college

team is the shit!"

"Language," Ben chides.

"I was, um..." Warmth creeps up my cheeks. "I was kind of a math nerd." I shrug. "I was on the math team and spent more hours than not tutoring others."

"So, no sports?" Brody asks.

"Nope."

"Parties?"

"Not really."

"How did you become friends with Brianne?" Ben chuckles. "I'm almost positive Lucas joked she majored in partying."

I nod and laugh, taking a sip of my crisp wine. "That's not far from the truth. She was my dormmate, and we hit it off. I guess it's true when they say opposites attract. Speaking of which... She's dragging me to poker tonight. She mentioned you're going."

"I am. It's been a while." He glances at Brody. "You okay with me going to Lucas's for a few hours?"

"I don't care," Brody says. "I'm not a baby. I've been left alone plenty, and he only lives one floor down."

"I know... Just checking." Brody takes a large gulp of his

wine. "Your mom will be back in town tomorrow."

"Yeah, she texted me."

"Which you ignored... She wants to know if you can come by and spend some time with her, maybe spend the night."

Brody's fork stills. "I have school during the week and football and homework."

My heart cracks, seeing the sadness in his eyes. At some point, they're going to have to all talk. From the comments he's made, I don't think the issue is with his mom but her fiancé. Since it's not my business, I keep my mouth shut, enjoying the dinner they made.

Ben looks like he wants to push Brody, but then he sighs. "All right, maybe this weekend. Ted's out of town, so it's just her at the house until Sunday. Then she's flying back out to meet him."

Brody nods his okay, then goes back to eating his food.

"What if instead of Brody going over there, you guys go out to dinner?" I suggest, going against my previous thought to keep my mouth shut.

Ben glares, but Brody's face brightens. "Will you go too?" Brody asks. "Please?"

"Oh, umm…" I glance at Ben to save me, but he just smirks, as if saying I walked into that one all on my own. When I look at Brody, he's eyeing me as if waiting for me to say no and let him down. "Sure. If she's okay with it."

"Cool," Brody says, snatching up his now empty plate.

"Dishes," Ben calls out as he walks away.

"I'll do them," I offer. "You guys cooked. It's the least I can do."

Ben clears his throat. "No, you're the guest. We got it."

Taking my plate up to the sink, I stop at the trash can to dump the little bit of remaining scraps into it. As I'm pressing my foot on the pedal to pop the top to the garbage, both guys yell, "Wait!" But it's too late. The open lid has exposed their lie.

"Seriously?" I accuse through a laugh, lifting the disposable aluminum dish. "You ordered food and pretended you cooked it?" Ben looks at me sheepishly while Brody cracks up laughing. "You both owe me a home-cooked meal!"

"THAT'S WHAT YOU'RE WEARING?" BRIANNE SCRUNCHES UP HER NOSE AT my jeans and hoodie combo paired with my favorite comfy UGGs.

"What? It's cold out, and I was in heels all day."

She sighs. "There are going to be good-looking guys there, Savy."

"So?"

"So, you need to move forward."

"Bri," I warn. "I'm going as *your* wingwoman. That's it. And I'm only staying for a little while, so whatever you need me to *wing* better happen quickly."

She rolls her eyes, returning back to her mirror so she can finish putting her makeup on. Once she's done, we head upstairs to Lucas's apartment, where the poker night is happening. When we arrive, a group of guys is sitting around a large circular table, drinking and laughing, with cards in their hands. I look around and count five guys total, all good-looking, just as Brianne mentioned.

"Geez," I mutter under my breath, making Brianne laugh.

"Told you. Hot guys flock together."

"Does that include your brother?" I joke.

She crinkles her nose. "I don't see him like that, but you

can't deny he isn't ugly."

"What are you doing here?" Lucas asks, glancing over at us, repeating the same question he asked me earlier today. Great... not off to the best start with my new boss. First, I'm hanging out with his best friend, and now I'm crashing his poker night.

"Hello to you too," Brianne snarks, walking over and hugging the one other woman who's here. "Savy, this is Laura, the saint who puts up with my brother. This is Savy, my best friend from college and—"

"And the new CFO of Sharp," Laura finishes. "It's nice to meet you. I've heard wonderful things about you from Lucas."

"Thanks," I mumble, glaring at Brianne. How did I not think about the fact that coming here meant hanging out with my boss?

"Oh my God, stop!" Brianne scolds. "Lucas, your annoying attitude is scaring Savy. Tell her it's okay to be here."

Lucas's face softens. "It's okay to be here."

"Damn right it is," Ben says. "Drinks are in the kitchen." He shoots me a playful wink before going back to his card game.

"Which one is Marcus?" I ask Brianne once we're in the kitchen, and she's mixing us each a Jack and Coke.

"The one on the right of Ben. The other two are Ian and Scott. Ian owns an investment firm, and Scott's a divorce attorney. Both single." She waggles her brows.

When I glance behind us to check them out, my eyes land on Ben instead. He's laughing as he slams his cards on the table and claims the chips as the other guys give him shit.

As if he can sense me staring, his gaze ascends, and he locks eyes with mine. His lips quirk into a soft smile, and butterflies that have no business residing in my belly spread their wings and fly.

"Oh my fucking God!" Brianne shrieks, making me jump.

"What?" I wait with bated breath for her to call me out on the way I'm reacting to Ben, but instead, she turns her phone around so I can read what's on the screen.

It's a picture of Lois and Neil with their hands on her stomach. The caption reads: **Baby on board! #16weeks**

Lois is pregnant... with Neil's baby. And based on how far along she is, he knocked her up while we were still married. I stare at the picture of the two of them. Lois is smiling at the camera, looking as if she's just won the lottery. But Neil... he doesn't look like a man in love at all. No, he looks like a man who cheated on his wife and mistakenly got his mistress pregnant and has to make it right.

And now the rushed divorce makes sense. He's from a Catholic family. It was one reason he pushed for us to get married—said his mother would be disappointed if we were living together out of wedlock. I'd bet his parents found out about Lois being pregnant and threatened his life and job if he didn't make it right. His parents are all about appearances. Although, anyone with a brain will be able to do the math and know she got pregnant while he was married to me.

I click on the next photo, and it's of the ultrasound. My hand instinctively goes to my stomach, and my heart clenches in my chest. When Neil insisted that we try for a baby right away, and month after month, I found myself unable to conceive, Lois was there. I cried to her, worried something was wrong with me. And when I had a feeling my husband was cheating on me, she's the person I whispered my fears to.

After over a year of not getting pregnant, the doctor didn't have any answers as to why I couldn't conceive and referred us to a fertility specialist. The next day, I found out Neil was cheating on me, so I didn't bother following up. I guess between me refusing to stay home and not giving him the family he so desperately wanted, he replaced me with someone he thought would be better suited to meet his needs. In hindsight, it was a good thing I couldn't get pregnant because had I succeeded, I would be stuck in a loveless, controlling marriage with a cheating husband and a baby. But it still hurts to know she could get pregnant so easily while I'm... broken.

"Hey," Brianne says, knocking me from my thoughts. "You're not seriously upset about them, are you?" And then, as if the light bulb in her head clicks, her face falls, remembering every time I cried to her over the phone. "Shit." She pulls me into a hug. "Your time will come."

"Maybe." I shrug. But based on Lois being pregnant, it obviously wasn't Neil who was the problem—it was... *is* me.

"No, not maybe. It'll happen. You dodged a bullet, Savy. That guy is a grade A douche. That kid is so fucked with the two of them as parents."

I laugh under my breath at her attempt to lighten the mood.

"You know what you need, right?" She backs up and raises a single brow. "To get laid." Her face lights up as if her answer is the cure to world hunger.

Typically, this is when I would argue with her and tell her that's not who I am, but as I stare at my lying and cheating ex-husband and ex-best friend on the screen, I can't help but think maybe she's right. As I was growing up, my world revolved around my parents—trying to be the perfect daughter so they would want me. And when nothing I did made them want to keep me, I focused on trying to make a foster family want to adopt me—which of course never happened.

Next came school. I worked my entire way through college to create a future for myself. I was the model student, afraid if I slipped, I would end up failing and be on the streets. And then there was Neil—my entire sham of a marriage was all about him—his wants, his needs, his desires.

I've been so focused on everyone else, I never focused on *me*. I made it through the years with my parents and in foster care, I graduated college and have the job of my dreams, I'm living in a beautiful home with my best friend in the city that doesn't sleep, and I'm single.

"You know I'm right," Brianne says with a knowing grin. "What you need is to find some hot guy to have some no-strings, no-emotions sex with. A few mind-blowing orgasms, and you'll be saying, 'Neil who?'"

Before I can respond and tell her I'm already over him, a deep throat clears behind me. When I spin around, Ben stands there with his cup in his hand, his gaze searing into me. "Needed a refill." He holds up his glass while his eyes remain on me as if Brianne isn't right next to me.

"Friday night," Brianne continues, refusing to be deterred. "We can hit up a club."

"Bri!" Laura shouts. "Where's my drink?"

"Coming!" Brianne yells back, snagging her phone from me and pocketing it before grabbing two of the drinks she made and heading out of the kitchen. "Friday night, Sav, it's on!"

"What was that all about?" Ben asks once Brianne is gone.

"Like you didn't hear." I roll my eyes playfully.

"I was just wondering if I heard her *correctly*." The corner of his lips quirks into a sexy smirk. "You looking for some no-strings sex, Savannah?" The way my name rolls off his tongue sends a shiver down my spine.

"What if I am?" I volley, trying like hell to come across as nonchalant while knowing full well I'm playing with fire. Ben is the type of man who picks up the gauntlet when it's dropped.

And his next statement proves me right. "Then I'll tell you if stringless orgasms are what you want, you don't need to leave this building to have them."

I pop a brow, silently asking him to clarify while I swallow thickly at the thought of Ben pleasing me over and over again.

He sets his cup down and backs me against the counter, one of his hands landing on the countertop next to me and the other on the curve of my hip. His breath is warm against my face as he murmurs, "You already know I have no desire to commit, and I have no doubt that the number of orgasms I could give you would have you forgetting about that asshole ex of yours."

His tongue runs across the seam of his lips, and my brain turns hazy, imagining his tongue on my body... until his phone rings. He pulls it out and frowns, taking a step back.

"Brody, you okay?" His son's name on his lips clears the fog from my sex-filled head. Ben is Brody's dad. My friend. My neighbor. He's best friends with my boss. Brianne was right. I do need to get laid, but not by him. He might not do commitment, but with everyone we're linked to, he's the definition of strings.

"I'm actually with her. Let me ask." Ben looks at me. "Can

you do dinner Friday night?" It takes me a second to understand what he's asking, and then it clicks. I agreed to go to dinner with Brody, Ben, and Paola.

"Umm, yeah, sure... I can do dinner."

"Did you hear her?" he says to Brody. With him momentarily distracted, I skirt past him, grabbing my drink and heading for the exit. "Okay, I'll be home in a couple of hours." Before I can make it out of the kitchen, strong hands grip my hips and spin me around, backing me up against the fridge.

"No," I blurt out before Ben can say a word.

"No?" He says the word as if he's never heard it before, and I'm sure he hasn't. He's a beyond good-looking, wealthy man. I'd bet women throw themselves at him all the time.

"No," I repeat, my tone firm. "We're friends, neighbors... I care about your son. There are already strings. So, no. No stringless sex."

He opens his mouth to argue, but before he can, I duck under his arm and run out of the room to safety.

Ten

Benjamin

SHE SAID NO. I OFFERED HER STRINGLESS, UNEMOTIONAL, ENDLESS orgasms—just like she wants—and Savannah Cartwright flat out said no. It's been three days since she looked me in the eyes and told me no, and I can't stop thinking about it. Of course, she lightened the blow by mentioning all the reasons the sex wouldn't be stringless, and her reasons make sense. I'd already thought about those same reasons when I considered making a move on her. We do live in the same building, we have become friends—good friends actually—and she has gotten close with my son. But when I heard them discussing their plan to find

Savannah a guy to get her laid, all those reasons went out the window because even though I know I shouldn't, I want her. In my bed, screaming my name. But her turning me down is for the best.

At least that's what I keep telling myself.

I thought after our conversation, Savannah would pull back, but every morning she's been at the gym working out—*if you can call it that.* We haven't ridden to work together since Brianne got back to town because they've been going in together. But we've had dinner both nights with Brody at our place, and the entire time, she acted like I didn't proposition her with sex, and she didn't tell me no. Hell, she even stayed after dinner and watched a movie with us last night.

Now, we're at Three Amigos, Brody's favorite Mexican restaurant, waiting for his mom to arrive for dinner, and I can't take my eyes off her as she talks to Brody about his day. I can tell he's nervous about meeting with his mom, but Savannah keeps him talking and laughing. She's good at making people feel comfortable around her.

We're going out after dinner tonight to Lush. I insisted we go there since the women want to go out, and I offered to show

Savannah my club. She'll have no problem picking up a stranger to fuck. She's beautiful, sweet, genuine… She'll have guys lining up a mile away, and unless I can come up with a good reason to stop it from happening, there's not a damn thing I can do.

"What do you think?" Brody asks.

"Huh?" It's then I realize I've spaced out, staring at and thinking about Savannah.

"Can we take Savy skiing? She's never been." His face lights up in excitement. Fuck, how the hell did I go all these years without this kid in my life full-time? I might've been running from Paola, but really the only one who was affected and hurt was Brody and me. I can't take back the past fourteen years, but I'll make damn sure all the years coming up count.

"Yeah, for sure," I tell him. "That'll be fun."

We're discussing the different places we can go when Paola arrives. To be cordial, I stand and give her a hug before introducing Savannah as Brody's and my friend. Paola looks like she wants to ask questions but wisely doesn't. Instead, she shakes Savannah's hand and then gives Brody a hug.

"How are you?" she asks, sitting next to him.

"I'm good," he says softly—very unlike him. Aside from the

day I picked him up from his mom's, this is the first time in years we've all been together. When Brody was younger, they were close, and it seemed they remained close as he got older, so I was shocked when she told me how bad things have gotten. He's started to see a therapist, and although he's only gone to one appointment so far, it seems like it went well. I don't know what they talked about since it's about Brody, but he seems to like the guy, so that's good.

"How's school?" she prompts, wanting to catch up.

"Good." The kid was talking up a storm before she got here, but now it's like he's shut down.

As if sensing the same thing as me, Savannah jumps in. "Tell her about football."

Brody's gaze goes to Savannah, and he grins, his face full of pride. "Coach says I have a good chance at starting QB."

"What's that?" Paola asks.

As Brody explains the ins and outs of football, his mom gives him her complete attention. Savannah and I stay quiet, only adding to the conversation when Brody includes us. We order dinner, and the conversation switches from sports, to school, to the girl Brody's dating—which in teen speak means they meet by her locker in the morning, and he walks her to class. By the time dinner is over, Brody's a lot more comfortable with his mom, so much so that when she asks if he'll spend the weekend with her, he agrees.

"She seems nice," Savannah says when we get into the Uber I called for.

"Yeah. Thank you for coming."

"Of course. Brody is awesome. It was my pleasure."

"What time did you want to head to Lush?" I ask once we arrive and are in the elevator.

"I'll text you once we're ready," she says as the elevator doors open, and she steps out. I consider grabbing her by her hand and pulling her back in, begging her not to do this, to go back to my place with me and let me take care of her, but I don't do any of that. Instead, as the doors close, I watch as she walks down the hall, praying for the strength to get through tonight. It's for the best, I tell myself. But even I don't believe a word I'm saying.

"HOLY SHIT," MARCUS CURSES, MAKING ME LOOK AROUND TO SEE WHAT has his attention. We're standing in the lobby of the building, waiting for the women to come down. Since a bunch of us are going out tonight, I ordered a Navigator to take us and pick us up so we wouldn't have to deal with snagging several cars.

My eyes follow Marcus's line of vision, landing on the three women walking our way. Brianne and Laura look beautiful, but Savannah has my attention.

With her honey-blond hair down in waves, her face full of makeup that makes her blue eyes pop, and her lips looking fucking edible, she's a far cry from the woman—in her southern shirts and work attire—I've come to know.

Her dress is a glittery silver number with chains for straps and a plunging neckline that exposes her ample cleavage. The dress stops short, with slits on both sides, showing off her toned thighs, with her tall black heels that have me imagining what it would be like to fuck her while wearing only those.

As she takes her coat from over her arm and puts it on, hiding her sexy as hell body, her eyes momentarily lock with mine. She smiles sweetly before looking at Brianne and throwing her head back in laughter at whatever she's just said to her.

"Fucking hell," Marcus mutters under his breath. I know he isn't looking at Laura since she's with Lucas, so that only leaves Savannah and Brianne.

"Savannah is off-limits," I tell him point-blank, not giving a shit that it makes me sound like a caveman.

"Oh yeah? You calling dibs?" He laughs, knowing damn well I wouldn't do that. For one, I'm not in high school, and two, I haven't *claimed* a woman since Paola.

"She's off-limits," I repeat, refusing to give him anything more.

"Got it, but she isn't who I'm looking at... Although, I kind of wish I was. You're a scary bastard, but if I'm honest, I'm more scared of Lucas."

Hold up. "You like Brianne?"

"What's not to like? Look at her." He nods toward the women who are almost over to us. "I've tried to push her away, but I don't know if I have it in me to resist anymore."

"You're both grown adults. Just tell Lucas." Marcus isn't the type to fuck over a woman, so if he's saying he likes her, I'm sure he has good intentions.

"Tell Lucas what?" Lucas asks, stepping over to us.

"Uh..." Marcus stammers like a fucking teenager. "That your girlfriend is walking over."

Lucas glances at Marcus, ready to call him out on his bullshit, but then Laura wraps her arms around him, and he forgets the conversation as he tells her she looks beautiful.

When Savannah makes her way over, I grab her hand and pull her toward me, not giving a shit at the look of shock on her face. "You look gorgeous," I tell her, kissing her cheek.

We pile into the SUV, and twenty minutes later, we arrive at Lush and are seen to the VIP section I had Val book for me. The club's two levels are sectioned off into different areas. On the first floor is an upscale restaurant and bar as well as a lounge. On the second floor is a nightclub, but unlike most clubs, Lush is chiller and more laid-back. The music isn't as loud, isn't thumping as hard, and it doesn't play the garbage most clubs play. Big names such as The Chainsmokers, Calvin Harris, and JB have performed at several of my clubs. The cost for VIP is over a hundred dollars a person, and bottles start at four figures, going up as high as six. People know that when they come to Lush, they're getting a high-class experience only a few other places can provide.

When the bottle-service girl—Nadine—who's been assigned to us, comes over to take our order, I ask Savannah what she drinks.

"I don't know!" She laughs. "This place is too fancy for this Southern girl. I doubt you'd even have what I drink."

"Nonsense," I tell her, pulling her into my side. "We have anything you want."

"Umm…" She averts her gaze to think, then looks up at me. "I like Grey Goose."

Out of the corner of my eye, I notice Nadine scrunches up her nose at the mention of the cheap vodka, but when I raise a single brow, she smooths her features.

"Grey Goose for the ladies," I tell Nadine, not giving a shit about anything other than giving Savannah what she wants. Most women would rattle off a bottle way more expensive just because she knows she can but not Savannah. She's as real as it gets. "And a bottle of Macallan 25 as well," I add because there's no way I'm drinking that shit.

Nadine smirks at the difference in prices between the two bottles before she quickly schools her features *again* and scurries away to put in our order.

"What's Macallan?" Savannah asks as I guide us over to one of the couches in our section to have a seat.

"Damn good whiskey."

While we wait for the drinks to arrive, some of Brianne's friends show up, along with a couple of Lucas's and my friends. Introductions are made, and then a few minutes later, Nadine returns with the bottles and glasses, asking everyone which bottle they'd like so she can pour the drinks.

"To great friends and even greater women," Lucas says, raising his glass and locking eyes with his girlfriend. Everyone agrees and clinks glasses before downing their drinks. It's been a while since I've drunk, but the whiskey flows smoothly down my throat.

A few more friends of Brianne's join our table while everyone talks and drinks. Eventually, the women make their way to the dance floor while the guys stay put.

I sit back and watch as Savannah dances with Brianne to the beat of the music. At some point, she lifts her hair on top of her head and turns her back to me, and I damn near choke on my drink. From the front, she's gorgeous, but from the back...

fuck. The chains holding her dress up wrap around her slim neck, leaving her entire back on display, and the material picks up again at the top of her ass. She's stunning, and I'm positive, before long, some asshole will be hitting on her.

The guys bullshit about various topics, catching up on sports and business. I keep half my attention on their conversation while keeping an eye on Savannah, watching as she lets loose. The women eventually come back for another drink and then head back out to continue their dancing.

My restraint is about gone, and I'm considering joining Savannah on the dance floor when it happens... a guy approaches her. I wait with bated breath for her to tell him no, but instead, she extends her hand and allows him to guide her away from her friends and over to the VIP bar. Fuck, he's buying her a drink. She doesn't need a drink, but of course she doesn't tell him that. I can't see what she orders, but a minute later, the bartender hands her a glass. She turns toward him, her body way too fucking close to his, and smiles, no doubt thanking him.

"You going to let him slide in on your woman?" Marcus says.

"She's not my woman." I grab my drink and drain it in one fell swoop.

But fuck if I don't want her to be.

Eleven

Savannah

the gentleman in front of me. His name is Dexter, and he's a CEO of some big company that he's spent the past twenty minutes bragging about while I nurse the disgusting drink he bought me. He insisted on buying it for me after I told him I was drinking Grey Goose, telling me we could do better than that.

He hasn't once asked me anything about myself, and if his self-involved personality is any indication as to how he'd be in bed, I'd be better off using a toy than counting on him to give me a single orgasm, let alone countless ones.

"I think I see my friend calling me over," I say to him when his mouth stops moving long enough for me to get a word in. "But, um, thanks for the drink." He opens his mouth back up to say something, but before he can get a word out, my back is to him—and I've left my drink on the bar top.

I'm searching for my party when another gentleman stops me.

"Are you here alone?" he asks, his Spanish accent on the strong side.

"I'm here with some friends."

"Can I buy you a drink?"

I'm about to tell him no thanks—been there, done that—when my eyes land on Ben. He's sitting in the same spot with his glass of whiskey in his hand and his gaze locked on me, drinking me in and waiting for me to fail so he can swoop in and seduce me. *Not going to happen...*

"Sure," I tell the guy, plastering a fake smile on my face.

He grins and places his palm on my back, guiding me back over to the bar where I just left Dexter. Thankfully, there's no sign of him. The bartender—the same one who took Dexter's order—comes over and raises a single brow as if silently judging me.

"Two glasses of your finest champagne," the gentleman requests, not even bothering to ask me what I want. Seriously, what is up with these men thinking the key to a woman's pants is through expensive alcohol?

Once she disappears, he turns his attention on me. "I'm Javier."

"I'm Savannah."

"A beautiful name for a beautiful woman," he says, laying it on thick.

We stand in silence while we wait for our drinks, and I use that time to assess Javier. He's a good-looking man with inky black hair and tanned skin, but the way he carries himself is kind of... stuffy. His face is freshly shaven, and he's dressed in a pin-striped suit complete with a tie and a watch that all scream, "I'm loaded."

My gaze flicks over to Ben, who's still sitting... and watching. Tonight, he's dressed in a suit as well, but unlike Javier's stuffy one, his gives off an *I don't give a fuck* vibe. His gray pants are sexy casual, and as soon as we got here, he shed his jacket, leaving him in only a white dress shirt, sans tie, with the top few buttons undone, exposing a small spattering of chest hair. As he sits back in his seat with his ankle crossed over his knee, his sleeves are now rolled up, showing off his ink. He scrubs his few-days-old scruff with his palm, his eyes never leaving me.

It's not that I don't want him. I do. But I'm also happy for the first time, and he and his son are a part of the reason for that. When I first met him, I thought he was some stuffy asshole, but he quickly shed those tough layers and showed me the real Ben he keeps hidden underneath. And that man is someone I enjoy having in my life. I look forward to our lunch dates and dinner plans with Brody. He's become someone I can talk to and have a good time with. Crossing that line with him will only complicate things, and is it really worth it for a few minutes of sex?

"Here you are." Javier hands me a glass. "To meeting new people," he toasts. We spend the next several minutes at the bar while he tells me about himself. By the time I finish my glass of champagne—which I must admit is delicious—I'm bored out of my mind. If I'm going to meet someone, I think I'm going to need to be a bit tipsier because doing this sober sucks.

"Would you like to dance?" Javier asks, gesturing toward the dance floor. I run my eyes over him again, trying to imagine this going anywhere, but I can't. Because he isn't who I want... not by a long shot.

"No, I'm sorry, I don't," I tell him, not wanting to lead him on further. "It was nice talking to you, though. And thank you for the drink."

His brows furrow, but he doesn't argue as I give him a small smile and then walk back toward my friends. Brianne spots me walking over, and I catch the pitying look on her face.

"Another dud?" she asks, obviously having seen me talking to the guy before him.

"Why are men so egotistical?" I grab the bottle of Grey Goose and pour myself a shot, quickly throwing it back, then pour another one and down that one just as fast. "They both couldn't stop bragging about themselves long enough to even ask me about myself." I roll my eyes. "I was already married to one selfish asshole. There's no way I'm wasting my time on another. I'd rather get drunk and Savy myself."

Brianne cracks up laughing, understanding the *One Tree Hill* reference—we spent countless hours watching reruns of it in our dorm—but Ben gives me a confused look, so I explain.

"It means to pleasure myself."

His eyes fill with mirth. "Now that's something I'd like to see."

"Of course you would because it would mean not having to do anything!" I huff, taking my annoyance out on him. "Typical man. Would rather watch a woman please herself than do it himself."

Ben's gaze burns a hole into me, but I ignore him because I'm on a roll.

"I'm over it," I announce, pouring myself another shot, ready to drink it down. "I'm oh for two in the men department tonight, and I'm not sure my liver can take much more."

I raise my glass, toasting the air—because I'm obviously tipsier than I thought I was—but before I can down it, Ben stands and grabs my drink, dropping it onto the table. I stare at him in shock for a quick beat before he takes my hand in his and drags me away from the table, up a hidden set of stairs, and through a door marked PRIVATE.

When we enter what looks like an office, he swipes the papers off the desk and sets me on it.

"Ben," I breathe, meeting his lust-filled eyes. "We can't go there..."

"We definitely can," he argues. "You want no-strings sex, and I want to have sex with you. It's that easy."

I shake my head, trying to remember my argument, but one of his hands is now gliding up my thigh, making it hard to think clearly. He grips my legs and spreads them wide, stepping between them.

"Ben," I groan when he pushes my hair to the side and places soft kisses along my neck. "Nothing about us would be stringless."

"Savy," he murmurs into my ear. He's never used my nickname before, and the way he says it is such a turn-on. "I promise you, no strings." He sucks on my earlobe, causing my entire body to shiver in anticipation.

"I'm serious. I... I can't do commitment. I already did that with Neil and—"

He pulls back slightly to meet my eyes and presses his finger over my lips to silence me. "I'm a man of my word, and the only thing I'm committed to is making you come... several times if you'll let me."

His last words are my breaking point, and before I can second-guess myself, I'm fisting the front of his shirt and pulling him toward me for a desperate, needy kiss. He tastes like expensive whiskey, and I find myself sucking on his tongue, wanting to get drunk off him.

He moans into my mouth before he pulls back, gripping my nape and exposing my neck. He slowly trails open-mouthed kisses along my overheated flesh, stopping with each one to suckle on my skin. When he draws a full-body shiver out of me, he chuckles lightly.

"Stand," he demands, stepping back. I find myself pouting when his touch leaves me, but I do as he says, completely under his spell.

"Turn around."

Again, without question, I follow his command, turning on my heel to face his desk. He steps behind me and dusts my hair to the side. Then he unclasps the chain straps holding my dress up and unwinds it from around my neck. When he unzips the bottom half—since nothing is holding it up anymore—it drops to the floor, making a clanking sound. Because the dress is revealing, I'm left in only my heels and a tiny black thong.

Ben groans under his breath as he runs his palms across my shoulders and sides, over the swells of my ass, and then down the backs of my thighs. When he reaches my ankles, he has me lift each foot, so he can pick up my scrap of a dress off the floor. "Now, put your hands on the desk."

My palms hit the top of the sleek wood, forcing me to bend slightly due to the height of my heels. I'm completely on display for Ben, but I don't care because when I glance back through my lashes, the look on his face is pure unadulterated lust, and at this moment, I've never felt sexier. He could have any woman he wants, but he wants me.

"Fuck, Savy. Do you have any idea what the sight of you like this does to me?" He doesn't wait for a response—and it's a good thing because I have no idea how to respond to that— before he closes the space between us. He plants a kiss on my shoulder as he spreads my legs with his thigh. His hand glides up my back, pushing my shoulders down until I'm flush with the desk. My ass is in the air, my breasts are smooshed against the cold, hard wood, and my legs are open for him.

Since he's put me in the perfect position to fuck me, I'm expecting him to do just that—get right to it—so I'm confused when his touch disappears momentarily and then reappears between the apex of my legs. *He must want to make sure I'm wet first...*

But I dart my eyes behind me and find him on his knees. I can't see what he's doing, but his lips kiss my left butt cheek and then my right. His fingers slide under the thin material and enter me with ease, causing me to release a groan I attempt to muffle.

"No way. Nobody can hear you. I want to hear every noise, every scream when I make you fucking come."

My thighs clench at his words, and he chuckles softly, going back to what he was doing. He pumps his fingers in and out of me, and this time, when I moan, I don't hold back, enjoying the feel of him. He peppers kisses across the globes of my ass, then pulls his fingers out and tugs my panties down my legs, helping me step out of them. A second later, my legs are widened, and his hot, wet tongue slides across the seam of my center. My forehead hits the hard wood, and I moan in pleasure.

With languorous strokes, he licks me from back to front. I can feel my arousal dripping down the insides of my thighs, but I just don't have it in me to care. His tongue feels too damn good. He adds his fingers back to the mix, hitting something deep inside me, building up the most delicious orgasm, and within seconds, I detonate around his fingers and tongue. My pussy clenches, my body trembles, but Ben doesn't stop until I'm begging him to, telling him it's too much and that it feels too good.

"Fuck, yes," he growls, turning me around and crashing his mouth to mine. Our tongues mingle, and I taste myself on him. I just came, but the scent of me on him has me wanting more. My fingers find the buttons of his shirt, and with shaky hands, I undo each one until they're all separated, and I can remove his shirt. Without breaking our kiss, I find the button to his pants next and pop it open, unzipping his fly.

As if the sound snaps him out of whatever trance he's in, he breaks our kiss and shakes his head. "No, this is about you."

"But—"

"Multiple orgasms," he murmurs against my lips. "Now, how about while I work on making you come for a second time, you play with those pretty tits since I won't be able to?"

Before I can argue, he lifts me onto the desk, spreads my legs, and then drops back onto his knees. He spreads my lips apart, and his tongue lands directly on my clit.

"Oh, God," I breathe as my eyes roll to the ceiling. The vibration of Ben chuckling while he sucks on my clit sends sparks through my body, and I find myself doing as he asked—grabbing my breasts and rolling my nipples between my thumbs and forefingers.

My climax is already on the precipice, and when he glances up and sees what I'm doing, his tongue still licking my clit, the heat in his gaze sends me over the edge. My elbows hit the desk, my eyes closing—black specks of pleasure blurring my vision—and if the music wasn't thumping through the place, I'm positive everyone would hear me coming undone.

When I reopen my eyes, I find Ben standing over me with a satisfied smirk on his face. With his shirt off, I take a second to appreciate his body. I knew he worked out daily, but holy shit, he's a sight. With a chiseled chest and rock-hard abs, I mentally pout that I won't get the chance to explore every inch of him more closely.

"I say we go for one more," he deadpans, his eyes trailing my body as if trying to decide how to accomplish the task.

"Only if it's with your dick inside me."

"Not tonight. You've had too much to drink."

"Yes, tonight," I argue, refusing to accept what he's saying. I'm a grown-ass woman and capable of making my own decisions.

I grab his pants and pull him toward me. "I need you to fuck me right now," I demand, yanking his hard as steel dick out of its confines. There's no way I'm ending this night, this one time with Ben, without him fucking me.

I stroke his shaft a few times before he groans and gives in, grabbing my ankles and yanking me to the edge of the desk. In one hard thrust, he enters me and bottoms out, making us both groan.

"Wrap those gorgeous legs around me," he growls, his palms smacking against the wood on either side of me. I do what he says just in time because, in the next second, he's fucking me fast and deep, and had my legs not been linked together, holding me to him, the force of his thrust would've damn near sent me flying.

My arms snake around his neck, my nails digging into his back as our mouths connect once again. Ben kisses the way he fucks—passionately and thoroughly, giving me every ounce of himself.

All too soon, a climax I'm not sure I'm capable of experiencing pushes to the surface, and with one final drive into me, I'm soaring high with Ben following.

As I come down from my orgasm, I know I'll never be able to be with Ben again. Three mind-blowing orgasms and I'm already addicted. There's no way we're ever doing this again.

No strings, my ass. He might be able to keep things stringless, but I have no doubt if I have another night like tonight, I'll be asking him to marry me and make me come every damn day for the rest of my life.

Twelve

Benjamin

FOR THE THIRD DAY IN A ROW, I STEP INTO THE EMPTY GYM. NO SAVANNAH on the treadmill, wearing her cheesy-ass shirts, drinking her coffee while eating her crap food. On Saturday, before I went for my run, I stopped in during her usual workout time to see her, only to find the place empty. I chalked it up to her wanting to sleep in. We were out late, and she did have a good amount to drink. Later that day, after Brody got back from his mom's, he texted her asking if she wanted to go bowling with us, but she said she wasn't feeling well.

I thought for sure I would see her yesterday. She might not

actually work out while she's at the gym, but she's been down there every day... until now apparently, because once again, the gym was empty. When Brody asked her to join us for dinner and a movie, and she said she still wasn't feeling well and needed to catch up on work, I knew something didn't sound right, but I let it go.

But now it's Monday, and she's once again not here. Something tells me she's avoiding me—though, I'm not sure why. When we parted ways Friday night, she didn't seem like anything was wrong—quite the opposite actually. She was sated from the multiple orgasms I gave her and had a blissed-out smile on her face the rest of the night. After we cleaned up and met our friends back at the table, we drank and danced until the early morning.

Brianne shocked the hell out of her brother by leaving with Marcus and, after saying bye to everyone, Lucas, Laura, Savannah, and I took the SUV back to our place. I walked her to her door, and after a kiss good night, I told her I would see her tomorrow. Everything in me wanted to ask her back to my place or worm my way into hers, but since she looked exhausted and mentioned passing out as soon as she rinsed off,

I didn't push it.

Now I'm wondering what the hell happened, or if I did something to upset her. I know damn well she enjoyed herself, and she definitely got off several times. Those screams of pleasure couldn't be faked, and neither could the way her cunt squeezed my dick as she came for the third time.

I attempt to work out, but I can't stop thinking about Savannah the entire time. The woman drives me nuts, stealing my treadmill every damn day, yet when she isn't here, I miss her.

Fuck. No, I don't miss her. I'm worried. Yeah, I'm worried something could be wrong. Because that's what friends do. They worry and care. She mentioned not feeling well on more than one occasion. Maybe she really is sick but didn't want to make a big deal about it. Did Brianne even come home this weekend? For all I know, Savannah could've been home all weekend alone, sick in bed with no one there for her.

When I can't stand another minute of not knowing what's going on with her, I turn off the treadmill and head back upstairs to take a shower and get dressed so I can catch her before she leaves for work—if she's even going. If she's sick, she might still be in bed, in need of medical attention.

Brody is dressed and ready for school, sitting at the table eating his breakfast when I come out dressed for work. "I'll be right back," I tell him as I head out the door and straight to the elevator.

When I get to Savannah's place, I knock several times, but there's no answer. Dammit. I knock again, but when there's still no answer, I go back up to my place, finding Brody still eating and staring at his phone.

"Have you talked to Savy?" I ask nonchalantly as I grab a muffin and join him at the table.

He looks up from his phone and raises a brow. "Since when do you call her Savy?"

"I didn't—" Shit, he's right. I called her Savy. I shake my head. "Have you talked to Savannah?"

"Not since yesterday." He goes back to watching whatever stupid videos he's watching on his phone—that are undoubtedly killing his brain cells by the dozen.

"Do you have practice after school?"

"Yep," he answers, not bothering to look up.

"Want to order in dinner and watch a movie afterward?"

"Sure." He still doesn't look up.

"You should invite Savannah."

"All right."

"Text her now," I urge. "Before she makes other plans."

I eat my muffin in silence, waiting to see if she responds. His phone vibrates a few minutes later, and then he looks up at me, wearing a scowl on his face. "Something going on with you two?"

"No," I scoff.

"Really?" He turns his phone around for me to see. "First, she bails on bowling, then on dinner... Now, when I ask her to join us for dinner tonight, she tells me she'll be stuck at the office late. Dammit, Dad, what did you do?"

"Don't speak to me like that. And I didn't do anything." But even to my own ears, I can hear the guilt in my words.

"Yeah, right," he mutters. "I gotta go. Whatever you did, fix it." He hits me with a pointed glare before slinging his backpack over his shoulder and stalking out of the house.

Damn, why does it feel like I've just been reprimanded by my damn teenage son? Oh, right, because I was.

I consider texting Savannah but figure it's probably best

to just show up unannounced. That way, if she's avoiding me, she won't have a chance to run. I have my Monday morning meeting, and I'm meeting my dad for lunch since he's back in town, but afterward, I'll head over to her office.

"SON, HOW ARE YOU?" MY DAD ASKS, SITTING ACROSS FROM ME AT THE table in my office. I give him a once-over and note that he looks tired. He's getting up there in age, and I wonder if maybe life is catching up with him. He's close to retirement age. I don't want to throw that out there and risk offending him, so I store it away for later when I can broach the subject without it coming across like I want to push him out. I would never do that to my dad. He's the only parent I have left, and he's been through hell.

After Amalia and I lost our mom, I thought for sure we'd also lose our dad. We watched him hit rock bottom, and it was a hard, long journey to help him get back on his feet. He's told me on numerous occasions his family and work are all he has left, so I wouldn't want to take that from him, but if it means taking the stress off his shoulders, I'll do what I have to do to keep my dad around as long as possible.

"I'm good." I hand him his sub and drink from Rosario's, our favorite sub shop that's been around since my father was a kid. "Brody seems to be back on track. He's back at his school and is playing football. He spent the night at his mom's Friday night, and it seemed to go well. We went bowling Saturday, and he kicked my ass." I chuckle, remembering the way he rubbed it in my face every time he rolled a strike.

My dad smiles, but it seems forced, and that has me worried. "I'm glad to see you home and in his life. He needs you."

"Yeah, he does. And I need him." I never realized how much so until recently. Now I can't imagine him not being in my life. "I fucked up, and I'm lucky he's making it easy for me to make shit right."

Dad nods. "I'm happy for you."

"How did your trip go?" I ask, still having no clue where he went and why.

"Good," is all he gives me.

"Was it for Fields?"

"Uh, no. Just a personal trip." When he doesn't say anything more, I consider pressing him on the subject, but then his phone rings, and he tells me he needs to get it. I expect him to take the call, but instead, he gathers up his food and drink and stands. "I'm going to take this in my office. Let's do dinner soon, all of us."

Confused, I stand as well. "Dad, is everything okay?"

Without answering my question, he pulls me into a hug. "I love you, Benjamin. I know I don't tell you enough, but I'm so proud of you. I fucked up when you were growing up. I didn't get your mom the help she needed, but instead of you and your sister letting it keep you down, you both soared."

"Dad," I choke out, worried as fuck. "If something's going on..."

"It's nothing I can't handle," he assures me. "You focus on that boy of yours, you hear me? I got this." And without giving me a chance to argue, he walks out the door.

Since my meetings are done for the day, I finish eating, then let my assistant know I'm heading out and not to call unless it's important. I take the elevator down to Sharp and go straight to accounting. Savannah's secretary is at her desk, and when she sees me, she lets me know that Savannah is alone, and

I can go right in. If she knew Savannah was avoiding me, she probably would've had a different answer.

I walk in without knocking and find Savannah at her desk, eating a sandwich while typing on her computer. She glances up, then does a double take, her eyes going wide when she realizes it's me. I close and lock the door behind me so we're not disturbed, then walk over to her desk and drop into the guest chair.

"Glad to see you've recovered." When her brows pinch together, I shake my head. "You know... because you were sick."

She swallows thickly. "I—"

"Save the lie. We both know you weren't sick, so you want to explain the real reason you blew Brody off all weekend?" Yeah, I'm hitting her with a guilt trip. You gotta use what you got. And she may be avoiding me, but she has a soft spot for my son.

Her face falls. "It's not that... You know I care about Brody."

"Then what is it?" I lean forward and shoot her a hard look that hopefully conveys I won't tolerate being lied to.

She closes her eyes for a moment, inhaling a deep breath before she releases a harsh exhale, reopening her eyes. "I needed some time alone to get my head on straight."

"Because of what happened between us Friday night?"

"Because while I was under the influence, I made reckless decisions."

"You're a grown adult, Savannah. I'd hardly call what we did reckless. People do it all the time."

"Do they also have unprotected sex while not on any type of birth control?" she asks, raising a brow.

It takes several seconds for her words to sink in, but once they do, I damn near lose my shit because holy fuck, we had sex without a condom.

I never have sex without a condom. Ever. Not since Paola tricked me into impregnating her.

This can't be right...

She has to be confused. She'd been drinking and...

I stand, my heart thrumming in my chest, and pace the room, trying to recall the details from Friday night. Unlike Savannah, I had barely drunk anything. A couple of glasses at most. My mind goes back to us in the office.

The clothes coming off.

The orgasms.

Her begging me to fuck her.

Me telling her no.

Me giving in.

I not only had sex with her without a condom, but I also came inside her.

My eyes land on her midsection that's hidden behind her desk. I fucked up, and I only have myself to blame. She didn't force me or trick me. I willingly fucked her bare.

"I'm clean," she says, mistaking the reason for my look of panic. "My husband was the last man I slept with without a condom, and after I found out he was cheating on me, I was thoroughly tested."

"I was... I've never..." I stammer, unable to finish a damn thought. Fuck! I had sex without a condom.

I stop in place and look at her. "*I always* use protection."

"I'm sure you do," she says dryly.

"I'm serious." I step over to her. "I'm always careful. I can't believe..."

"It was both our responsibility," she says. "Like I said, I made reckless choices Friday night, and I needed time to sort through my head. I wasn't avoiding you... I just..." She shrugs.

"I've scheduled an appointment with my gynecologist."

"Are you pregnant?" I blurt out, my eyes dropping back down to her stomach, which is stupid since it's only been a few days. Even if she is pregnant, she wouldn't be showing yet. Hell, I don't even think they can tell this early.

"Probably not," she says, and if I'm not mistaken, she almost sounds sad. "But I'll find out for sure in a couple of weeks. Either I'll get my period or the doctor will run a test."

My skin goes clammy, my insides turning ice-cold. There's a chance she could be pregnant. We only had unprotected sex once, so she's probably not, but there's still a possibility. It only takes one time.

"Look," she says softly. "I know you're freaking out, but the chances of me being pregnant are slim." She averts her gaze over my shoulder, and I notice her eyes are now glassy. "Neil and I tried to conceive for well over a year and couldn't. Then he got my ex-best friend pregnant, so I'm almost positive I was the problem."

She blinks several times before she releases a harsh breath. "So, don't worry. You couldn't have fucked up with a better person than me," she chokes out, forcing a watery smile. "I'm broken."

Oh shit. I'm over here freaking out that she might be pregnant, and she's sad that it's most likely not a possibility because she can't get pregnant.

"No." I close the gap between us. "Come here." I pull her up into my arms for a hug, and she lets me. Her face lands against my chest, and I can feel her body shaking with silent sobs. "Shh, it's okay," I murmur. "You're not broken."

She sniffles then backs up, wiping her tears away. "I am, but it is what it is." She shrugs. "We're quite the pair, aren't we?" she says with a humorless laugh. "I'd give anything to be pregnant because it would mean I'm able to be, and you're praying to God that I'm not." She releases a shaky sigh. "If by some chance I am pregnant, I won't ask you for anything, I promise. I knew from the get-go how you felt—"

"Stop," I say, cutting her off. "Do I want to have any more kids? No, I don't. But I was there in that office on Friday night, and I know how it all went down. If you are pregnant, I'll one-hundred-percent be there for you and this baby." And I mean that with every ounce of my being. "I'm not the same boy I was fifteen years ago. I'm not going to run. I am just as responsible, if not more so, for what happened, and I'll be there every step of the way."

Savannah sighs in relief. "I was scared you'd think I tricked you."

"I don't think that at all." Had it been any other woman, I might've jumped to that conclusion, but from the beginning, something about Savannah made me feel at ease. She's not the kind of woman who would trap me into impregnating her.

"Thank you." She laughs softly. "This just got real deep for a Monday afternoon."

She's telling me... I came over here to call her out on avoiding me, only to find out I could be a dad *again*.

"I better get back to work. Please tell Brody I'm not avoiding him, and I'll see him soon."

"You can tell him yourself when you come over for dinner tonight," I find myself saying.

Her eyes widen, clearly shocked by my suggestion.

"Savy." Reaching out, I brush a wayward strand of hair from out of her eyes. "We're friends, and I don't want what happened Friday night to change that. I meant what I said about it being stringless. If we find out you're pregnant, we'll go from there, but nothing needs to change between us until then. Besides," I say with a laugh, remembering my conversation from this morning with my son. "Brody knew you were blowing us off, and he's blaming me. Practically threatened me to fix it."

Savannah's face lights up. "He's a good kid."

"He is. And it would mean a lot to him if you'd come over for dinner tonight so he can see everything is okay."

"All right. I'll see you guys tonight."

When she forces a too bright smile, telling me she's still worried, I lean over and kiss her forehead. "It will all be okay," I promise her. And for some crazy reason, even though I should be freaking the hell out, I actually believe that.

Thirteen

Savannah

"WHERE ARE YOU GOING?" BRIANNE ASKS FROM THE DOORWAY, EYEING ME as I put the finishing touches on my face. I considered going straight to Ben's after work but instead made a detour home first so I could change into something more comfortable, which turned into me rinsing the day off, fixing my hair, and then reapplying my makeup.

I glance in the mirror and note she's dressed in a gorgeous slinky dress, and her hair is done in beach waves. I saw her earlier today, and she wasn't wearing that at work.

"I could ask you the same."

A huge grin spreads across her face. "Marcus asked me to dinner."

"So does that mean I can expect you out all night again?" I ask with a laugh. Since Friday night, when Marcus gave in and admitted to Brianne that he wants her—and told her brother as much—she's been gone more than she's been home.

"If it goes well, I hope so," she replies with a saucy wink. "And where are you going?" she asks again.

"Just over to Ben and Brody's for dinner." I turn around in time to see her brows kiss her forehead.

"What happened to no strings?" Sunday morning when she got home after her weekend sexcapade with Marcus, I told her what happened between Ben and me in the back office— leaving out the part about not using protection. Not everybody needs to know about my lack of brain cells.

"I'm going over as a friend. Brody invited me."

Brianne side-eyes me but doesn't comment. "All right, well, one night with Ben was good, but we need to get you back out—"

"Nope," I say, cutting her off. "That one night was good enough to last me a while." Total lie. That night only has me wanting more—specifically more of Ben—but I'm not going there. "I'm not a one-night stand kind of girl," I admit, not lying. "For right now, I just need to focus on work and me, and if or when the right guy comes around, then he does."

"So, you're *not* opposed to dating?" she asks, confused, and I can see why she would be. The entire reason for my no-strings sex was because I said I didn't want anything serious, but being with Ben made me realize I don't want to have sex with some stranger. At the very least, I want to know and like the person I'm engaging in sexual relations with.

"I think it's safe to say one-night stands aren't my thing."

"Was Ben that bad?" she jokes, making me laugh. "Or that good?" she adds at the last second.

I'm saved by a knock on the door, which has Brianne squealing in excitement. "Have fun at dinner," she says, kissing my cheek. "And don't wait up."

"YOU LOOK BEAUTIFUL," BEN SAYS, OPENING THE DOOR FOR ME. LIKE ME, he's changed out of his work attire and is sporting a pair of navy-blue lounge pants and a white Henley, his feet bare.

"Thank you." I step inside, the smell of something delicious hitting my senses. "Did you guys cook again?" I joke when I see the Japanese food spread out on the table.

"No." Ben chuckles. "I ordered in, and since Brody ended up going to his mom's house to spend the night, there's way too much food."

Wait... "He's not here?"

"I might've forgotten to tell him you agreed to come over," he admits, at least having the decency to look apologetic. "Paola is heading back to Seattle tomorrow, so when he asked if he could spend the night and go to school from her house in the morning, I told him okay, realizing I forgot to tell him you were coming over. I didn't want to make him feel bad or cancel on his mom, so I just left it alone."

"Oh, well, we can just"—I wave my hand in the air—"do this another night."

"No way. We have tons of food. Please, stay."

There *is* a lot of food on that table, and it would be a shame for it to go to waste.

"Okay, sure," I agree, walking over and having a seat at the table. "You got all the good stuff." I grab a pair of chopsticks and load my plate up with some sushi, pad Thai, rice, and shrimp tempura while Ben pours us each a glass of white wine.

"How was your day?" I ask, making conversation as I dip my sushi into the soy sauce.

"It was good," he says with a lazy smile. "Although, I'm not sure my assistant knows what to do with me being at the office all the time. I've been working remotely for so long..." He laughs out loud, and I try and fail to ignore the way his throaty laugh shoots through my veins like the best kind of drug, giving me an instant high.

"Since my team has everything under control, I've been focusing my attention on Artfully Delicious," he adds.

"I bet your sister and her husband are excited."

"Yeah. She loves handling the PR and event planning for Lush, but her passion has always been art." He takes a bite of his food, and I'm so distracted by the way his throat bobs as he swallows, I don't hear what he says next. It must've been a question, though, because he's looking at me as if he's waiting for me to answer.

I nod and shove a mouthful of food into my mouth, hoping

that was the correct answer, but when he throws his head back in a laugh, I know it wasn't.

"I zoned out," I mutter, embarrassed. "What did you ask?"

"I *said* you're staring at me like you want to eat me instead of that sushi."

"You did not!" I fling a piece of rice at him.

"No, I didn't." He leans over and runs the back of his knuckles down my cheek, sending a shiver up my spine. "If you want a repeat of Friday night, all you have to do is say so," he murmurs, taking a sip of his wine.

"Not happening," I say with more force than I feel.

Ben nods in understanding, but the way his gaze heats up feels like a direct contradiction. As we talk about our day, he keeps his eyes locked on mine, only glancing down briefly to see what he's eating. The action feels intimate as if he's so enraptured in our conversation he can't stand to look away for longer than a second. When my glass of wine is empty, he pours me some more, moving closer.

"What is that?" I point at the white strips on his plate.

"Calamari." He picks a piece up with his chopsticks. "Have you ever had any?"

When I shake my head, he brings the piece of food up to my mouth, feeding me a bite. I chew slowly, tasting the meat. It's chewy yet also tender and has a mild flavor to it.

"Good?"

"It's... different."

He chuckles. "It's an acquired taste."

We finish our plates, and then Ben pulls out a box of colored circles. "What is that?"

"You've never had Mochi?"

"Never even heard of it." Tonight is clearly a night for trying new foods.

Ben picks up the pink circle and brings it up to my mouth. "Take a small bite," he instructs when I open my mouth. The circle is cold as my teeth bite down, breaking it apart. Inside is... ice cream, I think. It's strawberry and refreshing. The outside is kind of chewy, but the inside is soft and so good.

"What do you think?" Ben asks, popping the other half into his mouth.

"It's delicious." I finish chewing and swallowing, already glancing into the box to see what other ones he has. When I reach my hand out to grab a white one, he pulls the box back and shakes his head, making me pout.

"Uh-uh." He grabs the white one I was eyeing. "This is vanilla." He brings it up to my lips. "Take a *small* bite."

This time, when I open my mouth, I make it a point to chomp down on his fingers, taking the entire piece of Mochi into my mouth just to mess with him. It's super cold, and the inside of my mouth damn near freezes, but it's worth it when Ben's eyes go wide in shock, making me laugh.

"Now you're gonna get it," he warns just before he flies out of his chair and scoops me into his arms. He takes us over to the couch and drops onto it with me in his lap. "That was my favorite." He tickles my sides as I chew the delicious dessert, laughing so hard my belly hurts.

"Sorry!" I say through a laugh, but because my mouth is full of cold vanilla ice cream, it comes out muffled.

He stops suddenly, his gaze landing on me, and then his mouth collides with mine, his tongue demanding entrance. I part my lips, allowing him access, and he swipes his tongue across mine, moaning into my mouth.

"Mmm," he murmurs against my lips, "my favorite." I open my eyes and find his already open, staring at me with his intention clear.

"Ben," I breathe. "We can't do this."

"Why not? We want each other... We both know the score. Wouldn't you rather be with someone you know than with some strange guy you have no idea about?"

I nod in agreement. That's exactly what I was talking to Brianne about earlier, but...

"I'm scared of getting attached," I admit. "Of mixing sex with emotions."

"I'll remind you every day that you can't get attached to me. That I'm not the guy for you. I promise you, Savy. You're safe to have your no-strings sex with me. And then, when you're ready to give that whole family plan a go again, I'll let you go so you can find the man you're meant to spend your life with."

He makes it sound so simple, so easy. And maybe for him it is, but for me... I don't know if I'm capable of this. Of not getting attached.

But then he drags his tongue across the seam of his lips, and I let my hormones, instead of my head, do the talking. Because my lady parts, they're begging for Ben, begging me to throw caution to the wind and, for the first time, live a little.

No analyzing, no planning, just having some fun.

His hazel eyes bore into mine, begging me to say yes, and before my head can talk my hormones out of it, I pull Ben to me for a hard kiss, silently communicating my decision. He pulls back slightly, raising a brow. "You sure?"

"Yes, I want you. Just... please, don't let me get attached."

"Not a problem," he growls, lifting me so I'm now straddling his lap. Because I'm in a jersey dress, when my legs land on either side of him, my center rubs against his hard length. I moan into his mouth, the friction of his sweatpants and dick turning me on.

In one fell swoop, Ben removes my dress, leaving me in only my bra and panties. He reaches behind me and unclasps my bra, sliding the straps over my arms and then tossing it to the side.

He cups one of my breasts in his large hand, and his lips latch onto my nipple, bringing the hardened peak into his mouth and between his teeth. When he bites down, scraping my sensitive flesh, the mixture of pleasure and pain damn near send me over the edge. I've never come like this, but based on the way my body is humming, I almost think it's possible.

When he does it again, this time rougher, I grind my pelvis against his, making him groan.

"I need you inside me," I beg, not caring how desperate and needy I sound.

"Nuh-uh," he murmurs, releasing my breast and taking the other into his hand. "We have the place to ourselves and nowhere else to be. I'm going to enjoy every single inch of you."

He picks me up and walks us to his room, laying me out on the middle of his bed. With one hand, he reaches behind and pulls his shirt off, and I take a second to appreciate the sight in front of me. He pulls his pants down, leaving himself in only a pair of black Calvin's, and joins me on the bed.

Spreading my thighs, he drags himself between them and wastes no time exploring my body. He nips and sucks and kisses along my breasts, across my torso, and down the apex of my legs until he gets to my center, where he eats me like *I'm* his dessert. I come loud and hard, tugging on his hair and begging for him to fuck me.

Thankfully, Ben is thinking straight because Lord knows my brain is hazy from my orgasm. He grabs a condom from his bedside drawer, rolling it over his dick before he climbs on top of me and enters me in one fluid motion.

His lips brush mine, and his fingers tangle in my hair as he fucks me. It's different from the other night, though. It's not hard or fast. It's slow and methodical. He takes his time, hitting all the right places deep within me until we're both flying off the edge together.

After we're done cleaning up, Ben pulls me back into his bed, wrapping his arms around me from behind.

"Should I go?" I murmur, unsure of the protocol when you have stringless sex with someone who isn't a stranger.

"No." He tugs me closer so my back is flush with his front. "You should stay right here."

With two mind-blowing orgasms at the end of a long Monday, I sigh into his embrace without arguing. But as my eyes flutter closed, I can't help but wonder if maybe I'm making a huge mistake because as Ben holds me in his arms, it feels an awful lot like strings are holding us together.

Fourteen

Benjamin

MY ALARM GOES OFF PROMPTLY AT SIX, AND I QUICKLY SHUT IT OFF. HALF-asleep, I reach over to pull Savannah to me and consider skipping the gym in place of a better way to get some cardio in, only to find she's gone and the sheets where she was sleeping have gone cold. Hoping she's still here, I search my entire condo without luck, then shoot her a text, asking if she's okay since she apparently skipped out sometime last night after we fell asleep.

When she doesn't respond, I throw on my workout clothes and head down to the gym. She hasn't been down in a few days, but now that we're talking again, maybe she'll be here. I walk in, and sure enough, she's on the quiet treadmill with a coffee in her hand and earbuds in her ears, no doubt jamming out to some country song.

Either she doesn't notice me walk in or she's ignoring me, so I walk around the back, checking out her peach of an ass in the tiny purple cotton shorts she's wearing. She's in her usual UGGs—today's color gray—and walking at a snail's pace.

I step onto the treadmill, wrapping my arms around her from behind in a sneak attack, and she squeals in shock, quickly shutting the machine down and removing her earbuds.

"What in the—"

"I don't appreciate you running this morning," I murmur into her ear. Her hair is up in a messy bun, giving me access to her slim neck, so I take advantage, bringing my lips to her warm flesh and suckling on the area just under her ear.

"Ben," she groans, her body doing that full-body shiver thing it always does when I touch her.

"I rolled over, hoping to wake you up with my tongue"—I run my hand up the side of her smooth thigh and then, spreading her legs, glide it over to the inside and straight up—

"only to find you were gone."

A whimper escapes her lips as my fingers slide under her shorts and underwear, finding her cunt ready for me. "I'm... I'm just trying to make sure no strings—"

Her words are cut off when two of my fingers plunge into her heat. "Fuck, Savy, you're so fucking wet." I grab her mane with my other hand and twist her head to the side so I can kiss her. "Stop running." I crash my mouth against hers, tasting her sweet as hell coffee.

I fuck her mouth with my tongue while I fingerfuck her tight pussy until her body begins to tremble under my touch. "That's it, baby," I coax against her lips as she rides my fingers, seeking out her pleasure. "Come for me." My words seem to be her undoing because several seconds later, she's doing just that—moaning into my mouth while she comes all over my fingers.

I'm just pulling my fingers out of her when she pushes against me, wiggling her ass.

I'm about to tell her we can't do that here—hell, I shouldn't have even fingered her here—the gym might be empty, but anyone can walk in at any time—when she twirls around and drops to her knees, pulling my shorts down and grabbing my dick. Of course it's hard as hell since I was just knuckles-deep in her pussy, and she wastes no time wrapping her plump lips around the head and taking me all the way into her mouth.

When my dick hits the back of her throat and she gags slightly, glancing up at me with glassy eyes, I damn near shoot my load. But there's no way I'm coming without feeling her tight cunt wrapped around my dick.

So when her mouth slides off my shaft and her tongue swirls around the tip, teasing the shit out of me, I pull her up, yank her shorts and underwear off, and lift her onto the edge of the treadmill so I can get a grip on her.

"Wrap your legs around me," I growl. Using the treadmill as a backboard, I lift her on to my dick. With her body clinging to me, I palm the bottom of her thighs and enter her in one fluid motion.

"Oh my God," she breathes when I bottom out in her. "Fuck me," she moans, throwing her head back. "Fuck me hard."

Needing something sturdier, I turn us around and step off the treadmill. Her back hits the wall, giving me a grip to fuck her how we both want—hard and fast and deep. Her fingers tug on my hair, and our mouths collide as I fuck her like I'm possessed. I can't remember ever wanting a woman as much as I want Savannah. The thought scares the shit out of me, so I push it to the side, refusing to focus on anything but the here and now.

Her orgasm hits her quick, and when her walls choke me like a fucking vise grip, I have no choice but to follow. Once she's milked me dry, she releases a harsh breath, then opens her eyes.

"Well, that's one way to start the day," she murmurs, a small, sated smile gracing her lips.

"That's the *best* way to start the day," I correct, ignoring the deep truth mixed in my words.

I lift her off me and set her on her feet, then grab her shorts and underwear so she can put them back on. I'm tucking my dick back into my pants when she gasps, her eyes going wide.

At first, I assume someone's come in and she's freaking out, but then my gaze hits her still bare thighs, the ones that are dripping with my...

"Fuck!" I look at Savannah, who seems to be in shock. "I'm so sorry."

I grab a bunch of paper towels from the holder and hand them to her.

"It's like I can't think when it comes to you," I grumble, scrubbing my hand down my face. "I didn't mean to... *fuck*." I don't even know what to say.

"It's okay." She quickly cleans up and puts her clothes back on. "I'm sure it's okay. I wasn't kidding when I said I had issues getting pregnant. We even charted and did temperature checks, but nothing worked." She grabs her crap off the treadmill and then stops at the door. "Maybe this wasn't a good idea. Lines feel like they're being crossed..."

She's probably right. I can't seem to keep my head on straight when I'm around her, but for the first time in a while, I'm happy and in a good place, and I know it's because of her. She brought Brody back to life, and she's easy to talk to and be around. And maybe it's selfish as hell, but I'm not ready to give her up yet. The smart thing to do would be to cut the sex out of it and go back to being friends, but the thought of going days without being inside her has me thinking like an idiot.

"Things got a little carried away, and for that, I'm sorry." I close the distance between us. "But I'll make sure that from now on, I'm more careful. I'll use protection, and we'll stick to sex only at night and in my condo. That way, the lines are firmly in place."

She looks like she wants to argue, but thankfully, she just nods, forcing a smile. "Okay." She juts her chin toward the door. "We should probably get going, or we're going to be late for work."

I don't point out that I usually work out longer than this because it's clear she's just trying to make her escape.

"All right. Let's go."

"DID YOU FIX SHIT WITH SAVY?" BRODY ASKS WHEN HE WALKS THROUGH THE door, throwing his backpack and gym bag on to the couch.

"Watch your mouth," I say over my shoulder from the kitchen where I'm putting together a salad to go with dinner. I have a few pieces of salmon and potatoes baking in the oven. It's weird getting home early enough to make dinner, but it's nice getting to spend my evening catching up with Brody, especially since he's been busy all week between football practice, going to his mom's, and hanging out with his friends.

He texted asking if he could have dinner at his friend's after practice, but I told him I was already making dinner and to come home. I've barely seen him all week, and I miss him. It's crazy to think I ever went weeks, sometimes months, without seeing him, and now I'm whining like a little kid about him being busy all week.

"Well, did you?" he asks, walking into the kitchen and bringing his foul body odor with him. "I want to invite her to my birthday party."

"Damn, kid, you stink." You'd think with it being cold as fuck outside, he wouldn't sweat as much, but clearly, he does. "Go jump in the shower. Dinner will be ready soon," I tell him, ignoring what he's said about wanting to invite Savannah to join us for his birthday festivities. The fact is, I haven't spoken to her all week. At first, my goal was to give her some space so she wouldn't question our arrangement and end things. I even skipped the gym, opting to use the treadmill in my office instead, so I wouldn't crowd her. But with every day that has passed, I'm wondering if I'm being stupid, and by not texting her, creating more of a rift between us. I promised her nothing would change between us, yet here I am making shit awkward by not texting her.

"I will," he says. "But first answer me." I should've known he wouldn't drop it.

"Yes, I fixed things. It's all good." I mean, technically, nothing's wrong... so it's not exactly a lie.

He eyes me speculatively, not buying what I'm saying. "You sure?"

"Yes."

"Prove it. Invite her over for dinner tonight."

I bark out a laugh. This fucking kid is too much like me it's scary.

"There's not enough food," I lie.

Brody opens the oven, then slams it closed. "Fix it," he barks, stalking out of the kitchen.

"In case you forgot, I'm the parent!" I yell after him.

"Oh yeah? Then act like it!" he shouts back, slamming the bathroom door behind him.

I finish cutting the veggies and set the salad on the table, then text Savannah.

Me: Brody thinks you're not speaking to us.

Savannah: Why would he think that?

Me: He hasn't seen you since last Friday.

Savannah: I'll text him.

Me: Or you could come over for dinner...

Savannah: Can't.

Me: Why not?

Savannah: I'm busy.

Me: Doing what?

Savannah: I'm on a date.

I drop my phone into the sink, and it clangs against the dirty dishes, cracking a plate. This can't be right... She can't be... I grab my phone and wipe it down, chuck the plate into the trash, and then type out a response.

Me: What do you mean you're on a date?

Savannah: Bri asked me to double with her and Marcus.

Me: Who are you on a date with?

Before I hit send, I stop myself, realizing my text sounds a lot like a jealous boyfriend. Although, if Savannah were my girlfriend, you can bet your ass she wouldn't be on a date with another guy.

I delete the text, then pull up Marcus in my contacts.

Me: Hey, how's it going?

Marcus: Good, you?

Me: Chilling. What are you up to?

Marcus: Out to dinner at The Cove with Bri, Savy, and Scott.

What in the actual fuck? They set her up with Scott? The guy is a womanizer. He's a divorce attorney who doesn't believe in marriage. Of all people, him?

As I'm about to text back, another one comes in from Savannah.

Savannah: I have to go. I'll text Brody later and let him know everything is okay.

I stare at my phone, wondering what the fuck just happened and how we went from fucking in the gym to her agreeing to go on a date with another guy. I'm still staring at my phone when Brody comes out and informs me that the oven has smoke coming out of it.

"Food's ruined." I switch the oven off and grab the pan from inside, throwing it onto the stove.

"Great, what are we going to eat? I'm starved."

"I'll make—" But then an idea hits me. "Let's go out to eat."

"All right." Brody shrugs. "Where?"

"The Cove."

"Can we invite Savy?"

"No, she's out with some friends tonight. But you never know... maybe we'll run into her."

Fifteen

Savannah

"IT'S A SHAME I DIDN'T KNOW YOU DURING YOUR DIVORCE," SCOTT DRONES on, refusing to drop the topic since I made the mistake of telling him about it. In my defense, he asked me what prompted my move to New York, and I gave him the abridged version. Only I didn't think about the fact he's a lawyer, and my vagueness would turn into him questioning me like I'm on trial. Next time Brianne suggests we double, I'm going to laugh at her and then politely decline.

"I could've gotten you a nice settlement, even if you were only married for a short time..."

As he rambles on about how much money he could've gotten me and how my situation is a perfect example of why couples should never enter a marriage without a prenup, I zone out, thinking about Ben's texts to me. I might be overthinking it, but it seemed like he was almost jealous. Which doesn't make any sense since he hasn't contacted me all week. I figured, after our slipup—times two—he was second-guessing our arrangement and had moved on—and I wouldn't blame him. He made it clear he doesn't do commitment, and possibly knocking up your stringless hookup is kind of the definition of commitment. Yet when we were texting, he seemed way more invested in what I'm doing and who I'm with than he should've been.

"Savy? I thought that was you."

My name being called shakes me from my thoughts, and when I look around to see who the owner of the voice is, I find Brody and Ben standing at our table.

"Hey," I say to Brody, getting out of my seat to give him a hug. "How've you been?"

"Good. Haven't seen you in a while." I don't miss the way he side-eyes his dad, who rolls his own like a teenager.

"We'll have to change that soon," I promise, needing him to know I wasn't purposely avoiding him.

"What are you guys doing here?" Brianne asks.

"Dad burned dinner," Brody answers, "so he suggested we come here."

"Quite the coincidence," Marcus says with a chuckle.

When I look over at Ben, he's glaring at Marcus. *There's no way... He wouldn't have...*

"I asked Dad to invite you over for dinner tonight, but he said you were out," Brody says. "My birthday is this weekend, and my friends and I are going to the arcade. It has laser tag and shit—I mean stuff... You should come."

"That sounds like fun," I tell him noncommittedly since I'm not sure where Ben and I stand, and I'm not about to make things awkward.

"We're doing a family dinner for him Sunday," Ben adds. "Lucas and Laura will be there..." His gaze flits from Brianne, to Marcus, then to me—skipping over Scott like he's ignoring him. "You guys are welcome to join. We'll be eating at Dragon Fusion."

"Hibachi's my favorite." Brody grins. "Savy, you'll come,

right?" His features morph into a frown. "My mom can't make it because Ted needed her back in Seattle." He shrugs, trying to play it off, but it's obvious his mom choosing her fiancé over her son has hurt his feelings. I've never been in her situation, and I hate to judge people, but I can't imagine missing my child's birthday. Maybe it's because I spent too many birthdays alone, wishing my parents would simply remember, let alone actually care enough to celebrate.

"I'll definitely be there," I tell him, no longer giving a shit how things are between Ben and me. "I wouldn't miss it for the world."

When his face lights back up, I know I made the right decision.

Everyone's silent for a few seconds, and then the hostess walks over and tells Ben their table is ready. Of course it's in the same area as ours, not just nearby, but close enough that we're in direct line of each other and able to lock eyes.

Thankfully, our meal arrives, and I'm able to focus on eating my dinner. Several times, though, my eyes find their way over to Ben's table and catch him looking at me.

Ben: I'm making pancakes for Brody's birthday. Join us?

I STARE AT MY SCREEN, CONFUSED AS ALL HELL, BUT KNOW I'M GOING TO say yes. For one, it's Brody's birthday, and I got him the best gifts ever. I've been chomping at the bit to give them to him, and I won't be able to wait much longer. And two, I'm curious to see how Ben acts around me. Aside from the brief conversation when they just *happened* to run into us at dinner, he didn't say another word to me all night. Not even after we finished eating and stopped by their table on the way out to say good night.

When Brianne and I got home, she confirmed my suspicions. Ben had texted Marcus, asking him what he was up to, and Marcus replied that we were out to dinner at The Cove. Brianne proceeded to tell me that it was obvious Ben was jealous and making his claim on me, and while I totally got that vibe, I waved her off, saying that Ben isn't the claiming type.

Me: Sure. What time?

Ben: 10:00 after I get back from my jog. He should be awake by then.

I climb out of bed and jump in the shower, then get dressed and do my hair. Once I'm ready to go, I wrap Brody's present, then head up to their place. I knock once, then again when no one answers. *He did say 10:00, right?*

I'm about to text Ben to let him know I'm here, thinking maybe he's still out for his jog when the door swings open. My jaw drops, and I'm almost positive drool drips from the corner of my mouth as I take in an almost naked Ben. His hair is shaggy and wet, and his shoulders and torso are dripping with fresh droplets of water. Around his waist is a plush towel slung low, revealing his happy trail that leads down, down, down to what's become one of my favorite spots.

"Sorry," he says with a knowing smirk, not sounding sorry at all. "I was in the shower. Have you been knocking for long?"

"No, I just got here. I take it the birthday boy isn't up yet?" I step inside and try with everything in me not to let my gaze descend.

"No, not yet. I'm going to wake him up soon, though." He eyes the present in my hand. "You didn't have to get him anything."

"I know, but the gift kind of fell into my lap. I mean, I had planned to buy him something. But then this happened." I shake the box, giddy inside. "So, yeah."

"All right. Well, I hope you didn't spend too much. The kid's already spoiled."

"I actually didn't spend anything."

Ben eyes me curiously but doesn't ask about it. "I have fresh coffee in the kitchen if you want some. I'm going to get dressed." I expect Ben to retreat to his room, so I'm momentarily stunned when instead he closes the distance between us—his body so close to mine I can smell the fresh masculine scent of his body wash. "You look beautiful this morning." He leans in and kisses my cheek. "I'm glad you came."

And with those parting words—which leave my head spinning—he retreats to his room, shutting the door behind him.

I'm making myself a cup of coffee when Brody enters the kitchen. "Hey," he says, his voice still gruff with sleep. "What are you doing here?"

"Your dad invited me over for breakfast." I finish stirring

my coffee and drop the spoon into the sink. "Happy Birthday."

"Thanks." He leans against the counter and grins. "Dad said once I turn fifteen, even though I can't get my permit until I'm sixteen, he'll take me to practice driving in one of his badass cars outside of the city."

"That sounds like fun." It also reminds me that I need to put my SUV up for sale. Brianne was right. There's no need for a vehicle while living here in the city. I might as well bank the money instead of dishing out hundreds every month for insurance.

"You're up," Ben says, walking out, dressed in a pair of dark wash jeans and a hunter green collared shirt that makes his hazel eyes pop. "Happy Birthday." He pulls Brody into a hug.

"Thanks. Savy mentioned breakfast?"

"Yep, I'm making chocolate chip pancakes. Your favorite."

Brody beams, like *literally* beams. "Cool."

"I brought over your gift," I tell him, handing him the wrapped box.

"You're not coming to the arcade later?" Brody asks with a small pout.

"I'm not really much of a video game person," I admit. "But

I'll be at dinner tomorrow night."

"I'm not either," Ben says. "You can keep me company while Brody and his friends spend all my money playing."

Brody laughs, playfully punching his dad in the arm. "It's *gaming*, Dad, not playing." He takes the box from me and unwraps it, pulling a football jersey out. "Thanks, Savy." He grins. "Jennings is my favorite." He's referring to Toby Jennings, the quarterback for New York.

"I know," I tell him. "You mentioned that at dinner with your mom. Flip it over."

He does as I say, and when he spots the signature, he gasps. "Holy shit. How'd you get this signed?"

"He offered. He's using Sharp to remodel his home, and when I was in a meeting with Lucas, he stopped by to pick something up. He introduced himself, and when I asked if he was the same guy you mentioned, he said he was. I told him how much you loved him and wanted to play like him one day, and when he came back to drop something off, he brought that for you."

"Wow." Brody sighs. "I can't believe you met him, and he signed this. This is awesome. Thank you."

"You're welcome." If he loves the jersey, he's going to freak out over the next part of the gift. "There's something else in there."

Brody pulls the envelope out and tears it open. After a few seconds, he glances up at me, his eyes bugging out of their sockets. "Are you freaking serious? Four tickets to the first home game of next season? Thank you!"

"You're welcome."

"I gotta go tell Sam and Ishmael! Thank you!" He hugs me quickly before he sprints out of the kitchen.

Once Brody is gone, and the sound of his door being slammed closed echoes, Ben cuts across the kitchen, cornering me against the countertop. "You must've made quite the impression on this guy."

"Or he's all about his fans."

"Maybe..." He tucks a strand of hair behind my ear. "Or he saw a beautiful woman and wanted a way in." His eyes land on my mouth, and he wets his lips. The action has my lady parts clenching in memory of what his tongue is capable of. "Can't blame him if that's the case. If I would've seen you strutting around at Sharp in your sexy work attire, I damn well wouldn't be able to resist."

With his finger and thumb, he pinches the tip of my chin and raises my face, placing a lingering kiss to the corner of my mouth. "...ask you... number...?" I'm trying to focus on what he's saying or whatever it is he's asking, but my head is fuzzy. He kisses the other corner of my mouth, and I swear my brain literally turns to mush. "Is that what happened?"

"Huh?" I can't focus on what he's saying with him this close to me, with his hands and mouth on me.

"Did he ask you out? Ask for your number?"

"Yes," I breathe, unable to lie to him.

"And what did you say?" He kisses my cheek this time, then trails his lips downward, along my jaw.

"I... I said no to dinner..."

He hums his approval, then works his way up my neck. "But you gave him your number, didn't you?" His teeth close around my earlobe, sending shocks of pleasure through my body.

"Yes," I whimper, shifting my head to the side to give him better access.

He peppers kisses along my neck and back over my jaw, stopping at my lips. "You seem to have quite a few men courting you..."

"No, only two." I'd hardly call that quite a few.

He takes a step back, and his eyes meet mine. I'm waiting to see what he's going to say, but instead, he simply swallows thickly and nods. "I better get started on the pancakes."

He walks away, taking his warmth with him, and I'm left standing here wondering what the hell just happened.

Sixteen

Benjamin

SAVANNAH HAS TWO MEN COURTING HER…*TWO*. NOT THREE. TWO. BECAUSE

I'm not courting her. And I need to remember that. Because she obviously has. And that's the way it should be. I'm not the settling down, commitment type. Commitment leads to expectations, like babies and families, and with those expectations come the inevitable disappointment—I witnessed it firsthand with my parents. The fact that Savannah gets it and accepts it and knows I'm not trying to court her should make me happy.

So then why the hell am I so goddamned jealous of the

fact that when I mentioned she has several men vying for her attention, she didn't include me in that scenario?

I whisk the pancake batter a bit too hard, trying to get myself under control. Out of the corner of my eye, I can see Savannah standing there, watching and assessing, wondering why I went from being all over her to giving her the cold shoulder. She wants to ask but doesn't want to cross over that stupid invisible line that we have to stay behind.

No, it's not stupid.

It's smart.

It keeps us in our place.

Reminds us what we're doing...and not doing.

"Do you want any help?" she finally asks softly, making me feel like an asshole for the way I reacted.

"If you want to make the eggs, I won't stop you." I make sure my voice is playful so she understands I'm not being cold to her. She did nothing wrong and doesn't deserve my shit just because I'm stuck in my own head. When she visibly sighs and smiles, I know it's worked.

We work side by side getting breakfast ready, neither of us saying a word, and when I can't take the silence anymore, I turn on some music—a country playlist since it's Savannah's favorite. A song comes on that Savannah must really like because she starts to sing along, knowing all the words, shaking her ass and using the spatula as a mic.

"I wouldn't quit your day job," I joke, bumping her hip with mine.

"Hey!" She pouts. "I'm a good singer."

"Maybe to the tone-deaf…"

She glares my way, then grabs a pancake from the pile on the plate without a second's hesitation and throws it at me. It smacks the side of my face, then falls to the floor with a plop. I glance at her, shocked as hell that she just hit me with a hot pancake. She tries to hide her smile by grabbing another one and taking a bite of it. "Mmm." She moans dramatically. "These are yummy."

"I wouldn't know," I say dryly.

Her attempt at tampering down her smile fails when an adorable giggle bubbles out of her.

"You think that's funny, huh?" She's so busy laughing that she doesn't see me grab the bottle on the counter and quickly shake it before I aim it at her. "How about some whipped cream to go with your pancake?"

Her eyes go wide, her head already shaking back and forth, but it's too late. I press down on the top, and white shit shoots out all over her face.

"Oh my God!" She shrieks, coming after me to steal the can. I turn away from her, and she jumps on my back. "You're so dead!" she yells through her laughter.

I carry her on my back over to the living room, then shake her off so she falls onto the couch. She hits the cushion, her face dripping with white cream, and before I can back away, she grabs me by my neck, pulling me to her. I'm not sure what she's going to do, but when she rubs her face all over mine, transferring the cream onto me, I crack up laughing.

When she finally stops, our eyes meet, and I drink her in. She should look ridiculous with white stuff dripping all over her nose and mouth, yet she looks gorgeous. Her eyes are filled with mirth, and her cheeks are stained pink from laughing.

I plant my hands on either side of her head and press my lips to hers. The kiss is meant to be chaste, but it quickly turns heated. Our tongues tangle with each other, tasting, coaxing... until I hear the sound of Brody's voice getting closer.

"Mmm," I murmur against her lips, repeating the same sound she made a few minutes ago. "Delicious."

I push off the couch and step back just in time because a second later, Brody enters the living room, his phone still pressed up against his ear. He stops in his place, looking at us like we've lost our minds. "What's all over your faces?" he asks, his nose scrunched up in disgust.

"Whipped cream," I tell him with a shrug. "We were hungry."

He quirks a brow. "Did you at least save me some food?"

Savannah snorts out a laugh. "In the kitchen, just don't eat the pancake that's on the floor."

Brody gives us both another look before he shakes his head and walks away.

"ARE YOU FREAKING SERIOUS?" SAVANNAH SHOUTS. "I SWEAR YOU'RE cheating."

"How?" I laugh, throwing my arms up in victory.

"You just... are!" She drops the striker onto the air hockey table and glares. "I want a rematch."

"Again?" I round the table and pull her into my arms. "I already beat you four times." I kiss the tip of her nose. "You gave it your best shot, Sav, but I think you need to know when to cut your losses."

"I hate you," she mutters as I kiss her chin.

"No, you don't." I kiss her lips, tasting the sugary sweetness from the cotton candy she was munching on a little bit ago.

"Hey, Dad!" Brody yells, causing Savannah to jump back like I'm on fire. "There you are!"

We've spent the afternoon hanging out in the arcade, eating, drinking, playing games like air hockey and Whac-A-Mole while Brody and his friends run rampant through the place. Shortly after we arrived, I loaded them up with credits and told them to let me know when they're hungry. They disappeared and haven't returned once... until now.

I clear my throat. "You hungry?"

He gives me an odd look, telling me he saw how close Savannah and I just were, but he doesn't call me out on it. "Yeah. Can we get some pizzas?"

"Of course. I'll order them and call you once they bring them out."

"Cool, thanks."

He and his friends take back off, leaving Savannah and me alone again. "What kind of pizza do you like?"

"Pineapple." She smirks. "But I doubt they have that, so anything is fine."

I take her hand in mine and guide her over to the counter to order, then head back to our table and have a seat while we wait for the food.

Since the table is in a private room and the boys won't be back until I call them, I pull Savannah into my lap so she's straddling my thighs.

"What are you doing?" she squeals, wrapping her arms around me. "We can't have sex here!"

"Who said anything about sex? I just want to kiss you." I fist the back of her hair and pull her face toward mine. We stay like this, kissing like horny teenagers until the server drops the pizza and drinks off.

When we separate, Savannah looks at me curiously.

"What?"

"I'm just... confused."

"About what?"

"This..." She gestures back and forth between our bodies. "Us... What we're doing."

"I'm pretty sure we were just kissing." I'm only half-joking since I know she means something more than that, but I'm not sure what she's talking about.

She rolls her pretty blue eyes to the ceiling. "I'm not an expert on stringless sex, but I don't think people who have it go around making out and holding hands."

She isn't wrong. I've had plenty of stringless sex, and never once did we hang out and act like we're dating. But I'm not about to tell her that—and I'm not about to think about why I'm not about to tell her that.

"There are no rules," I tell her instead. "We're grown adults, and we can do whatever the hell we want. And what I want to do is kiss you." I press a hard kiss to her lips.

When we break apart, her eyes flutter open, and she hits me with a hazy smile. Her lips are slightly puffy, and her cheeks are tinged pink. Fuck, she's so goddamn beautiful.

As I stare at her, wanting her back in my arms, in my lap, kissing me, a truth I haven't been wanting to admit hits me like a freight train doing a hundred with no working brakes. This no-strings shit isn't going to fly much longer...because I want Savannah Cartwright. Every goddamn part of her.

"YOU LIKE HER, DON'T YOU?" BRODY GLANCES AT ME FROM THE OTHER SIDE of the couch where we're watching Breaking Bad, a show that has become part of our nightly routine after he got me into it one night.

"Who?" I ask dumbly. There's only one woman he would ask about. The same woman who's been on my mind since we dropped her off at her place a few hours ago, agreeing to meet back up tomorrow afternoon to ride to dinner together. I wanted to ask her to come back here to watch a movie or something, but at the same time, I needed some space to think about shit. My head is all over the damn place since I've come to the realization that just sex with Savannah isn't enough for me.

"You know who." He throws a pillow at me. "Savy. I saw you kissing her." His tone isn't just a statement of fact. It's an accusation.

"Is that a problem?" I don't technically need his permission to kiss someone, but I find myself wanting his approval for some reason.

"Depends on what your intentions are," he says, sounding older than his newly fifteen-year-old self. "If it's just to fuck her, then yeah, it's a problem. Because she deserves better than that."

I blink once, twice, taking in what my son just said, because holy shit, when the hell did he grow up? I mean, I know how old he is, but I guess I didn't think about what that means. He's fifteen and in high school. The same age I was the first time I stuck my dick into a woman.

"Have you had sex?" I ask, ignoring his foul language.

This time, it's his turn to blink several times while I wait for him to answer. "No," he finally says, making me sigh in relief.

"You planning on it?"

"Sure not planning to stay a virgin for life," he deadpans, making me chuckle. Fucking asshole.

"Soon?"

A shrug. Shit, he's planning to have sex soon.

I think for a moment about how to respond. I have two

options: tell him not to, or use this moment to be real with him. I'm not sure what the right way to go is, but I'm learning there are no instructions when it comes to being a parent. You just have to go with your gut, and my gut is telling me that he's going to have sex—just like I did—whether I give him permission to or not, so it's probably best to make sure he's safe about it when he does do it.

"Sex isn't something you should take lightly," I begin. When his brows rise to his forehead, I internally cringe at my choice of words—it's clear my son knows how I've been living my life. "What I mean is, while sex can be good, damn good, there's a lot more to it than just getting your dick wet..." Jesus, I'm fucking this up. "What I'm trying to say is you need to think about STDs, pregnancy..."

Brody groans. "Dad..."

"Don't 'Dad' me. If you're old enough to have sex, then you're old enough to discuss it." Damn, I sound like a dad. "When you have sex, you need to use protection. If you don't have any, I'll buy you some. I don't give a shit if she says she's on birth control. Things happen, and the last thing you need is to get her pregnant while you're in high school. Also, STDs are no joke. Some have no cure and can be life-threatening."

He swallows thickly but nods.

"When you have sex, remember to be good to her. Women, by nature, are romantic. Make sure she gets off first. No woman likes a selfish lover."

Another audible swallow and nod.

"Do you have any questions?"

He shakes his head.

"All right, well, if you do, I'm here."

We go back to watching Breaking Bad for a few minutes before Brody clicks pause and looks at me. "You never answered my question."

I quirk a brow in confusion.

"What are your intentions with Savy?"

"I like her," I admit out loud for the first time.

"So why don't you ask her out?"

I laugh at that. "Because I'm not fifteen."

He rolls his eyes. "Well, maybe you should be...because I'm fifteen, and I have a girlfriend."

Point well made, kid...Point. Well. Made.

"DAD, THIS IS SAVANNAH CARTWRIGHT. SAVANNAH, THIS IS MY DAD, OLIVIER Fields."

"It's nice to meet you," Savannah says, shaking my dad's hand.

"You too," he says back.

I assess him for a moment, noticing the black circles under his eyes. He looks tired...more than the last time I saw him. I make a mental note to talk to him soon—demand to know what the hell is going on with him. Not today, though, since this is about Brody's birthday.

"There he is!" Amalia saunters in with her husband, Gerald, on her heels, carrying a stack of gifts. She grabs Brody and hugs him. "Happy Birthday, my favorite nephew!"

"I'm your only nephew," he points out, making everyone laugh.

More introductions are made, and then we're shown to a private room with a long rectangular grill situated in the center. Several chairs are surrounding the outer perimeter with a wooden bar-like table attached. This restaurant is one where the chef cooks your food in front of you.

Brody sits in the middle, and I sit to the right of him at the same time my dad sits to the left of him, leaving a seat empty for Brody's girlfriend. He asked me last night if she could join us, and I didn't see why not. Her parents had to first confirm with me that I would be there and they wouldn't be left alone, and once I agreed, they allowed her to come. Next to my dad is Amalia and her husband.

"Sav, sit next to me," I insist, pulling her into a seat. Lucas and Laura sit next to Gerald, leaving two seats open next to Savannah for Brianne and Marcus.

"Sariah's here," Brody says. "I'm going to go meet her in the front."

"Who's Sariah?" Amalia asks once he's gone.

"His girlfriend," I tell her.

"What?" She shrieks.

"Don't embarrass him," I warn. "I've never met her either. They only started dating a couple of weeks ago."

A few minutes later, Brody walks in, holding hands with a cute little blonde. She's dressed nicely in an appropriate dress and flats, and her makeup isn't done up too much. When he introduces her to everyone, she smiles shyly and waves, then follows him to the table to sit down.

"She seems sweet," Savannah murmurs into my ear.

I turn my head, and our faces are close...so fucking close. I want to kiss her right here, but it would raise questions. "Yeah, she does."

Dinner is loud but fun, with everyone talking and laughing over each other. I didn't realize how much I've missed doing shit like this. It reminds me how long I've been away and that we need to do this more often.

At some point, my hand finds Savannah's knee, and I spend the entire meal massaging circles into her flesh. I've never been like this with a woman before, needing to touch her in some way at all times, and it only helps to cement my newfound truth: I want more with Savannah.

Seventeen

Savannah

I WAKE UP TO CRAMPS STRONG ENOUGH TO MAKE ME DOUBLE OVER IN PAIN.

I tuck my legs up to my chest and stare at the wall, not wanting to get up, because I know that when I do, I'll sit on the toilet to go pee and wipe crimson.

My period has arrived.

I'm not pregnant.

I should be ecstatic.

Ben and I played a game of Russian roulette and dodged the bullet.

Yet my heart hurts.

Because as a woman who has wished and hoped and prayed to one day start my own family, I was hoping by some miracle I was pregnant. I knew the chances were slim, and really, it's for the best since Ben isn't the man I'll be spending my life with—but a part of me still wanted to be pregnant. To carry a baby in my womb, to feel him or her kick, to see the creepy yet beautiful skeletal face and body on the ultrasound screen, and at the end of the nine months, give birth to the most precious baby in the world.

The pain in my lower belly worsens—like a subtle reminder that I'm not pregnant—and I squeeze my eyes closed, wanting to go back to sleep and wake up in five days when my period is over. For most women, a period is a necessary annoyance, but for those like me who can't conceive, it's like a flashing neon sign that points out month after month that I'm broken.

And with that thought, I find myself lying here, wondering where the hell I'm going and what I'm doing with my life. What kind of person am I to wish for a man, who has no desire to have any more kids, to impregnant me? And of course this is the same man I'm falling for—hard and fast.

No strings, my ass.

My thoughts go back to the past few days, to the way Ben held my hand and kissed me. We haven't had sex in over a week, not since our gym session, yet somehow after this weekend, it feels like we're closer than ever. I'm not sure how kissing and holding hands can feel more intimate than the act of sex itself, but with Ben, it does.

I should break things off, tell him I'm done, but every time I think about doing so, sadness blankets me. Because with every kiss, every touch, every look he gives me, I'm falling deeper and deeper. I know it's going to end with my heart broken, but I just can't find it in me to walk away. God, I'm such a masochist.

The alarm goes off on my phone, and I shut it off, not wanting to get up but knowing I need to. Until I take some pain reliever, the cramps won't lessen, and I don't want my clothes and sheets to be stained red. I roll out of bed and head straight to the bathroom.

Sure enough, my period has started, and my underwear is coated red. I peel them off and throw them into the sink so I can try to keep them from staining. Then I jump in the shower to rinse off. Once I'm out, I pop a couple of pain pills. I can already tell this month's cycle will be bad, and mixed with my feeling sorry for myself, I'm in no mood to go to work. After pulling up Sharp's employee website and putting in for a sick day, I crawl back into bed, tucking myself under the blankets, and go back to sleep.

I WAKE TO BEN STARING DOWN AT ME, HIS FEATURES MARRED BY A DEEP V in the middle of his brows.

"I was worried about you. What are you doing in bed?"

I glance around, taking in my surroundings. "How did you get in here?"

"Brianne. She let me in on her way out." She was still asleep when I decided to stay home, so I didn't tell her, not wanting to wake her up. "You didn't show up at the gym this morning. You okay?"

I think about his question for a moment... Am I okay? Physically, yes... Emotionally, not so much. But how do I explain that to him?

No, Ben, I'm not okay. Remember when we had unprotected sex? Well, I didn't get pregnant, and now I'm heartbroken. That's one way to push him away. Hell, if I told him that, he'd probably run the other way.

When I don't answer right away, lost in my head and heart, he sits on the edge of the bed and tips my chin up so I'm forced to look at him. "What's wrong, Sav?"

"I'm not feeling well. I'm..." I take a deep breath. "My period started, and I have bad cramps."

He nods once, then dips down to kiss my forehead. "I'm sorry, baby."

"It's okay," I mutter. "Only the first day is bad. I took pain pills and—"

His eyes lock with mine. "Not about that."

I was already on the verge of crying all morning, so his words—the fact he's apologizing I'm not pregnant when he should be throwing a party—push me over the ledge. Hot, fat tears well up, blurring my vision, and then spill over, sliding down my cheeks.

"Hey," he coos, sliding his thumb across my cheek to swipe a tear away before he stands, kicks his shoes off, and then climbs onto the bed next to me—still dressed to the nines in his business suit.

He pulls the blanket off me, envelops me in his arms, and then throws it back over us. I nuzzle my face into him, and in his warmth and comfort, allow myself to cry.

He doesn't say a word the entire time, just rubs circles on my back and holds me tight while I cry for the baby I want and may never get. For the family I never had and crave. For the love I desire and wonder if I'll ever truly experience.

When I've cried all the tears and have calmed down enough to think rationally, I tense up, embarrassed I've just spent who knows how long crying on Ben's shoulder—literally.

"I'm sorry," I mumble into his chest. "This isn't what you signed up for."

His thumb and forefinger pinch my chin, lifting my face so I'm looking at him. "Maybe not, but there's nowhere else I'd rather be."

His words confuse me, but I'm too exhausted—mentally and physically—to ask him what he means, so instead, I just nod once and slide out of his arms. "I need to use the restroom."

I spend several minutes in there, using the bathroom, taking some pain pills, and washing my face, and once I feel like I'm halfway decent, I go back out. My bed is empty, and I find Ben in the living room talking on his phone.

"I won't be in today. Grab the permits on my desk and have a courier drop them off." He pauses to listen to whatever is being said on the other line, and then he says, "Yes." Another pause. "Perfect, thanks. Only call if it's an emergency."

Without so much as a goodbye, he hangs up and glances over at me. "You okay?"

I shrug. "I will be. Who was that?" I nod toward his phone as he's putting it back into his pocket.

"Lenora." His assistant. Bless her heart, I don't know how she's worked for him as long as she has. "She sounded a bit too happy when I told her I won't be in today," he says dryly.

I snort a laugh. "She probably needs a break from seeing your grumpy ass every day."

Ben glares. "I'm not grumpy. It's called running a business."

I roll my eyes. "You are *totally* grumpy. That day I ran into you during your meeting, you were all growly. If I were working for you, I would've quit after the first day."

Ben stalks forward, and shocking the hell out of me, he scoops me into his arms bridal style, walking us back to my bed. "I bet I could convince you to stay." He sets me down and crawls over me, his muscular arms framing my head.

"And how would you do that?" I breathe.

"I can be very persuasive." He drops a kiss to the side of my neck.

"Oh, really?" I turn my face to the side, giving him access. "And what would you do to persuade me?"

He runs his tongue across my pulse point, then nibbles playfully on the skin above my collarbone. "For starters, I would buy you coffee. The vanilla latte mocha frappe shit you love."

I bark out a laugh. "Oh, baby. Coffee *is* the key to my heart." I flutter my lashes dramatically. "What else?"

"That lemon pound cake crap you love...The one with the frosting on the top... I'd buy you an entire loaf."

"Mmm...now we're talking. Tell me more," I say as butterflies flutter in my chest over the fact that while he's joking around, he knows exactly what I eat and drink—because he pays attention.

Ben kisses his way along my jaw, stopping at the tip of my chin and nipping at it. "I would bring you lunch every day, alternating between Italian, Thai, and the sub shop since those are your favorites." He sucks on my bottom lip. "And for dessert, I'd give you... me."

His lips brush against mine in a soft, sensual way... and then my stomach growls, making both of us laugh.

He pulls back, holding himself up so none of his weight is on me. "You stay here, and I'll go get us coffee and breakfast."

"You don't have to do that," I tell him, not wanting him to miss an entire day of work because of me.

"I want to." He kisses me again before he climbs off the bed. "Besides, I already told Lenora I was taking the day off... Don't want to disappoint her."

A half an hour later, he returns with a carrier filled with coffees, orange juice, and water. "I know you love coffee, but you also need water to stay hydrated, and orange juice is good for you." He sets it on the nightstand, then starts pulling stuff out of the bag he's carrying. He produces an entire loaf of lemon pound cake, a box of Godiva chocolate, and a bottle of pills—specific for menstrual cramps. My heart soars at his thoughtfulness.

"Thank you."

He nods and kicks off his shoes, and it's then I notice he's no longer in his business suit but in a pair of gray sweats and a T-shirt. He must've stopped by his place to change. He climbs over me, onto the bed, and rests his back against the headboard. "So, what are we watching?"

I hand him his coffee and click on Netflix. "Only one of the best shows ever..."

AT SOME POINT, DURING THE THIRD...MAYBE FOURTH EPISODE OF *HART OF Dixie*, I must conk out because sometime later, I wake up to Ben still watching the show, only he's a lot further along. My head is in his lap, and his fingers are combing through my hair.

"Good morning," he says with humor laced in his tone.

I sit up next to him and grab the bottle of water to wet my parched throat. "How long was I asleep?"

"A few hours. How're you feeling?"

"Okay... I'm sorry—"

"Stop, you have nothing to apologize for. I enjoyed watching you sleep until you shifted onto my lap. I can't remember the last time I took the day off and relaxed. It's been nice."

His phone goes off with a text, and he reads it before typing out a reply. "Brody will be home soon. They're expecting some heavy snow to come through this evening, so they canceled practice. Why don't we go over to my place, and I'll order dinner in for all of us?"

"That sounds good, but I need to take a shower first." I rinsed off earlier, but I need a good scrub down and to wash my hair.

"I can get on board with that." Ben waggles his brows playfully. He edges off the bed and pulls his shirt over his head.

"Wait, you're joining me?"

He pauses, his shirt already off and his fingers dipped into the waistband of his pants, ready to push them down. "Is that okay?"

"Yeah, I guess... but I'm on my period," I remind him.

"So? What does that have to do with us taking a shower together?"

"Umm... Well, for one, we can't have sex." Which is kind of the entire purpose of our arrangement.

"We *could*..." he points out. "But that's not why I want to shower with you."

Without any further explanation, he finishes undressing and saunters into the bathroom, leaving me standing and staring at his sculpted ass and back. My God, the man is sexy.

"Sav, let's go!"

His words snap me out of my mental drooling, and I join him in the bathroom. He already has the shower turned on, and the steam is billowing over and fogging the mirror.

As I watch him, completely naked, move around my bathroom with ease, I hold back from getting undressed, suddenly self-conscious.

When he notices, he sets the towels on the sink and stalks toward me. "Raise your arms."

I do as he says, and my shirt comes off. Since I'm without a bra, my breasts are exposed, and despite the warm air, my nipples harden. He glances down, and a look of lust crosses his features.

"You're so beautiful," he murmurs, reaching for my sweats and tugging them, along with my underwear, down my legs. Once I'm naked, he kisses me softly, making me squirm under his touch.

"I need to use the bathroom," I mutter when the kiss ends.

As if he knows why, he nods and steps into the shower to give me some privacy.

After I'm done, I join him in the shower. It's not a big area, but there's enough room for us to fit comfortably. I stand under the spray, wetting my hair and body, and then move over to wash my hair. Before I can grab the shampoo, though, he stops me.

"Turn around," he says, pumping some shampoo into his hands. I do as he says, and then a second later, his fingers land on my head. He massages the soap into my scalp, and it's probably one of the best things I've ever felt in my life.

When I sigh into him, my back hits his front, and he presses an open-mouthed kiss to the top of my shoulder, sending a spark of desire through my body.

"Rinse," he tells me in a soft yet demanding tone.

Once my hair is soap-free, he squirts the conditioner into my hair, then proceeds to massage my scalp all over again. My eyes close as I get lost in the relaxing feeling of his fingers. All too soon, he finishes, though, and I rinse my hair out.

As I'm reaching for the bodywash, he grabs it first, his eyes locking with mine, making his intentions clear. I consider telling him that's too intimate, too... much, but he's already squirting the rose-scented liquid into his palm and rubbing his hands together.

Not needing to be prompted this time, I turn around on my own. His hands start on my neck and shoulders, kneading the tension knots out. Then he descends, massaging my arms and back. It's so relaxing I damn near fall asleep standing. While he works his way down my thighs, avoiding the apex between my legs, I wonder if other men are like this... this attentive and caring. Neil sure as hell wasn't.

Ben turns me around, so we're facing each other. "What's wrong?" he asks, his brows dipping in concern.

"How did you know...?"

"I could feel your entire body tense."

I sigh. "Sorry, I was just thinking about my ex-husband."

His brows fly up to his forehead, so I quickly explain. "You're being so nice... and I was wondering if this is how it's supposed to be. When I got my period, Neil would complain I wasn't pregnant and that he'd have to deal with days of my emotional roller coaster. A lot of times, he would work late..." I flinch, realization dawning on me. He would come home late...

He was probably screwing someone else during that week.

"Neil's an asshole," Ben says flatly. "I don't know what other men do, and to be honest, I've never done this with another woman before, but…" He swallows thickly. "I've also never felt like this before."

Before I can question what he means by that, his mouth is on mine, kissing me, devouring me. It's not sweet or soft, but hard. As though he's trying to tell me something he can't voice through words. His tongue plunges past my parted lips, tasting, caressing.

My hands slide up his wet chest and snake around his neck. His hands grab my ass, lifting me. My legs wrap around his waist, and my back hits the cold wall, sending a chill up my spine.

Ben reaches between us and finds my clit. He strokes and massages it, and my body bows against his, grinding and silently begging for the relief I know is coming. With a couple more strokes, I let go, flying high as my entire body trembles in pleasure.

"That's it, baby," he murmurs against my lips. "Fuck yeah, come for me." He doesn't stop coaxing my orgasm out of me until I've completely come down.

He gently sets me onto my shaky legs, which feel like Jell-O, making it hard to even stand. But when I glance down at his erection, all thick and veiny and protruding outward proudly, my wobbly legs are forgotten as I drop to my knees so I'm eye level with his dick.

"Savan—" he begins, but his words are cut off the moment my mouth wraps around his shaft. I take him all the way in, sucking and licking, working to get him off. It doesn't take long until he's coming down my throat, his fingers tangled in the back of my hair and his head thrown back as he groans through his climax.

Once I've milked him completely dry, swallowing every last drop, I stand. His eyes pry open, looking hazy and satiated, and he pulls me into his arms, crashing his mouth against mine for a quick yet punishing kiss.

"That is *not* why I wanted to shower with you," he says, a boyish grin splayed across his lips.

Eighteen

Benjamin

WE FINISH OUR SHOWER, THEN GET OUT AND DRY OFF. I GET DRESSED IN her room, leaving Savannah to handle her woman business in the bathroom. The shower didn't go as planned, but I can't lie and say it didn't go better... Any time I'm with her, I can't get enough. I just want to touch her and kiss her and fucking be with her. When she asked if other men treat their women the same way I was treating her, I couldn't be anything but honest when I told her I didn't know because I was never like this until her. It's her—she makes me want to take care of her, be there for her.

She steps out of the bathroom in nothing but a towel, and I have to remind myself—specifically my dick even though it just got plenty of attention thanks to her perfect mouth—to chill out. She's not feeling well, and the last thing she needs is me constantly attacking her because I can't seem to keep my hands off her.

Once she's dressed—in a pair of sweats and a shirt that reads, "*When a Southern woman says 'Oh hell no,' it's already too late*"—we head up to my place. We're on the couch with Savannah tucked into my side, deciding what to order, when Brody plows through the door like a tornado, throwing his bags on the floor.

He stops in his place and eyes us. "So you guys finally started dating, huh?"

"What? No!" Savannah squeaks out.

At the same time, I say, "Not yet."

Brody barks out a laugh. "You guys might wanna figure that out."

Savannah moves to the other side of the couch like my touch is suddenly contagious. "There's nothing to figure out," she says through clenched teeth, glaring at me. "Tell him... Tell him we're just friends."

"You don't have to pretend for me," Brody says. "I'm not a kid… and I'm okay with you two dating. Hell, I'm okay with you getting married. It just sucks my mom couldn't find someone nice too." He shrugs and walks through the living room, already pulling his phone out of his pocket. "I'm calling Sariah. Let me know when dinner's here."

The second his door closes, Savannah bolts to her feet. "What the hell was that?"

"That was my kid," I say, knowing full well that's not what she was referring to.

"Ben…" she warns.

"I've actually been meaning to talk to you." When she takes a step back, I stand as well. "I know we agreed to no strings, but—"

"Don't do this…"

"Savy." I sigh, stepping toward her. She takes another step back. "Things have changed."

"No, nothing has changed!" she whisper-yells. "You promised me no strings. You said you were a man of your word."

"That was before…"

"Before what?" she barks, her chest rising and falling in quick succession.

"Before I started to fall for you."

"No... No. No. No. You promised!" Tears fill her eyes and quickly spill over, shattering my heart. This isn't what I had in mind when I imagined telling her I want to be with her. "You promised, Benjamin!" She throws her arms in the air. "I need to go."

Before I can beg her not to leave, she's out the door, slamming it behind her. I'm stuck in place for a few seconds, unsure what to do, when Brody makes his presence known.

"What are you waiting for? Go after her."

Shit, he's right. I run out the door and down the hall, catching her while she's waiting for the elevator. Tears are running down her face, and she's sniffling loudly.

"Savannah, wait," I call out when the elevator opens. I sprint in front of her and block the doors. "Please talk to me."

"There's nothing to talk about."

"Yes, there is." I close the space between us as the doors close since nobody got in. "Over the past several weeks, my life has changed drastically. From Brody moving in to meeting you.

When I agreed to no strings—"

"You didn't agree," she hisses. "You offered."

"I did, and at the time, I had every intention of keeping it that way. I've been single for the past fifteen years and have had zero interest in anything more... until you."

"You don't mean that," she whispers. "You think you do, but you don't."

"I do." I cup her face in my palms. "When we hang out, I can't stop touching you, needing to be close to you. When we're not together, I miss the hell out of you. I'm always wanting more... more of your smile, more of your laughter. You make me a better person. You make me want everything I never thought I wanted."

"You don't know what you're saying," she breathes shakily.

I use my thumbs to wipe the liquid emotion from under her eyes, hating she's so upset. "When you thought you might be pregnant, I didn't freak out, and when you got your period today, a part of me was sad."

"Stop it," she begs. "Don't do this. You might think you want more, but this isn't who you are, and when you change your mind, you're going to break my heart." Her voice cracks on the last three words, and I vow at this moment to never let them be true. "Please... if you care about me at all, stop saying this stuff. We can cut the sex out of it and be friends."

"I don't want to be your friend." My hand moves to the back of her head, entangling my fingers in her hair. "I want you, Savy. All of you. Your mind. Your body. Your heart."

"No." She shakes her head back and forth emphatically. "You can't have me because I don't want you."

My heart drops at her admission.

She doesn't want me... not the way I want her.

Did I read this all wrong?

"I tried to pretend I was okay with all of this," she says. "Bri told me stringless, emotionless sex would be good for me. And I thought she was right. I'd been so focused on trying to create a perfect life that I forgot to focus on me... on my wants and needs. But this..." She points back and forth between us. "This isn't who I am. And as much as I want *you*, I want to find love more. And not just love... I want it all. The doting husband, the crazy kids. The cliché white picket fence. I want a home that's filled with toys and family and love and laughter..."

A choked sob breaks up her words, momentarily stopping

her from speaking, and I use that moment to cut in. "And I can give you all that if you give me a chance."

Her eyes go wide. "But that's not what you want. You said so yourself. It's why you left Paola. Why you stayed away from Brody all these years."

"I was scared," I admit. "And she tricked me. She lied and manipulated me. But you're not her, and I'm not the same guy I was back then. For so long, I told myself this was how it had to be, and by keeping every woman at arm's length, it made my decision easy. But then you walked into my life with your Southern accent and crazy shirts and Starbucks coffee and your goddamned fluffy boots on *my* treadmill...and everything changed."

She laughs a watery laugh, mumbling, "It's not your treadmill," and I know I have her in my grasp.

"I don't want to allow my fear of history repeating itself to keep me from being with you. My mom was sick, I know that now, and even though my dad loved her, he didn't get her the help she needed. But that won't be us... I won't allow that to be us." I lock my eyes with hers, silently pleading for her to understand. "I want everything you want, Sav. The family, the house... And I want it all with you."

With my fingers in her hair, I tilt her face up slightly. "Now, the question is, do you want it with me?"

After several long as fuck seconds, she answers me with a single nod, but that's not enough. "I need to hear you say it. Do you want it with me?"

"Yes," she breathes. "I want it with you. The house, the babies...Brody... I want it all with you."

Fuck, this woman. Of course she includes my son, and that only solidifies what I've known since I admitted to myself that I was falling for her: she's the one. She's the goddamn strings attached to my heart.

My mouth crashes down on hers in a quick but bruising kiss. "I'm going to give it all to you," I murmur against her lips. "Every goddamn thing."

We stay in the hallway kissing for several minutes until my phone chimes with an incoming text, breaking the moment.

Brody: I'm starving! There's no food here.

I turn the phone around so Savannah can see it.

"C'mon, let's go back in," she says with a laugh. "I'm hungry too. I'm craving some Mexican...Oh! And chocolate cake."

"You got it." I kiss her one more time, then take her hand in mine and guide us back to my place. When we open the door, Brody pops his head out of the kitchen.

"Oh, good. I thought I was going to have to eat like a sandwich or something."

Savannah snorts out a laugh. "You poor thing."

Brody's eyes descend to our adjoined hands. "Looks like you guys figured it out…"

"We did," I tell him. "Savannah and I are dating."

"And how did you come to that?" he asks with a smirk, turning his attention on Savannah. "Did my dad ask you out?"

Savannah giggles. "He did."

"Good job, Dad." He walks over and pats my shoulder. "Looks like dating isn't just for teenagers." Little shit. "Now that we got that handled, what's for dinner?"

"DO YOU NEED ANY HELP AT THE OFFICE?" BRODY ASKS, CLOSING HIS NOW empty box that held his mountain of nachos—chicken, cheese, beans, sour cream, piled high on a shitload of tortilla chips—

that looked like it was meant for three people. The kid is like a damn bottomless pit, and not only does he eat a shit ton but he also practically inhales it, leaving me to wonder if he even tasted his food.

"Why?" I ask, stabbing a piece of my cheesy grilled chicken and extending it toward Savannah so she can take a bite. Her plump lips slide the food off my fork, and she moans in appreciation.

She couldn't decide between chicken and steak. I told her just to order both, but she didn't listen, and the second she eyed my food, I knew she wished she had. I offered to switch with her, but she shook her head, insisting she was fine with what she got. *Liar.* She's eaten half my food through my feeding her while we watch some chick flick she picked out that she's cried through.

"Valentine's Day is coming up, and I want to buy Sariah something, and umm..." He shrugs. "Maybe take her to dinner and a movie."

Savannah grins wide. "You're so sweet. What do you want to get her?"

"I guess it depends on how much money I can make between

now and then."

"I'm sure we can find something for you to do...Maybe you can clean the bathrooms," I joke, making Savannah slap my chest.

"Be nice," she says, opening her mouth to take another bite of my food. Brody laughs, having noticed as well that she's eaten more of my food than her own. "Do you have somewhere, in particular, you want to take her? First dates are important. They set the tone for the entire relationship."

Brody's eyes go wide. "Umm...I don't know. I haven't thought that far ahead, and her parents are kind of strict, so I don't even know if they'll let her go out with me."

"We're having a Valentine's Day party at Lush," I mention. "You're too young to attend, but if you're okay with double dating with your old man, we can have dinner there."

"Who are you going out with?" Savannah sasses.

"You." I pull her into my side so I can kiss her temple.

"Funny, I don't remember being asked." She leans forward and grabs her glass of wine, taking a sip.

She sets it down, and I tip her chin to look into her ocean blue eyes. "Savannah Cartwright, will you be my valentine?"

A mischievous grin curls her lips. "Hm..." She taps her chin in mock thought. "Exactly what does being your valentine entail?"

"For starters, dinner at Lush." I kiss the tip of her nose. "Followed by an evening of dancing and drinking." I peck her cheek and lean in so only she can hear my next words. "And afterward, a night in my bed." A shiver wracks her body, making me chuckle.

"You guys are gross," Brody says with a gagging sound. "I'll have dinner with you guys since Sariah's parents are more likely to let her go if my parent is there, but try to tone it down a notch, will you?"

"Hey, don't act like you don't kiss your girlfriend by your locker," I taunt.

He stands and shakes his head. "I do, but not in front of my dad. So about making some money..."

"We'll figure it out." I'm sure I can give him something to do to earn some money.

"Thanks, Dad."

He throws his trash away, then disappears into his room, leaving Savannah and me alone.

"Want another glass of wine?" I ask, seeing hers is empty.

"No, thanks." She yawns. "I'm exhausted. I think I'll head home—"

"Let's finish the movie first," I suggest, not ready for her to leave yet.

She yawns again but agrees, and I pat my lap so she can lay her head down. I click the movie back on, and within minutes, the sound of her soft snores fills the room. I pull my phone out, checking and replying to a bunch of emails I neglected today. Then I check my calendar for the rest of the week. I do all this one-handed while I use my other one to play with her hair.

"Is Savy okay?" Brody asks when he comes out of his room a couple of hours later. The movie has ended, and the screen is paused.

"Yeah, she's not feeling well."

"Is she sick?"

"No, she's on her period." I could lie, but what's the point? He's fifteen and has to learn about this shit sooner or later.

Brody's nose scrunches up. "Oh. Sariah said when she's on hers, she cries a lot."

I chuckle. "Yeah, it makes women emotional." Savannah

shifts slightly, snuggling closer to me. "You done with all your homework?"

"Yeah. Sariah's mom said she can go to dinner with us."

"What about the movie?"

"Only if you guys come...but I know you have that party afterward, so..."

"I don't have to be there the entire time. I won't be at any of the others. I'll make a quick appearance, and then we can go to the movies if that's what you want to do."

His face brightens. "Yeah? That'd be cool. Thanks."

"No problem. Get ready for bed. It's getting late, and you need to get up early tomorrow."

"I'm gonna jump in the shower."

"All right, if I'm not here when you get out, I'm walking Savannah home." As soon as I wake her up...which is hard to do when she's sleeping so peacefully.

"Or she can just spend the night," Brody suggests, shocking me. "It's not like Mom doesn't have that asshole living with her."

"Watch your mouth." I side-eye him. "Why don't you like Ted, anyway?" He's made several digs at the guy, and his mom mentioned they used to fight. I don't know the guy, but I'm not sure how I would feel if Brody didn't like Savannah.

"I just...I just don't like him," he mumbles. "But Mom loves him so..." He shrugs. "I'm just glad I don't have to live with him anymore...as long as you're here."

"I'm not going anywhere," I assure him. "But at some point, you're going to have to see your mom...and not just when he's out of town." We have fifty-fifty custody, but she's always had him the majority of the time because of my dumb choices. "Maybe we should sit down and talk to your mom—"

"No!" Brody barks. "Just leave it alone, please." Something more is going on, but I don't know what it is.

"What about your therapist? Would you consider talking to him about it?" We still have three and a half more years of him being home until he goes to college, and there's no way his mom will let him avoid staying at her house that long.

He averts his gaze, looking past me. "I guess."

Not wanting to push him, I leave it at that for now. "All right. Go jump in the shower. You have school in the morning."

"Unless it snows enough for schools to cancel," he says as he walks down the hall toward his bathroom.

Once he's gone, Savannah rolls over onto her back and looks up at me. "I don't think I like that Ted guy," she says, obviously having heard at least that part of our conversation.

"Yeah, me neither," I agree, dipping my face to kiss her. "Want to spend the night? Unlike Ted, Brody likes you and said he doesn't mind." I waggle my brows, making Savannah smile.

"As tempting as that sounds, I think it's best if I sleep at home. All my stuff is there, and I think we should take it slow... not just for us but for Brody too. He's been through a lot, and he might be okay with it, but it doesn't mean we should take advantage of that."

"You're amazing," I tell her, kissing her when she sits up. "I'll walk you home."

"Such a gentleman." She grins, kissing me back.

Nineteen

Savannah

isn't going to know what hit him."

I turn around and glance at myself in the mirror, taking in my appearance. Since the Valentine's Day party at Lush is a black-tie affair with a red, pink, and black theme for the occasion, I'm dressed in a bright-red velvet minidress that's covered in shimmering sequins and ruching at the waist to accentuate my curves. The front dips low, showing off the swells of my breasts while keeping it classy with long sleeves, yet it has an off-center slit up the side. My dirty-blond hair is down in waves with one side pinned back behind my ear. Since it's been snowing on and off, I'm wearing red suede closed-toe heels with an ankle strap.

Not wanting to wear a dress bought by another man, I bought this dress for tonight during Brianne's and my shopping trip. She needed something new as well, so we made a day of it. It was nice since we haven't had a lot of girl time between dating and working.

"Me?" I say back. "Look at you."

Brianne went with a sexier, shorter, more formfitting blood-red dress, and she looks amazing. Her hair is up in a tight ponytail with the ends spiraling down her back, and her lips are a matching matte crimson while mine are a bright red glossy color.

"We do look gorgeous, don't we?" She grins. "Benjamin picking you up?"

"Yeah, he and Brody should be here soon. We're going to pick up Brody's date and then head to Lush."

"I can't believe how much he's changed in such a short time. Although, it shouldn't surprise me."

"Why is that?"

She shrugs. "I guess I'm just learning that when the right person comes along, it doesn't matter if it's hours, days, or weeks... if they're the one, they're the one."

"Are you trying to say Marcus is the one?" Since the night they left together from the club, they've been inseparable, but she hasn't mentioned how serious they are.

"Yeah," she says with a smile. "I think he is. What about you and Benjamin? Is he the one?"

I think about her question for a few long moments before I answer. "It's hard because at one point I thought Neil was the one, but looking back, it was actually the *idea* of him that I was caught up in. You know? The idea of getting married and being in love and having a family. I didn't think about the fact that he wasn't actually the kind of person I wanted to spend my life with.

"So, this time, I'm trying to be more cautious and pay attention to the details. I told Ben I wanted to take things slow, but it's hard when everything he does and every word he says seems so perfect. I think in the back of my mind, I'm waiting for the moment he does something wrong so I can convince myself he isn't the one for me."

"You can't do that to yourself," she says. "If you keep waiting for him to mess up, he'll eventually prove you right. Nobody is perfect, and one day he *will* say the wrong thing, *do* the wrong thing. But that doesn't mean he isn't the one for you. It just means he's human."

A knock on the door signals one of our dates is here, halting our conversation. "We need to have a girls' day soon," Brianne says. "Facials, pedis, manis, the whole nine yards so we can get some good girl talk in. Our shopping trip wasn't enough."

"That sounds perfect."

Another knock and she playfully rolls her eyes. "We better get that. Don't want to keep them waiting. They might die from impatience."

I grab my sparkling silver clutch and my overcoat with a laugh and follow her out to the foyer. She swings the door open, and standing on the other side is Ben, dressed to the nines in a black suit, complete with a bright red bowtie that matches my dress, holding a huge bouquet of roses. His hair is cut short on the sides with the top slightly longer and gelled messily in the way guys do to make it look like they just rolled out of bed yet still look perfect. His facial hair is trimmed short, and he's sporting a grin that conveys every ounce of emotion he feels—lust, want, need, desire.

We still haven't had sex since he took me against the wall that morning at the gym. Between my period and work and Brody, we haven't found the time to be alone. I'm hoping that changes soon.

"Happy Valentine's Day," he says, stepping over the threshold. "You look stunning." He presses a kiss to the corner of my mouth so he doesn't ruin my lipstick, then hands me the flowers that are already in a vase.

"Thank you. You look… well, like your usual handsome self." The man wears a suit every day. I do have to admit that tonight, his suit seems sharper, making him look extra sexy.

It's then I notice Brody standing there, also dressed in a suit and holding a bouquet of pink tulips. Dressed similarly, with his hair also freshly cut, he looks so much like his father. "New suit?" I ask. "It looks great."

"It's a tux," Ben corrects. "Suits are for work. Tuxes are for romantic nights out with your woman… and weddings." He winks playfully, making me laugh.

"Oh, I'm sorry," I say, sarcasm dripping in my words. "Your

tux looks great."

Brody chuckles. "Dad said every man needs a tux just in case. It's tailored to fit me." The pride in his voice makes my heart soar. They've come a long way in a short amount of time, and that makes me so happy.

"You both look extremely handsome in your tuxedos. Let me put my flowers in the kitchen, and then we'll go."

I'm filling the vase with water at the sink when a pair of strong arms encircle me from behind, and a masculine, fresh scent I would recognize anywhere hits my senses. "That dress looks fucking delectable on you," Ben growls, kissing the side of my neck. "If I don't get you alone soon, I might combust."

I giggle at his dramatics, set the flowers on the counter and turn the water off, and twirl around, remaining in his arms. "Well, maybe if you're a good date, I'll *consider* letting you take this dress off me later." I kiss him chastely on his lips. "We wouldn't want you to combust now, would we?"

"No, we definitely wouldn't want that." He runs the back of his knuckles down my cheek and sighs. "Thank you for going along with this double date tonight. I know Valentine's Day is supposed to be romantic and—"

"Whoa, stop right there." I cover his lips with my fingers that are freshly painted—bright red to match my dress. "Being a father should come first, always, and you choosing to go on a double date with your son tells me more about you than any romantic gesture ever could. That alone secures your spot in my bed tonight."

He chuckles softly and shakes his head. "I don't know what the hell I ever did to deserve you, but I need you to know how thankful I am to have you."

After saying goodbye to Brianne, who assures us Marcus is on his way up and they'll see us later at Lush, we head out. Parked in front of the sidewalk is a sleek all-black stretch Hummer limo Ben rented for the occasion. Apparently, Brody didn't even know about it because he freaks out and takes a million selfies in front of it—all of which I'm sure will end up on social media. Ben also has him take a few pictures of us, and then we take off to pick up Sariah.

Her house is on the way, so it doesn't take long, and once we arrive, Brody jumps out with his bouquet in his hand and runs up to her front door to knock.

"We should take a couple of pictures," I tell Ben as I watch

Brody wait for someone to answer the door.

"Or I can use this time to give you this." He pulls a small black box out of his pocket. "I was helping Brody pick out his gift for his girlfriend when I saw this and thought of you...of us."

I open the top and nestled inside the felt bedding is a white gold or maybe platinum pendant with a beautiful diamond in the center. It looks like it's a knot of some sort, but I'm not sure why. Or what it means. Maybe it's just something pretty...

When I glance up, silently asking for him to explain, he takes the box from me and pulls the pendant out, letting it dangle from the delicate chain. "Turn around."

I do as he says, lifting my hair up so he can clasp it on. The pendant lands on my chest just above the swell of my breasts.

"It's a love knot," he explains. "It's made up of two strings that are tied together to form one knot. Each string represents us. When we first started this, we agreed to no strings, but now everything is different, and those strings have come together to form a knot. Alone, they're fragile and easy to break, but together..." He locks eyes with me, and my heart thunders in my chest. "Together, they're strong and can withstand anything."

"Ben, this is so beautiful," I choke out. I've never been given a gift with so much thought and meaning put into it before. "Thank you." I entwine my fingers around his neck and connect my mouth to his, wishing we were alone so I could show him just how much this gift means to me.

The ride to Lush is filled with casual conversation. While we met Sariah at Brody's birthday dinner, she was quiet for much of the time around so many people. Tonight, though, she's chatting away, and I can see why Brody likes her. She's cute and bubbly and funny, and the way she talks about and looks at Brody is so sweet.

When we arrive at the restaurant, it's busy with everyone arriving for dinner and the Valentine's Day party. Outside, there's a black carpet where a photographer is taking professional photos of the couples, and since it's a high-traffic area for celebrities, several paparazzi are camped out, watching for anyone they can get their eyes on. The four of us get our picture taken together and then separately as couples. Ben is given a QR code where we can view and purchase the images once they're uploaded.

We arrive at the hostess stand, and she greets us, recognizing

Ben. She immediately walks us back to our table in a quiet area of the restaurant. There are red, pink, and black balloons in the corner, and a small vase of roses and candles decorate the table. I glance around and notice the other tables don't have all this, which means Ben had this done in advance. It's crazy that he's spent the past several years not in a relationship because he's naturally good at it. He pays attention to the details, which is probably why his business ventures are so successful. He's put all his energy into that instead of his relationships.

"This is beautiful," I murmur, kissing his cheek. "You really set the bar high."

He chuckles—no doubt remembering when I told Brody not too long ago that the first date sets the tone for the entire relationship—and takes my hand in his, threading our fingers together.

Dinner is fun, and the food is delicious. Brody and Sariah are adorable together, and when Ben tells them that we have to run upstairs for a few minutes to make an appearance before we take off to the movies, Brody asks Sariah if she'll dance with him, not caring that nobody else in the restaurant is dancing.

We take the elevator to the second floor, and then Ben

guides us through the club. The area is filled with large heart-shaped balloons, and the band is playing a slow, seductive number that couples are on the dance floor swaying to.

As we make our way through the crowd, several people stop Ben to say hello. He also makes it a point to seek out a few people, introducing me as his girlfriend and asking them if they're having a good time. It's the second time I've seen him in business mode since we've met, and a lot like the day in his office, he's attentive to each person he speaks with while also being unemotional and detached. He's completely different than the Ben I've grown to know, and I know this is the man who's spent the past fifteen years building up his successful business.

When we finally arrive at a roped-off area housing a group of about fifteen people, I notice they're everyone we know. Lucas and Laura are slow dancing in the corner. Amalia and her husband are sitting at a table, holding hands and talking. My eyes land on Scott, who thankfully seems to be on a date since he has a woman sitting sideways on his lap. He texted me once after our date, and not wanting to lead him on, I told him there wasn't a connection. I told the same thing to Toby

Jennings when he texted me—after Ben and I made the decision to date—and asked me to dinner.

I find Brianne standing and talking to a girlfriend of hers I've met once while Marcus has his arms wrapped around her from behind, his chin resting on her shoulder. We lock eyes, and she leaves the person she's talking to, to come over and hug me.

"What happened to your double date?"

"They're downstairs dancing while we make a pit stop. Ben wanted to come up before we head to the movies."

"Hey," Amalia says, giving her brother a one-arm hug because he's holding my hand and not letting go. "The event is running smoothly. I've already checked in with the other locations, and everything is going well."

"Of course it is," he remarks. "You're running it. I wouldn't expect anything less."

His sister lovingly rolls her eyes before her features turn serious. "Have you heard from Dad? Gerald and I have some news, and I wanted to tell you both at the same time, but he hasn't returned any of my messages."

Ben frowns. "He's probably busy with the quarterly reports

due soon." But as he speaks, I can see it in his features that he's worried.

"Yeah, maybe," she says, not sounding like she agrees. "But, um... he hasn't been in his office all week."

"What do you mean?" Ben's back goes ramrod straight.

"I stopped by, and his secretary said he hasn't been in all week."

"That can't be right..." He pulls his phone out and hits a few buttons, then puts it to his ear. A few seconds later, he hits end and pockets it. "He's probably out with some woman. It's Valentine's Day. I'll give him a call tomorrow and get it sorted out. What was it you wanted to tell us? Is everything okay?"

Amalia's lips curve into a huge grin, and Gerald wraps his arm around her. "Everything is perfect. Gerald and I found out we're expecting a baby!"

"Holy shit," Ben says, letting go of my hand and pulling his sister into a hug. "Congratulations!"

"Thank you. The timing probably isn't the best with the restaurant and—"

"What? Stop. We'll handle it. Family first. This is awesome news."

Amalia's eyes go wide as though she's shocked he's said that. While Ben shakes Gerald's hand and congratulates him, Amalia steps closer to me and wraps me in a hug. "Thank you," she murmurs. "Thank you for giving my brother back to me." When she pulls away, her eyes are glassy, but she's smiling brightly.

She turns back to her brother, and he asks her how far along she is, but I don't hear her response because Brianne tugs me gently to the side, giving me a knowing look. "Are you okay?"

"Of course I'm okay. I'm not so unstable I lose it every time someone announces they're pregnant."

"I know, but it's okay for it to hurt. I just don't want to see you bottling it up."

I give her a hug, loving that she cares enough to make sure I'm okay. "I promise you, I'm okay. I'm focusing on what I do have these days and not on what I may never have... Like an amazing job and a best friend like you...and Ben..."

"Oh my God," Brianne whispers. "You're in love with him."

My gaze goes to Ben, who's talking to his sister but looking at me with adoration in his eyes, and that makes my heart swell. All those years with Neil and not once did he ever look at me like that. And because I never experienced that look, I didn't know it was missing... until now.

"Yeah," I admit, "I am."

Twenty

Benjamin

AROUND THIS TIME LAST VALENTINE'S DAY, I WAS BALLS DEEP IN SOME woman I met at a party at one of my clubs for a quickie in the office. I couldn't tell you her name or even what color her eyes were. Once we both got off, I threw the condom away, zipped up my pants, and then we parted ways. I went back to my place and spent the rest of the evening getting lost in my work. That was the norm for me. The occasional hookup. Working too damn hard. Not being enough of a father to even know what my son was doing on a day supposed to be about love.

This year is different because not only do I have Brody but

I also have Savannah. We've dropped Sariah off, and Brody has headed up to our place to, I'm sure, call Sariah so they can continue their evening on the phone. I'm currently standing in front of Savannah's door, staring into her azure eyes as I thank her for tonight. For going along with the double date. For showing me that there's more to this life than faceless, meaningless sex and that it's okay to let someone in.

"Why does it sound like you're saying good night?" she asks with a soft laugh. "You don't really think we're going to end tonight out here, do you?"

She opens the door and tugs on my lapels, pulling me over the threshold. "Bri texted me and said Marcus booked a room for them tonight, so we have the place to ourselves." She waggles her brows playfully.

"I'm sorry I couldn't book a room—" I start, feeling bad that I couldn't give her the romantic night she deserves. Of course she cuts me off, not wanting to hear any of it.

"Stop. Tonight was perfect. The dinner and then the movie. The way you shared your popcorn with me. I don't think I've even been on a real date before like that. It was nice." Her lips curl into a smile that I swear could light up even the darkest of rooms.

She pushes me gently onto her bed so I'm sitting on the edge and she's standing in front of me. "But you know what will make it even better?" Instead of answering her own question, she unzips her dress on the side, pushes the thin straps down her shoulders, and lets the material pool at her feet, leaving her in some sexy as fuck red lingerie.

"Did you buy these for tonight?" I ask. Running my finger over the swell of her breast, I watch as goose bumps appear along her flesh.

"I did," she breathes, already squirming in anticipation. "You like?"

"I more than like." I pull both of the straps down, exposing her perfect tits. Her areoles are a dusty pink, and her nipples are pointed and hard, begging for my attention.

I glide my hands down the curves of her hips and over her plump ass, pulling her close to me. She comes willingly, groaning when I wrap my lips around her nipple and swirl my tongue around the beaded tip. I trail my mouth over to her other nipple, giving it equal attention, while Savannah runs her fingers through my hair. As I kiss and suck on her sweet flesh, I can't help but compare the intimacy of this moment to where I was a year ago. I can't imagine ever going back to being with someone I don't have this intense connection with.

I lift her to change positions, placing her on the edge of the bed, on her back, with her thighs spread for me. She arches her back to unclasp her bra and drops it to the floor once she slides it off. Her breasts fall slightly, exposing the pendant around her neck.

"It's starting to feel a bit one-sided." She pouts, nodding toward my still clothed body.

When I don't move quick enough, she sits back up and reaches to undo my bowtie, throwing it to the side. Piece by piece, she helps me remove each article of my clothing until I'm only in a pair of black boxer briefs.

"That's better," she breathes, pressing a soft kiss to the center of my torso.

I drop to my knees, so I'm eye level with her satin-covered cunt, and press a kiss to her mound, taking a moment to inhale her scent. When I glance up at her, I find her on her elbows, staring down at me with awe and lust in her eyes, and I know this woman is it for me. I can feel it. I want nothing more than to worship her every day for the rest of my life.

I tug her underwear down, revealing her neatly trimmed hair, and kiss her again. Everything about her is perfect. Separating her legs farther, I lick up her center, making her gasp. She tastes as good as she smells, like the best addiction. I get lost in her pussy, licking and sucking and eating her raw. In her sounds, every whimper of pleasure. I work her up until she's trembling under my touch, begging for a release. I push two fingers into her, and she explodes, screaming my name.

Needing to be inside her, I push my briefs down and crawl up her body, kissing every inch of her flesh I can get my lips on. Our mouths unite, tasting, caressing, nipping. She wraps her legs around my waist, and I sink into her tight warmth, our two bodies becoming one.

After we've both found our release and are lying in bed, Savannah's resting her head on my chest with her body wrapped around me like a warm blanket, and the mood seems to grow somber. It's getting late, and I have to go back to my place soon. I hate the thought of having to sleep apart from Savannah. She's become a necessity in my life, and every time we're apart, I crave her. But she won't spend the night with me, wanting to provide stability for Brody, so I doubt she'd be up for moving in with me—and holy shit, I can't believe I just suggested that in my head like it's no big deal, when we've only been dating for a short time. But the truth is, I want her all the time, and if she was willing to move in with me, I'm positive Brody would be on board with it. But in order to get there, I have to take baby steps with her... Start off small... But how do I get her to spend the night with me without spending the night?

And then an idea hits me...

"Let's go away this weekend." People take trips all the time. It's not technically spending the night if we're away, right?

"What?" She lifts her head. "Where?"

"To my house in Miami Beach."

"Miami? Don't we have to like... make flight reservations?"

"Something like that. We'll use the plane Sharp and Fields Enterprises share."

Her eyes go wide. "You own a plane?"

I chuckle. "With someone else. With all the flying I used to do, it was worth it. Now that I'm home, though, and don't plan to travel as much, I should probably reassess."

"What about Brody?"

"He'll be ecstatic. I promised to teach him how to drive, and the house in Miami has my Maserati. We can fly in tomorrow and spend the weekend, then fly home Sunday night. It might be too chilly to go in the ocean, but the pool is heated, and"—I lean forward and nip her bottom lip—"it's three stories. My room is on the bottom floor, and Brody's is on the top. We'll have plenty of alone time."

She looks like she's trying to think of an argument, but when she can't come up with one, she grins and nods. "Okay, let's do it."

Hell yes! Two steps forward...

"SLOW DOWN. IS YOUR FOOT MADE OF LEAD?" THE DAMN KID IS GOING TO get a ticket before he has a license. Is that even possible?

Brody side-eyes me but lets off the pedal. "Hilarious coming from you. Mom once said you got two tickets on the same day."

Fucking woman...Of course she did. And she isn't lying. It was our freshman year of college. Lucas and I rented a kick-ass McLaren for a weekend away with our girlfriends. The women were pissed because even though it was a four-seater, it was small as fuck, and we made them sit in the back while we reenacted *Fast and the Furious* the entire drive. I got pulled over twice during that drive in two separate cities. By the time we made it to the hotel, Paola was so mad that she refused to sleep in the same bed with me and banished me to the couch.

"I was young and dumb."

"And so am I." He shrugs, making Savannah laugh from the back seat.

When I showed her the small collection of cars I keep here since it has a decent-size garage, I expected her not to care—most women don't—but she shocked the hell out of me by knowing what each one was and arguing which cars and trucks are better. Since she's a Southern girl, she prefers American muscle over foreign. While I would beg to disagree, it was a turn-on to hear her talk cars. Apparently, one of the guys she grew up with in foster care was a huge car freak and taught her everything she knows.

"Reckless driving will get you killed," I tell him seriously. "You're fifteen and just learning. You want to drive fast, you do it on a track where it's safe."

"Oh! Can we do that?" Savannah squeals. "I've always wanted to do that. Go like two hundred around a track."

Fuck, I love this woman. The internal admission has me swallowing thickly because as much as I'd like to say those words were just a figure of speech, the truth is I mean them... It's probably too soon, but it doesn't change the fact that I mean them.

I glance back at her in the rearview mirror. Her hair is messy, and her cheeks are stained pink from having the windows down and the cold wind blowing in. She's never looked as beautiful as she does right now. Unable to help myself, I pull my phone out and snap a picture of her. She pouts playfully but doesn't hide.

"A friend of mine owns a track a few hours outside of the city. We can go one day for sure."

Both she and Brody whoop in excitement.

"Make a left at the stop sign," I tell him so we can head back to the house. After we arrived this morning, we spent the day alternating between the beach and pool. When everyone agreed we were sunned out, I told Brody we would go for a drive before I take Savannah out to dinner. I asked Brody if he wanted to go, but he said he'd rather hang back, order in a pizza, and talk to his girlfriend on the phone.

I'm almost positive the two of them see each other more on the phone than in person. Not that I'm complaining. Virtual dating means he can't get into too much trouble—at least none that will result in diapers or antibiotics.

We pull into the driveway, and Brody jumps out, already calling one of his friends to brag about driving.

"What'd you think?" I ask Savannah, opening the back door to help her out. "Not bad for a foreign car, right?"

"I guess." She grins, sliding out. Because I didn't move, her body is flush against mine. "I think I just prefer something a little... manlier." She glides her hand across the sleek paint job. "I've always wondered what it would be like to make out in the back seat. Too bad this back seat is too small."

I lift her and push her against the side of the vehicle, and her legs wrap around my waist. "You want to make out in the back seat?" I growl against her lips. "I'll buy whatever the fuck car you want, but I guarantee we'll be doing a lot more than just making out."

My mouth crashes against hers, and my tongue delves

between her parted lips, making her groan. We kiss for several minutes with her body grinding against mine, seeking pleasure.

"I want you now."

Her words create a haze in my brain, and the next thing I know, I'm walking us away from the car and over to the side of the house where there are no windows or doors that Brody can see out of and a huge fence with tall shrubbery, giving us the privacy we need.

Her back hits the wall, and she pushes her dress over her hips, giving me easier access. In seconds, my shorts are unzipped, her bikini bottoms are shoved to the side, and I'm inside her, filling her completely. As I fuck her frantically, driving into her over and over again, hard and fast, she peppers kisses all over my face, nipping along my jawline.

"Oh. My. G—" she begins as her climax overtakes her. Not wanting to risk anyone hearing, I slant my mouth over hers, swallowing down her screams as she comes, squeezing the fuck out of my dick and bringing forth my own release.

When we both come down, she sighs, dropping her head onto my shoulder. "God, that was so good."

I pull out and set her down, and she glances down then up

at me with a horrified expression on her face. "You realize we keep forgetting to use protection, right?"

"Yeah, I know." I pull my shirt off and use it to wipe the cum dripping down the inside of her thighs. Fuck, that's hot as shit.

"The chances of me getting pregnant are slim, but—"

"There's a chance... I know." I lock eyes with her. "But I don't care."

Her eyes go wide. We haven't discussed her getting pregnant, aside from me telling her I didn't want kids when we first met and me comforting her when she got her period. But I've been thinking a lot about it since the day she told me there was a chance she could be pregnant. I thought I'd flip my shit—not at her, because I knew it wasn't only on her, it was on us both—but just at the idea of doing the whole dad thing all over again. I'm so close to Brody turning eighteen, and Paola and I have made it through without anything bad happening, like what happened to my mom.

Yet when she told me she could be pregnant, my first thought was seeing her swollen with my baby. Of us discussing baby names, decorating a nursery... raising the baby together.

And I knew something in me had changed. I'm no longer the same guy I was back then. She's changed me, changed what I want in life, in my future.

"But Ben," she breathes. "Getting pregnant... it's forever."

Yeah, it is... which is exactly what I want with her because what I thought earlier in the car definitely wasn't a figure of speech. And before I can second-guess myself, I find myself saying exactly what I was thinking.

"I love you." But as the words leave my mouth, they don't feel like they're strong enough to describe the way I feel for Savannah, so I continue, trying to fully express the way I feel. "But more than that, I never want you to leave my sight." Her eyes bug out at my admission, and I fear I'm about to fuck everything up. But since I've already started, I figure I might as well keep going. "The way my body is constantly drawn toward you is like nothing I've ever felt. I crave you, desire you, need you. When you're not with me, I want you to be. You've come to own so much of my heart, and while the thought of a woman holding that kind of power over me used to scare me, with you, it makes me feel stronger and more alive."

I palm the side of her face, letting the words flow now, not overthinking what I'm saying. "I love you, Sav, and being with you makes me feel complete. I thought building my empire did that. I thought with every club I built, I would feel more fulfilled, but now I can see the difference, *feel* the difference. Those three words don't feel like nearly enough, but since they're what people use to express themselves, I need you to know that I love you so damn much, and yeah, having a baby is forever, but I'm okay with that because if it's up to me, you and me... we'll be forever."

Tears fill her eyes, and I worry I've said the wrong thing, or maybe it was at the wrong time. Or fuck, maybe it was too much too soon. But then a smile curls at the corners of her lips, and I breathe a sigh of relief.

"I love you too. And forever sounds really freaking good."

Twenty-One

Savannah

"I THINK I PICKED THE WRONG PLACE TO LIVE." I SINK MY TOES INTO THE cool sand and stare up at the bright moon hanging in the sky. I don't know the exact temperature here, but it's warm enough to have my feet in the water wearing a jersey dress while still cool enough that I'm not sweating.

After we finished eating a delicious dinner at a cute little seafood restaurant that overlooks the Atlantic, we stopped on our walk back to Ben's beach house to sit and watch the sunset. One of the things I love about Ben's place is that it's within walking distance to several shops and restaurants.

"You want to stay here?" Ben asks, his warm, supple lips kissing the side of my neck. I'm sitting between his legs, and he has his arms wrapped around my waist, holding me tight. I can't remember the last time—if ever—I've felt so safe and loved. "Just say the word." He nips the bottom of my earlobe. "We can stay as long as you want."

I know he's only joking, but the thought of staying on this beach with Ben with no end date is kind of tempting. It's not that I don't love my life, I do. But I also love the moments when we're in our own little bubble.

"As much as I—" My words are cut off by the sound of his phone ringing from inside his pocket.

"Hold that thought," he says, pulling his phone out. "It might be Brody..." When he glances at it, he hums. "I don't recognize the number. Probably spam."

"You should get it just in case."

"Yeah." He hits answer. "Fields." He listens for a moment, then, "Yes, this is Benjamin Fields." Another pause. "Yes." I can't hear what's being said, but Ben's entire body tightens in response. "How long ago?" He pushes away from me and stands, so I do the same. Something is wrong. I can feel it. He asks a few more questions and then says, "I'm on my way. Thank you," before hanging up.

"Brody?"

"No. My dad." He clenches his jaw. "He had a heart attack while he was at home. He was able to call the ambulance before he lost consciousness. When they got there, he wasn't breathing. They performed CPR, and he's alive, but he's in a coma."

"Oh, Ben." I wrap my arms around him. "I'm so sorry."

"We have to go." I can see his brain is in overdrive. Much like when he's in business mode, he's become detached. "Luckily, the jet is here, ready to go for tomorrow." He types away on his phone. "I'll call the company we use and see if they have someone available to fly us back tonight."

We speed walk back to his house, and on the way, he confirms a pilot and calls his sister to let her know the little bit of information he was given while demanding she stay calm because the stress won't be good for her pregnancy.

When we get back, he tells Brody what's happened. We pack quickly, and Ben has an Uber waiting to take us to the airport when we walk outside. He's quiet during the entire drive, as well as the plane ride to New York. Once we land, he insists Brody and I take a taxi home while he heads straight to the hospital. It's almost eleven o'clock, and even if his father can have visitors, visiting hours won't start again until the morning.

"Shit, would you mind staying at my place with Brody?" he asks at the last second just before I close the door. "His mom isn't home yet and—"

"Hey, stop. Go be with your dad. Don't worry about us. I have Brody."

He dips his head into the vehicle and kisses me. "Thank you."

Luckily, Brody has his key on him, so we can go to Ben's place when we get home. Using Ben's bathroom, I take a quick shower to rinse off and then change into my pajamas, and after telling Brody good night, I lie down in Ben's bed. It's the first time I've been in his bed, and it feels weird to be in it without him. I don't want to bother or distract him at the hospital, so I only send him one quick text to let him know we're home. Then I call Brianne to let her know about Olivier, so she can let her brother know since they're best friends and their fathers are friends.

I pull up a book on my Kindle app in an attempt to read myself tired, but after I've read the same line no less than a dozen times, I give up and pull up my social media. I never go on it, but I need a distraction. I notice a couple of messages so I click on them and find one from Lois.

Ugh. Not exactly the distraction I was going for. I consider deleting it, but my curiosity gets the best of me. It figures she would message me on here since I blocked her and Neil after they both texted, trying to apologize.

> Savy, I saw your posts, and it seems you've moved on and are happy. I'm hoping this will mean you are ready to forgive me. I miss you.

I roll my eyes and am about to block her when I change my mind.

> Lois, yes, I forgive you. You saved me years of being in a horrible, loveless marriage by sleeping with my husband, and for that, I thank you. With that said, you and I will never be friends again. I wish you the best.
> -Savannah

A bit petty? Sure...But it still feels good.

I can see when she reads it—like she was already on the app—and I quickly block her so she can't respond. The other messages are spam, so I delete them and then log out.

I'm not sure how long I toss and turn for, but eventually,

sleep must come because the next thing I know, I'm waking to a pair of strong arms encircling me from behind and the masculine scent of Ben as he kisses my bare shoulder.

"Hey," I croak out, turning to face him. He's still dressed in what he was wearing last night, and blackish purple circles are under his eyes. "How's your dad?"

He shakes his head, and I tense, fearing the worst. "He's alive," he says, making me sag in relief. "But it's not good. Because of the lack of oxygen to his brain, he slipped into a coma. The doctor said as of right now, it could simply be a matter of his body healing, but if he doesn't come around in the next couple of days..." His words trail off, but he doesn't have to say them for me to know. If he doesn't wake up soon, it could mean never waking up.

"He's going to wake up," I tell him with every ounce of positive energy I can muster. "Did you see him?"

"For a few minutes. My sister was there too with Gerald. But visiting hours aren't until eight o'clock, and because he's in the ICU, only one person can go in, and they limit the amount of time you're there. Nobody under eighteen."

"I'm so sorry." I wrap my arms around his torso. The words

are so pointless and won't change anything, but I don't know what else to do or say.

"If he hadn't called for help, he would be dead on his floor, and nobody would even know," he murmurs. "I could tell something's been wrong with him. He looked tired...I asked him about it because he's seemed off lately, but he blew off my concerns, telling me he loves me and that he's proud of Amalia and me. I should've pushed and made him go see a doctor. If I would've—"

"You can't play the what-if game. It's a waste of time."

He nods. "I just... fuck." His eyes turn glassy. "I don't know what I'll do if I lose him. He's..." He swallows thickly.

"He's your dad," I finish for him. "Don't think the worst." I run my fingers down his cheek. "You'll go back first thing in the morning and speak with the doctors to figure out a plan."

Ben rolls us over so I'm on my back, and he's hovering over me. "Thank you for bringing Brody home." His lips brush against mine once, twice, before he deepens the kiss, his tongue caressing my own. "I need to be inside you. I need to just... *fuck,* I need to get lost in you for a little while."

His tone is pleading, his eyes begging me to help him

momentarily escape. He's scared. He's already lost his mom, and now there's a chance he's going to lose his father as well.

I glance over his shoulder to make sure the door is closed, and when I see it is, I reach between us and pull his dick out. With my fingers wrapped around his thick shaft, I stroke him up and down, working him until he's nice and hard. He groans softly at my touch and dips his face, kissing along my collarbone.

As we kiss and touch, we shed our clothes, and then once Ben checks and sees that I'm wet and ready, he slides into me slowly, gently. He frames my face with his forearms and nuzzles his own into the crook of my neck, gliding in and out of me at an unhurried pace—doing exactly what he said: getting lost in me.

We make love, and then Ben wraps me in his arms, falling asleep with his face still buried in my neck. I want to get cleaned up, but I don't move, not wanting to wake him. He's been through a lot tonight and, if the fates aren't in his favor, will be going through more in the near future.

At some point, I doze off, only to wake up to him sliding into me again. This time, he fucks me quick and rough. He doesn't kiss me—instead nipping at the sensitive flesh between my neck and collarbone—and there isn't any foreplay. Ben always makes sure I get off first. It's as if he was drawn to me in his sleep and is barely awake. He doesn't last long before he finds his release and then falls back asleep.

This time, since he's sleeping on his stomach and not on me, I do get up and jump in the shower. After I'm dressed, I tiptoe out to the kitchen, finding it's almost seven in the morning. I make a pot of coffee and whip up some pancakes, bacon, and eggs.

I'm just finishing up when I hear Ben's phone ringing. I pad into the room and find him sitting on the edge of the bed with his head hanging down. My heart plummets into my stomach. This can't be good.

Closing the space between us, I kneel in front of Ben. He looks up, his eyes filled with unshed tears, and I know something is very wrong.

"He's gone," he whispers. "He's gone."

There are no words to say, so I do the only thing I can do and wrap my arms around him, hugging him as tight as I can while he cries against my chest.

Brody must hear him because he steps into the doorway, his eyes knowing. On the way home last night, he told me that even though his dad was gone a lot, his grandfather always made it a point to visit with him and check in on him. But in the past couple of months, Brody hasn't talked to him as often. He was worried he wouldn't get a chance to make sure they were okay.

"Come here, sweetie," I tell him, opening my arm.

Ben glances up and chokes back a sob. "Fuck... Brody."

Without saying a word, Brody joins us on the bed, and for the next several minutes, I hold my boys, wishing I could make this better for them. I've never known what it's like to lose someone I love. Both my parents abandoned me. And I've never had anyone else in my life close enough to miss, let alone mourn... until now.

I try to imagine what it would be like to lose Ben or Brody, but just the thought of it happening causes my heart to clench in my chest, knocking the oxygen from my lungs.

"I love you," I murmur to them both, needing them to know. Watching how quickly Ben and Brody went from laughing at the beach to crying over Olivier makes me realize how uncertain life really is, and at any moment, those you love can be ripped away from you.

THE NEXT FEW DAYS PASS IN A BLUR OF EMOTIONAL CHAOS. BEN GETS LOST in planning his dad's funeral while Brody stays close to me. I try to be there for Ben, but the more I push, the more he pulls away. We sit together at the funeral, but afterward, he takes off on his own and doesn't return until the next day. He doesn't even notice I'm there, and he reeks of alcohol.

When I call him, asking if he wants to meet for lunch or dinner, he tells me he's busy dealing with work. I go to the gym the following morning, but he doesn't show up. And the next evening when Brody tells me that his dad never came home, I head over to his place to stay with him, explaining that his father is grieving and we just need to give him some time.

"Can I move in with you?" Brody asks one night after we've had dinner and are sitting at the table while he finishes his math homework.

"What?" I ask in confusion.

"When my dad leaves, can I move in with you?"

"Brody…" I cover my hand with his. "Your dad isn't leaving. He's grieving… But he'll get through it. He just needs some time."

He nods but doesn't look like he believes me. "Okay, but if he leaves, can I move in with you? I don't…" He swallows thickly. "I really don't want to move back in with my mom and Ted."

"It's not going to come to that. I promise."

Ben isn't going anywhere… He said he wasn't. He told me he loved me and wanted a future with me… He's reconnected with his son… He wouldn't leave after all that… *Right?*

Twenty-Two

Benjamin

ONE MONTH LATER

"I DON'T GIVE A SHIT WHAT IT SAYS! I NEED YOU TO HANDLE IT, AND—" MY words are cut off by a knock followed by Savannah walking through the door.

"I could hear you yelling from the lobby," she says, coming to stand next to me.

"Well, I wouldn't be yelling if my employees would do their damn job."

Savannah flinches, and I feel like an asshole because she doesn't deserve that. I've been on edge since my dad died, feeling as though I've been pushed into the middle of the ocean with a weight attached to my ankle. I'm drowning, and no matter what I do, I can't come up for air. But regardless of how I feel, neither she nor my assistant deserves to be spoken to like that.

"I'm sorry," I tell her, taking a calming breath. "I just have a lot going on right now—"

"I brought lunch." She holds up a brown bag. "How about you take a break to eat, and then you can go back to yelling afterward?" she says dryly. I do a double take at her words. They sound like a joke, yet her face shows she's dead serious.

My assistant, of course, uses the moment to make her escape.

"I was actually in the middle of—"

"Working, I know, and it will *still* be there after lunch. But right now, you're going to sit your ass down and have lunch with your girlfriend, who brought lunch for her and her boyfriend. The same damn boyfriend she misses very much." Her words start off strong, but by the time she gets to the end, her voice is cracking, right along with my goddamn heart.

I cut across the room and pull her into my arms. Her shoulders slump, and her head drops against my chest. "I miss you," she murmurs. "I know you're grieving, and it's going to take time, but I miss you and so does Brody."

"Baby, what are you talking about?" I tip her chin up, confused as hell. "I'm right here."

"Your body, yes, but your head... your heart... it's like you're lost, and I'm getting scared," she whispers. "Every day, it feels like you pull further away, and I... I'm terrified I'm going to lose you."

Her phone goes off, and she quickly checks it, types back to whoever it is, and then pockets it.

"Who was that?" I ask.

"Brody."

"What did he say?"

"He said he wanted to make pizza for dinner."

"Oh...well, I don't know if I'll be home. I have a shit ton to do and—"

"Nobody planned for you to be," she snaps. "That's the problem. You're here." She backs out of my arms and spreads her own. "All the time."

"Excuse me?"

"Nobody planned for you to be home. Just like you haven't

been home a single night in the past month before midnight... if you come home at all. And when you do come home, you're back here at the crack of dawn. And you're not even going to the gym."

"What are you talking about?" I think back to the past several weeks. Yeah, I've been dealing with the shitstorm my dad left me, but...

"When's the last time we had sex?"

I try to remember, but I can't...

"Ben, are you going to leave?" she asks softly, hesitantly. "Because Brody asked, and if you are, I just... I need to know." Her words are the sword that cuts through the fog in my head. I've been so lost in my own grief that I've blocked everyone and everything out, focusing on what I can do without even thinking... work. And in doing so, I've pushed away the two people who mean the most to me.

"Fuck, Sav. No. No." I lift her by her ass and carry her over to my desk, not giving a shit about anything but showing her that I'm sorry and that I'm not going anywhere.

I pull her shirt up and kiss my way down the center of her chest. Pushing the cups of her bra down, I take one of her pert nipples into my mouth.

"Ow." She jumps slightly.

"You okay?"

"Yeah, it's just been a little while..."

"Too long," I agree, bringing my mouth to hers. "I'm so sorry," I murmur against her lips, needing her to know that. Needing her to understand.

I break our kiss to give her breasts some more attention. The harder I suck, the louder she groans, begging me for more.

She hikes her skirt up and frantically grabs for my pants, unbuttoning and unzipping them quickly. Within seconds, her legs are spread, her underwear is moved to the side, and I'm thrusting into her cunt that was made for me.

Fuck, I've missed this woman. What the hell was I thinking pushing her away? *I wasn't...* and instead of her letting me, she pushed back, bringing me back to her. Every day since my dad's death, she's made sure I'm fed, leaving me food on the counter, taking care of my son when I was too fucked up in my grief to do it myself. For the past month, she's stayed at my house, slept in my bed, and not once given up on me. She was afraid I was going to leave, and I need her to know that's never going to happen. She's it for me. The woman I want to spend the rest of my life with. She should never go a single day without knowing that, without knowing how much I love her and how much she means to me.

I find her clit and massage it in small circles until her body is trembling under my touch, her cunt contracting and choking my dick. I lose myself in her, burying my face in her neck, inhaling her sweet scent, tasting her warm flesh. She's mine. And I'm hers. And fuck if she'll ever doubt that shit again.

I lift my head and look into her satiated gaze. There's so much I want to say, but now isn't the time. Not with me buried in her pussy anyway. So instead, I kiss her softly, keeping us connected for a little while longer.

"I love you," I murmur against her lips when our kiss comes to an end.

Her entire body sags in relief, and I hate myself for allowing her to doubt that for even a second.

"No matter what happens, I'm not going anywhere. I'll always be here."

She nods but doesn't say anything back, and that's okay. I fucked up this last month. Put my grief above her and my son.

It's going to take time, but I'll show them that I'm not going anywhere. They're my number one priority, and I'll make sure they know that.

After we clean up, Savannah grabs the bag of food and sets it on the table, handing me a box and a can of soda and placing hers in front of her. We're sitting across from each other, but I need to be closer, to touch her and feel her. I can already feel my head starting to fog up again with shit about Dad, and I can't let that happen.

I walk over to her and lift her off her chair, grabbing the box of food, and bring it with us to the couch, where I situate her on my lap. "What are you doing?" She laughs, the beautiful sound hitting my heart.

"That's better." I give her a quick kiss. "You were too far away."

She opens the box of food, the smell of chicken lo mein wafting in the air, and scrunches her nose. "Ohh, I think it's bad." She closes the box back up. "We must've had it sitting too long when you distracted me with your dick."

It doesn't smell bad to me—in fact, it smells delicious—but when she drops the box onto the table and brushes her lips against mine, rearranging herself to straddle my lap, all thoughts of food evaporate. After all, Savannah is my favorite thing to eat.

"FUCK." I SLAM MY LAPTOP DOWN AND GLANCE AT THE TIME. IT'S AFTER six, and I need to get going so I can make it home in time for dinner. Savannah and Brody are making pizza—Brody's favorite thing to make—and I'll be damned if I miss it again.

"I've walked in on you cursing twice in one day. Do you want to talk about it?"

My gaze swings to the doorway, and I find Savannah standing there leaning against the doorframe.

"I was just about to leave. Aren't you and Brody making dinner?"

"We were supposed to." She walks farther into my office. "But it's the last day of school before spring break so he's going to the movies with his friends, and we're going to make pizza tomorrow night. And before you freak out, he asked me because he's been worried about bugging you."

"Which shouldn't go through his head," I argue, feeling like shit. "My son should be able to come to me about anything at any time. We were finally getting somewhere, and now it's like I've pushed us backward twenty damn steps."

"No, you didn't. You were grieving. You lost your dad suddenly. Nobody expects you to just bounce back." She walks around my desk, and I grip the curve of her hips, pulling her in front of me. "We'll get through this... together."

"I didn't even realize Brody had spring break coming up." I sigh in exhaustion, feeling like a damn failure. "His mom texted she'd like to see him, and now it makes sense. He's avoiding her again because Ted's home, but she's done not seeing him. She wants him to go to her place for a few days. She must know he's going to be on break. I can't let him hang out at the house alone, so I'll probably have him go there or come to work with me." He's going to be pissed, but there's nothing I can do. I'm sure as hell not leaving my fifteen-year-old alone to get into all sorts of trouble—even if he's been behaving lately.

"I actually took the week off to hang out with him," she says, shocking the hell out of me. "We can come have lunch with you, and maybe you can take a day off, and we can do something fun."

"You took off work?"

"Yeah... I hope that's okay. I didn't mean to overstep. You've just been kind of out of it and—"

"Whoa, stop. I just can't believe you would do that. Thank you." I reach up and kiss the tip of her nose. "I'd say we should go away, but I'm swamped. My dad..." I swallow thickly, hating what I have to say next. "My dad must've been sick because he left me in a bind. None of the books are current, and he handled everything... and with quarterly reports due..."

Savannah frowns. "Let me help you."

"What?" I heard her, but she already has a job.

"Ben, I took the week off anyway. I can help you sort out the mess, and we can go away for a few days." Her face lights up, and even if I thought it was a horrible idea to leave right now, there's no way I can say no to her. Because while I should be here, handling the mess my dad left me, Savannah and Brody need me more.

"All right. Let's do it. If you don't mind."

"I don't. You can show me everything tonight since Brody won't be home until ten, and I'll get it all sorted for you next week."

"Well, in that case, there's only one thing left to discuss. Where do we go for vacation?"

Twenty-Three

Savannah

"NOPE, IT'S NOT HAPPENING." I SHAKE MY HEAD. "YOU GO, AND I'LL SAFELY stay right where I am… with my feet firmly on the ground."

Ben and Brody laugh.

"C'mon, Sav," Brody whines. "It's not that bad. Trust me, you're going to have fun."

"That's what you said about the Tower of Terror! I almost died. That freaking elevator…" I shiver in remembrance. "The way it went down and my body went up!" I shriek. "Nope. Not happening."

More laughter.

"You'll be belted in tight," Brody argues.

"Yeah, because it goes fast and upside down, and did I mention fast? You go, and while I'm waiting for you, I'll sit my ass down and eat one of those delicious Mickey Mouse ice creams… and maybe a pretzel." Mmm… yeah, those sound yummy.

"You're going," Ben says, grabbing my hand and pulling me toward the long line. "We'll sit next to you, and I'll hold your hand. And when you have fun, and you will, I'll even go on it with you again."

"Yeah, let's go," Brody adds. "We didn't fly all the way to Orlando so you could go to Disney and Universal for the first time and not ride all the good rides."

"Fine." I huff, knowing he's right. When we discussed where to go away, and Ben and Brody learned I've never been to a single theme park, they insisted that's where we go. This is our second day and fourth park, and all the other ones were great, but of course they saved the scariest ride for last.

"Besides," Brody says. "Tomorrow is Universal and Islands of Adventure, and the roller coasters there are way faster."

Ben elbows him in the ribs, making Brody grunt in pain.

"They get faster than this?" I hiss.

"You'll be fine. Let's go. And afterward, I'll buy you an ice cream and pretzel, and we can go find some more animals to take pictures with."

Brody snorts out a laugh, and I glare. "Keep it up, and I'll make you take more pictures with all the princesses again."

The line goes slow, and finally, we make it to the front, where it lists off the millions of reasons you shouldn't ride this ride and what will happen if you do.

"Great, you see this?" I point at the sign. "This is their way of saying, 'If you die, it's not our fault.'"

Both guys laugh.

"It's only for people who have heart trouble, problems with motion sickness, or are pregnant," Brody says. "Are you any of those?" He quirks a playful brow, not knowing that there's one thing on this list I wish I were.

"No," I murmur. "I'm none of those."

As if Ben knows what just went through my head, he pulls me into his side and kisses my temple.

It's finally our turn to get on the ride, and after meeting

a fake Aerosmith, we're prompted to get into the fake stretch limousine, which will take us to the fake concert—if we don't die on the way.

Once we're locked into place, Ben's hand finds mine, squeezing it so I know he's there. The music blasts into our ears, and then we rocket off into the dark. The second we hit the first turn, I'm screaming my head off, but they were right. It's fun! We're jolted left and right and upside down. Blurs of neon signs fly by while we jam out to some rock 'n' roll, and what feels like seconds later, we come to a stop—the ride over.

"So, what'd you think?" Brody asks, wearing a shit-eating grin on his face.

"I think that was freaking awesome, and we should go again!"

"Told you!" Brody says, fist-bumping his dad.

We go on the Rock 'n' Roller Coaster two more times before we call it a day and head back to the hotel. Ben booked us a cool room where we can watch the fireworks from our balcony, so he suggests we watch them tonight.

Like every day when we get back, we all go to our rooms to shower the day off, but unlike every other time, Ben says he needs to handle some business and leaves me to shower alone.

Once I'm clean and in comfy pajamas, I head out to find Ben and Brody talking softly.

"Everything okay?" I ask, making them both look over at me startled.

"Yeah, go ahead and head out, and we'll be right out," Ben says.

"Okay, but hurry." I open the French doors and head outside. "They always start promptly at nine o'clock." I glance at my phone and see it's almost time.

"We'll be right out," he says again.

It's a cooler day in Florida, in the high seventies, which compared to New York right now is like heaven. I inhale the fresh air and am staring up at the sky, waiting for the first explosion to go off when the French door creaks open. I'm expecting them to join me against the railing, so I'm confused when I glance over and find both of them standing behind me.

"What are you guys doing? Get out here."

But instead of moving, Ben extends his arm, popping open a tiny black box and exposing a... "Is that?" No, it can't be...

"The past few months have been the best of my life," Ben

begins, forcing my gaze to snap from the gorgeous ring to him. "Between Brody moving in with me and meeting you, my life has changed significantly, and I can't imagine ever going back to the way it was before. When we were in my office, you asked if I was moving, and I realized I never made it clear to you and Brody that I'm not going anywhere ever. I said I wasn't, but you need to see it for yourself. You both are my life. And while a ring can't force someone to stay, it symbolizes my commitment to you."

He gets down on one knee, and my heart pounds against my rib cage as tears well up in my eyes. "Savannah Cartwright, will you do me the honor of wearing my ring and spending the rest of your life with me?"

"And me," Brody adds with a shy shrug. "Well, until I move out and go to college." Ben grunts, making Brody laugh. "It would be really fuck—freaking cool if you would be my stepmom."

"So, what do you say?" Ben asks. "Marry me and get both of us?"

"Yes," I whisper, tears of happiness sliding down my cheeks. "Yes, I will marry you." I look at Brody. "And I would love nothing more than to be your stepmom."

Ben pushes the ring onto my finger and then stands, wrapping me in his arms and kissing me while he twirls me around. When he sets me down, Brody scoops me up into a hug, making my tears fall even harder.

The first explosion of the fireworks go off, but I barely notice them, too focused on what's in front of me—love, friendship, happiness… family.

"YOUR MOM WANTS YOU TO VISIT."

"And I don't want to."

We're on the plane ride home, and I'm lying with my head in Ben's lap, half-asleep, listening to Ben and Brody talk.

"We have shared custody."

"And I'm fifteen. I don't want to go. I told her to let me know when Ted isn't home, and then I'll come by."

"What did he do that made you hate him so much?" Ben asks, his tone is filled with concern.

Brody goes silent for a beat, then says, "He's just an asshole."

The plane shakes, hitting some turbulence, and my stomach does a flip-flop, making me tighten my body.

"You okay?" Ben asks.

"Yeah, I just felt…" Before I can finish my sentence, the plane shifts and dips, and I fly up, darting to the tiny bathroom. I make it there just in time to expel my entire breakfast and the coffee I consumed less than an hour ago.

I'm perched over the toilet when Ben arrives less than a minute later. He pulls my hair into a ponytail and rubs my back while I get it all out. Once I'm done, and my stomach is groaning in pain, he hands me a warm washcloth to wipe my mouth with.

"Thanks." I stand and flush the toilet. Grabbing a disposable toothbrush they keep on hand, I brush my teeth and then gargle some mouthwash.

"There's a storm so the rest of the trip might be rocky. Why don't you go lie in bed?"

"Will you lie with me?" I waggle my brows.

"Of course."

Thankfully, the rest of the flight is spent with us in bed cuddling and not with me cradling the toilet.

"THIS DOESN'T MAKE ANY SENSE." I GO THROUGH THE NUMBERS FOR THE fourth time, already knowing what I'm going to find but wishing somehow, they would change. Unfortunately, numbers don't change. They're constant. Two plus two always equals four.

I take a sip of my water, and my stomach gargles. When I woke up this morning, I wasn't feeling well, so I skipped breakfast, but now I think I'm feeling sick from not eating. I briefly wonder if maybe I'm coming down with something.

Needing a break from staring at the screen, I make myself some toast and coffee, but the second the Keurig begins to brew and the scent hits my nostrils, my stomach roils, and I end up in the bathroom with my face down in the toilet.

"Savy?" Brody calls out. "You okay?"

"Yeah! I think I have a stomach bug. You feeling okay?"

"I'm fine." He steps into the doorway. "Do you need anything?"

"No, I'm going to take a quick shower. Can you text your dad and ask him if he can bring dinner home? I don't think I'll be up for cooking."

"Yeah, sure."

After I take a shower and throw on some comfy pajamas, I head back out to the couch to go over the numbers again. I'm in the middle of running them again when a wave of nausea hits me, and I wonder if it's the stress of what I'm going to have to tell Ben that's making me sick.

"Dammit, this can't be right," I mutter to myself.

"What can't be right?" a masculine voice asks, making me jump.

"You're home early."

Ben smirks. "I am, and I've brought food"—he holds up a pizza box—"and roses for my beautiful fiancée." Butterflies warm my belly as I take in the pizza and gorgeous pink flowers in an elegant glass vase. "You were so caught up in whatever you were doing, you didn't notice me come in." He drops the pizza onto the table and sets the flowers down, then comes over to sit on the couch next to me, pulling me into his arms. "I missed you today." He brushes his lips against mine. "It was weird going all day without you."

"You probably shouldn't be this close to me," I warn. "I

think I'm coming down with something."

"Yeah, Brody texted me that you were throwing up." He smirks. "I'll take my chances."

"Thank you for the flowers."

"You're welcome." He glances around. "Where's Brody?"

"In his room."

He nods then kisses me harder, making me moan. His tongue darts into my mouth, the scent of cinnamon hitting my senses. I gag slightly and back up.

"What's wrong?" he asks, concern etching his features.

"I think I'm a little... or a lot nervous to talk to you, and my body is reacting to the stress."

His brows come together. "Does it have something to do with what you were intently focusing on when I got home?"

"Yeah." I sigh. "I spent the day sorting out your books, and..." I take a deep breath. "Ben, I've run the numbers several times, and you weren't wrong. You're missing a lot of money. Several thousand."

"So my dad messed up..."

"No, he didn't mess up." And this is what I've been dreading telling him. "He was stealing from the company."

Ben's face jerks back like he's been smacked. "Excuse me? What did you just say?"

"I started going through the books for Lush, New York, but in doing so, I found several errors that didn't make sense. So, to double-check them, I had Owen send me the information for your other properties."

"You called one of my employees behind my back?"

"I didn't want to have to tell you what I suspected until I knew for sure. You've taken your dad's death so hard and—"

"Of course I've taken his death hard," he barks. "He was my dad, my only parent left, and now he's gone."

"I know," I say, trying to remain calm, but my emotions are getting the best of me, and I can feel myself on the verge of crying. "After going through the numbers, I found that *someone* who has access to your business accounts has been skimming off the top for several months."

"This can't be right." He sets me onto the couch and stands. "My dad wouldn't steal from me."

I was afraid he would say that, so I open my laptop and send him my findings. "Over the course of six months, your dad moved thousands of dollars to his personal account. The exact figures are in the report I just sent over."

"You're wrong," he deadpans, not even considering what I'm saying. I know he's hurt right now, but I made sure I had all the facts straight, and eventually, he's going to have to deal with it. Fortunately, his business is thriving, which is why he didn't notice it missing until he went to run the reports. His dad knew what he was doing, taking a little bit from each account so a red flag wouldn't be raised. When I spoke to Owen, though, he told me he did notice, but when he tried to speak to Olivier, he was brushed off.

"I'm not wrong. I double- and triple-checked, and honestly, I kind of resent you accusing me of being wrong. Either you don't trust me, or you don't think I'm capable of doing my job. Either way, that's not okay."

"All I'm saying is that you could very well be mistaken. Hell, you told me you couldn't conceive, yet here we are, a few months later, and you're pregnant. So if you could be mistaken about that, maybe you're mistaken about this too."

It takes me a moment to wrap my head around what he's just said, and once I do, I take a step back, trying to get a handle on this new information. "I'm not..." I shake my head. I can't be… We tried for years, and it never happened. I'm broken…

"When's the last time you had your period?" he asks. "You've been throwing up, certain smells make you sick, and your body, especially your breasts, are sensitive. It doesn't take a rocket scientist to put it together."

"No… I…" Fuck, am I pregnant? I try to think back to when I got my period last, but my brain isn't working. Too much is happening at once, and all I want to do is cry.

When Ben quirks a knowing brow, my blood boils over, and I snap at him. "Even if I were, that has *nothing* to do with the fact that your dad stole from you, and instead of listening, you're accusing me of lying about it."

Hurt and confused and needing some space to think about everything that's just happened, I bolt out of Ben's place without looking back. It's only when I get to the elevator that I realize I'm without any shoes or keys or hell, even my cell phone. I've been staying at his place for so long that everything of mine is there.

Praying Brianne is home, I get on the elevator and press the button for our floor, all while blocking everything out that was just said. If I think about it, I'm going to lose it.

When I knock on the door, Brianne opens it, confused. "Did you lose your keys?" The second her eyes lock with mine, all the emotions bubbling to the surface spill over, and I throw myself into her arms.

"I think I'm pregnant."

"What?" She gasps. "That's amazing." She backs up and looks me in the eyes. "That's amazing, right?"

"Yeah, it would be, if my fiancé didn't just accuse me of lying about his dad stealing from him."

Her eyes go wide. "Oh, shit. Come sit down. I think we're going to need an impromptu girls' night, complete with ice cream and tea, because it seems you have some spilling to do."

Twenty-Four

Benjamin

"FUCK!" I POUND MY FIST AGAINST THE CLOSED DOOR AND THEN, WITHOUT thinking, swipe a bunch of shit off the table. When the vase holding the flowers explodes against the wood floor, shards of glass flying every which way, I release a harsh sigh, feeling as though that's the perfect representation of my life at this moment—fucking shattered.

This can't be happening. She was supposed to find the issue in the books that my dad left behind. She was *not* supposed to tell me my dad—my own flesh and blood—was stealing from me. It doesn't make any sense. He worked for me for years and was paid way beyond his pay grade. He has no reason to steal from me. She has to be lying. *She wouldn't be the first woman to lie to me.*

I'll be damned if I allow her to destroy my family and disgrace my father's name. But even as the thoughts emerge, I internally cringe because deep down, I know that's not who Savannah is. She doesn't lie or trick or play games. I saw the look on her face when she told me, and it was clear it hurt her to say the words almost as much as she knew it would hurt me to hear them.

My thoughts go back to the weeks leading up to my dad's death… The way he was sneaking around and hiding where he was going. I tried to ask him what was wrong, but he refused to confide in me.

"Pizza here?" Brody asks, stepping out of his room and snapping me out of my thoughts. He looks around at the sight of destruction, then glances at me. "Where's Savy?"

"She left."

"What happened?" He walks over and picks the pizza box up, setting it on the table and opening it. Because it was closed, the pizza is still intact, just a little jostled.

"We got into an argument."

He nods and picks up several of the roses, carrying them into the kitchen.

"Leave it," I tell him. "I'll clean it up." It's my fault, after all.

"I got this. You can go."

"Go where?"

His eyes meet mine. "Find her and fix whatever you broke." He holds up the flowers. "I'm assuming these were meant for her."

Dammit, this kid. He's never looked or sounded so old... or wise. But...

"It's not that simple," I tell him as my phone rings out. I grab it from my jacket pocket, hoping it's Savannah, only to find it's my sister. She's been down since Dad's death, and with her being pregnant, I don't want to ignore her call. I hold up a finger to Brody, indicating to give me a minute, then take the call.

"Hey."

"Hey," she says back, sounding worried. "Mr. Jeffreys called. He said he's been trying to get ahold of you, but you're not taking his calls. If you need me to handle it..."

I sigh in exhaustion. Mr. Jeffreys is the attorney our dad used to create his will. I should've met with him immediately following Dad's death to sort out his affairs, but I've been putting it off.

"I'll give him a call right now," I tell her, not wanting to cause her more stress.

"Okay. How are you?"

"I'm okay. You?"

"I'm all right. I haven't seen you in a while. I was thinking you and Savy and Brody could come over for dinner one night."

"Yeah," I choke out. "I'll let you know." My phone beeps in my ear, and hoping it's Savannah, I tell her I'll get back to her soon, then switch over without looking at who's calling.

"Benjamin." I cringe at the sound of Paola's voice. Shit, I should've checked to see who was calling.

"What's up?"

"I would like to see my son. You're back from your trip, so can you please have him come see me?"

"He has an issue with Ted…" I begin as the sound of a phone goes off.

Brody picks it up from the coffee table and shows it to me.

It's Savannah's. She left it here. Guess she won't be calling... He answers it and walks into the other room.

"Hello?" Paola snaps, reminding me I'm still on the phone with her.

"Yeah. Brody doesn't like Ted, and I think—"

"Ted isn't here," she says, cutting me off. "We're actually not together anymore. I've ended our engagement."

"Really?"

"He..." She clears her throat. "He cheated on me. It's over. He's out of town, with his mistress I imagine, but once he returns, he'll be getting his shit and moving out."

"Sorry," I tell her, unsure of what else to say. We might not be friends, but she's still Brody's mom.

"Thanks. So do you think I can spend the weekend with him?"

"I'll speak to him, but I'm sure that can be arranged." Plus, it'll give me time to sort my life out.

We hang up just as Brody is walking back out. "Your mom wants to spend the weekend with you. And before you argue, she and Ted broke up."

Brody's eyes widen. "Seriously?"

"Yeah. Are you okay to go over there for a few days?"

"Yeah."

"Who was on the phone?" I nod to Savannah's phone still in his hand.

"Bri. She's coming by to grab Savy's stuff. She said she tried to call you, but it kept going to voicemail."

"I had a call on each line."

"Why is she coming to get Savy's stuff?" he asks, glaring at me.

"Because she doesn't live here," I explain dumbly. "She's been staying here while I was dealing with my dad's death, to be here for me and you. But she doesn't live here."

"That's stupid. You guys are getting married. She might as well just stay here. And she wouldn't need her shit if you two weren't fighting." He drops the phone onto the coffee table. "Fix it," he says before turning to go to his room.

"You didn't eat," I mention.

"Not hungry." He waves his hand over his shoulder. "Guess I'll get ready to go to Mom's."

"I JUST WANT TO TALK TO HER."

"Not happening." Brianne blocks the door like a fucking guard dog. "She needs some space. You hurt her."

I know she's right, but at the same time, I need to talk to her. I was in shock by what she said. I never should've lashed out at her, and I definitely shouldn't have pointed out that she's most likely pregnant the way I did either. When Brianne came and got her stuff, I tried to get her to let me see Savannah, but she wasn't having it, and since it's the weekend, I can't even catch her at work. I've sent chocolates and flowers and her favorite pineapple pizza, but she still won't talk to me. I fucked up, but damn, I just need a chance to fix it.

"I've given her two days. I just want to talk to her."

"And when she's ready to talk to you, she knows your number."

She slams the door in my face, and I hang my head against the door in frustration. My phone rings, and I pull it out, hoping it's Savannah, but it's not.

"Lucas, what's up?"

"Nothing. Laura is having a girls' night with her friends. Just calling to see what you're up to? Want to grab a drink?"

"I'll meet you downstairs." I'm not really in the mood to drink, but being alone in the condo last night sucked. There was a time when I loved the silence, but now, it just feels lonely as fuck. No Brody playing his loud as hell video games. No Savannah binge-watching her stupid shows. I used to revel in the quiet, and now I despise it.

"Congratulations on your engagement," Lucas says when he sees me.

"Thanks. How'd you know?" Savannah and I haven't had time to discuss doing an engagement party since it just happened. Hell, we haven't even discussed when she wants to get married and what kind of wedding she wants. Then again, at this rate, there won't be a wedding.

"My sister told me. I haven't seen Savy all week since she's on vacation." He smirks, and I know something sarcastic is about to come out of his mouth. "Never thought you'd be engaged before me."

And there it is. "Never thought I'd meet a woman like Savannah."

He nods in understanding.

We spend the next few hours at Erwin's, a hole-in-the-wall

bar around the corner we frequent, drinking and shooting the shit. I'm probably a good four, maybe five scotches in when my phone rings.

It's late, after three in the morning, and it's Savannah. Something in my blood turns cold with worry.

"Sav."

"Ben, I need you to come home."

"Where are you?" I'm already standing and throwing down a couple of bills.

"I'm at your place...with Brody."

"I thought he was with his mom." What the hell is going on?

"Just come home, please."

Twenty-Five

Savannah

ONE HOUR AGO

"MMM, SO GOOD." I TAKE A BITE OF MY PHISH FOOD ICE CREAM AS MY favorite episode of *One Tree Hill* plays. It's the one where Nathan admits to Haley that even though he hated her leaving him to go on tour, he kept every article and photograph of her. They're standing in the rain, yelling at each other, and then he kisses her with such passion, goose bumps prick my skin and tears fill my eyes, making it hard to see the screen.

I let out a choked sob as I scoop another bite of caramel-chocolate-marshmallow goodness into my mouth. "I want a love like that," I say out loud, shoveling more ice cream into my mouth. When I dip my spoon in, and nothing comes out, I glance down and see the container is empty. "Figures." I drop my spoon into the container. "Looks like my *fiancé* isn't the only Ben fucking with my heart."

"Are you talking to your ice cream?" Brianne asks with a laugh. She must've just gotten home from Marcus's place. I told her she doesn't have to babysit me, but she's insisted on sleeping here for the past two nights.

"Yeah." I shrug, owning my craziness. "I was just pointing out that I've been heartbroken by two Bens in the past two days."

She quirks a brow. "Well, there's more of that Ben in the freezer."

My mood perks up. "You bought me more?"

"I did, but you can only have it when you talk to the other Ben."

My mood plummets.

"I think I'm done with both of these Bens." I drop the container onto the nightstand with a huff.

Brianne rolls her eyes. "You are not. You're just emotional

and hurt, and cranky because you're refusing to take a pregnancy test and find out if Ben was right and knew you were pregnant before you did."

"Whatever," I grumble as my phone rings. I grab it, ready to hit ignore, thinking it's Ben again. But when Brody's name shows up, I pause my show and answer it. No matter how mad and hurt I am at Ben, I'll always be there for Brody.

"Hey."

"Savy, I, umm, I need you." Brody's voice is nothing more than a whisper. Something is wrong.

"I'm here. Where are you?"

"I'm outside the building."

I don't understand why he's out there instead of at his dad's place, but it doesn't matter. "I'm at my place. Do you want me to come down, or do you want to come up?"

He's silent for a few beats before he says, "I'll come up... Wait, are you alone?"

I glance at Brianne. I should tell him she's here, but something tells me he might not come up if I do.

"Yeah, I'm alone. I'll come unlock the door."

"Okay."

He hangs up, and Brianne quirks a brow. "It's Brody. Something is wrong, and he needs to talk to me. Can you, umm, hide in your room?"

"I'll do you one better and go back to Marcus's, but if you need me..."

"I know. Thanks."

I hug her, then throw on a bra and leggings before walking her out so I can meet Brody at the door.

"I saw Bri at the elevator," he says, walking in.

"She's going to Marcus's. She was on her way out when you called."

He nods, and his gaze connects with mine, and it's then I notice he has a swollen eye like he's been punched.

"What happened?"

I step toward him to check it out, and he takes a step back, shaking his head. "I... I didn't know who else to go to." His hazel eyes, identical to his father's, meet mine. "I know I have my dad, but..."

"Hey, I'm here. Come sit down."

He follows me over to the couch, and we have a seat. I give him a few moments to gather his thoughts before I ask him to talk to me.

"I like girls," he starts, confusing me because I know he does—hence him dating Sariah—and I'm not sure where he's going. "But I also think I might like guys."

I nod but remain quiet since I'm sure there's more to come, and I want to let him get it all out.

"Shit, this is so embarrassing," he mutters, scrubbing his hands over his face.

"No, it's not. Whatever you have to tell me, I'm not judging."

He releases a harsh sigh. "One night I was in my room watching... porn." His cheeks tinge pink, and I have to swallow down my smile because it's so normal, but I can imagine how embarrassing it is for a teenager to admit. "I clicked on a video, and it was of a girl and some guys. The guys, they were..." He meets my eyes, no doubt praying I understand so he doesn't have to explain.

I nod my understanding, and he continues. "I was curious, so I found some with more guys. I was watching it when Ted barged into my room drunk. My mom was asleep. He liked to watch sports and drink after she went to bed. A lot of the time, he would pass out on the couch."

A lump, the size of a bitter lemon, fills my throat as I pray to every God what he's about to say isn't what I think.

"He, umm, he called me a queer and shit, and I told him to get the hell out. Every time he would get drunk, he would talk shit, but I ignored him. I didn't tell my mom because I didn't want her to think I was gay. I don't really know..."

"I get it," I tell him. "But there's nothing wrong with it if you are."

"Yeah," he breathes. "His taunting kept getting worse... and then one night, he told me if I want to find out if I liked guys, he could show me..." He clears his throat and looks down, refusing to meet my eyes as he says the next part. "He started unbuttoning his pants, telling me he could fuck me, and I would know if I was gay."

Needing to remain strong for Brody because he's trusting me with this, I swallow down the bile of anger burning my throat, patiently waiting for him to continue.

He glances up and looks at me, his eyes sad. "My mom used to say she was lonely, that my dad left her and she had to raise me alone. I didn't want to ruin her happiness."

Oh no. His getting into fights was his cry for help. He just didn't know how to handle it. It's why he never goes with his mom since he moved in with his dad.

"I don't know your mom, but I can tell you that there's no way she wouldn't want to know what Ted was doing. I saw her at dinner that day, and she loves you. What he did is wrong... so damn wrong."

"They broke up. My mom said he cheated. She didn't tell me that, but I overheard her crying to her friend on the phone."

I feel like what he's telling me is a lead-up to more, so I simply nod and wait.

"She said he moved out, so I went with her for the weekend. I was pissed at Dad for upsetting you and making you leave."

"He didn't make me leave."

"Whatever. He still upset you. I told him to fix it."

Oh, my heart.

"I guess Ted wasn't supposed to come back to get his stuff until later," Brody says, changing gears, "but he showed up tonight while my mom was asleep. He saw my light on because I was playing my PlayStation and came in. He started calling me names and shit, and then he tried to kiss me. I pushed him away and tried to leave, but before I could, he punched me in my face. I hit him back, and he hit his head on the edge of my bed. When I left, he was knocked out cold."

"You did the right thing. What he did is wrong and illegal on so many levels."

He nods in understanding. "I just didn't know where to go. I don't want to hurt my mom and my dad… What if I am gay?" The nervous look on his face damn near breaks my heart.

"Has your dad ever indicated he would be upset if you were?" I don't want to tell him he wouldn't care if he's nervous because of something his dad has said in the past.

"No." He shakes his head to emphasize his answer. "But I mean, he's always been about women. He even owned strip clubs."

"So? You're right. Your dad isn't gay, but that doesn't mean he would care that you are."

"True. I guess I just choked."

We're silent for a few minutes before I say what I hope he will understand. "We have to tell your dad."

He nods. "Yeah, I know. But can you be there, please?"

"Didn't you hear what I said?" I quirk a brow. "*We* have to tell your dad. I'll be there for you every step of the way that you want me there."

After I throw on a pair of shoes and a sweater, we go upstairs to his dad's place. Since Brody has a key, we go right in, but Ben isn't there. I'm not sure where he is, so I pull my phone out and dial his number. He answers on the third ring.

"Sav." His voice fills my belly with butterflies. I've missed him so much. But right now, we need to focus on Brody and fixing this situation.

"Ben, I need you to come home."

The second he walks through the door, he can tell something is wrong, and before he freaks out, I stand and walk over to him. "Stay calm," I whisper when I hug him. He nods into my hair and hugs me back.

The three of us have a seat in the living room—Brody next to me and Ben across from us—and then Brody begins telling his dad the same story he told me. And even though I've already heard it, I'm almost positive my heart breaks all over again.

Twenty-Six

Benjamin

I'M GOING TO KILL HIM. FUCKING KILL HIM. AS SOON AS I'VE EXPLAINED TO

my son how much I love him and don't give a shit if he's gay or

bi or a goddamned unicorn, I'm going to kill that motherfucker.

"You're not going to kill him," Savannah says calmly, making

me frown. *Shit, did I say that out loud?* "I can see it all over your

face, but you're not going to kill him because if you do, you'll

end up in jail."

Not wanting to lie to her—because I am most definitely

going to kill him—I look at my son, so I can focus on the

important part here. "I don't care if you're gay. I don't care who you like, who you fuck… You're my kid, and I'm proud of you."

He sighs in relief. "I don't really know."

"And you're fifteen. You have plenty of time to figure it out. I know I haven't been around as much as I should've been, and that's all on me, but you need to know I don't care. If you decide you're straight and marry a woman, great, but if you decide you're gay and marry a guy, that's great too. Either way, I'll be at the wedding."

I stand and open my arms. When he walks over, I give him a hug as tight as humanly possible, needing him to know I mean every word I say. "I love you, Brody, no matter what."

"Love you too, Dad."

We separate, and I catch Savannah wiping tears from her eyes.

"What now?" Brody asks.

"Now, I go kill that fucker."

"No, Dad, please don't," he says. "Mom already broke up with him, and technically, he didn't do anything except call me names and try to kiss me. I don't want to turn this into a thing. Please."

Fuck. Unfortunately, he's right, and since there's no

proof of anything other than him punching Brody, there isn't anything we can do. Thankfully, he's here and safe, and nothing physically happened to him.

"All right, I'll respect your wishes on it, but we have to tell your mom, and if he's anywhere in the vicinity, I can't guarantee I won't lay his ass out."

We call his mom, waking her up, and she comes right over. As Brody tells her, she cries, blaming herself for not seeing what was happening right under her roof and for him feeling he couldn't come to her. Once he's done, I tell her she can crash in my guest room. I'll call a locksmith in the morning to have her locks changed and help her move his shit out of the house.

Savannah hugs Brody goodbye, telling him she loves him and is about to leave when I stop her. "We need to talk. Please."

"I know, but not tonight." She glances over at Brody and Paola. "Tonight, they need you."

"COFFEE AND LEMON POUND CAKE, YOUR FAVORITE." I HOLD UP THE CUP and bag, hoping it will be the key to Savannah letting me in.

After making sure Ted and all his shit was gone from Paola's house, I could tell Paola was completely distraught from everything and needed some time alone, so I spent the day with Brody, going to breakfast and then hanging out and playing video games, just focusing on him. When I offered to let him stay home from school, he told me he wanted to go, so I confirmed his weekly appointment with his therapist and assured him we'll get through all of this together. Ted might be gone, but there's no way Brody is past what happened that easily... But he'll get there, and I'll be there every step of the way.

Since he took off for an early football practice, I ran to the coffee shop and snagged Savannah's favorites in hope of catching her at home before she left. I should probably wait until after work to talk, but I can't go another minute without apologizing for the way I treated her.

Savannah eyes the goods, then sighs, snatching them from me and letting me in. "Only because I'm craving coffee and sweets."

She sits on the couch, still in her pajamas, and takes a sip. "Mmm... so good. I read if I'm pregnant, I can only drink like one cup a day. This is going to be a long nine months."

"If you're pregnant?"

"I haven't confirmed it yet."

"Why not?"

"Because I was mad you knew before me." She shrugs a single shoulder. "And... kind of scared that if I was, I'd be doing it on my own." She takes another sip of her coffee to keep herself busy, but I take it from her, wanting to see her face, needing her to look at me.

"You're not going through anything alone." I take her hand in mine. "I was shocked by what you told me, and I reacted wrong, but I love you, and that hasn't changed. And neither has me wanting to marry you and have a family with you."

"Did you find anything out about your dad?"

"No, not yet. But I know you wouldn't lie to me. I don't know why he was stealing from me, and I'm afraid to find out. He's gone, and even though our family went through a lot, we came out okay, and we were close. What if what I find out makes me see him in a different light?"

"True, but like you told Brody. You're family, and I don't believe he could've done anything to make you love him any less."

I want to believe she's right, but it's hard when you don't know what you're dealing with.

"Will you come with me?"

"Where?"

"To my dad's. His attorney needs to meet me there to handle his estate and assets. I've been putting it off. If I'm going to find any answers, it would be there."

"Of course," she says with a soft smile. "Why don't you see if he can meet us after work?"

"All right, but before we go to work, there's something we need to do."

Her brows dip in confusion.

"Sav, you've been wanting a baby for years. How is it not killing you not knowing if you're pregnant?" It's been in the back of my mind every other damn second since I put the pieces together.

"I told you why. Plus, I think I wanted you to be there. I really thought I was broken. It feels like it's almost too good to be true."

"Or..." I bring her hand up to my lips and kiss each of her

knuckles. "It was meant to be."

"IF YOU'RE NOT PREGNANT, IT'S NO BIG DEAL," I TELL HER AS I WATCH HER nervously pace the bathroom. It turns out Brianne had already bought tests, so finding out was as easy as her peeing on a stick. Once she did, she began pacing. Back and forth. Back and forth. And when I saw how nervous she was, it hit me. What if I'm wrong and she's not pregnant—and I just put it into her head that she is. She's going to be devastated, and it's all my fault.

Shit.

"Sav, did you hear me?"

"Oh my God!" She grabs the stick and waves it in the air. "I'm pregnant!" She thrusts the test toward me so I can see the word PREGNANT, then throws herself into my arms. "Thank you. Thank you. I can't believe it." She steps back, tears flying down her cheeks. "I've wanted this for so long, and now I have it, and it's all thanks to you."

Jesus, this woman. She's actually thanking me for mistakenly knocking her up when I should be the one thanking her.

"Sav, you've got it all wrong," I tell her, palming her face and wiping away the liquid from her cheek with my thumb. "When I met you, I was broken and hanging on by a thread..." I finger her necklace—the one with the love knot. "I was going through life, but not actually living. Until I met you. It's me who should be thanking you."

"No." She shakes her head and kisses me softly on the lips. "It's like you said when you gave me the love knot. We were both broken, hanging on by a thread. But together, those strings formed a strong knot that will withstand the test of time."

She presses her lips to mine again, this time deepening the kiss, and I thank whoever was responsible for that annoying fucking treadmill. Had it not driven me nuts, I might never have given this Southern-accented, coffee-loving, weird T-shirt-wearing woman, who holds my heart in the palm of her hand, a second glance.

Epilogue

Savannah

THREE MONTHS LATER

"THAT'S THE HEAD…AND THE HANDS…THOSE ARE THE FEET…AND OH! IT seems your baby is not at all shy. Those little legs are spread wide." The doctor laughs, glancing at Ben and me. "Are we finding out the sex?"

"No," I say, giving her the answer Ben and I agreed on. Life only has so many surprises, so we decided to wait until our little alien is born to find out—yep, you read that right, our baby's nickname is Alien. Brody took one look at the ultrasound pics, having never seen any before, and said it looked like I was carrying an alien. Of course Ben thought it was hilarious, so, for the past three months, we've called our precious little miracle an alien.

The doctor goes about taking measurements, explaining the baby's right on schedule growth-wise, then we listen to the heartbeat.

Ben squeezes my hand, knowing I get choked up every time I hear it. He surprised me with an at-home doppler so I could listen to it any time I wanted. The fear of this being my only pregnancy, since it was so hard to conceive the first time, has me enjoying every step of this pregnancy—from weekly baby bump pics to journaling how I feel, I'm not leaving anything out.

"Everything looks good. Here are some pictures." She hands us a strip of black and white images. "And you can view the video on the portal. You can check out and schedule your next appointment for four weeks from today."

"Thank you."

After I get dressed and check out, we head out. I scheduled the appointment late in the afternoon so we could take the rest of the day off.

When Ben tells his driver a different address, I look at him confused. "We're not going home?"

"We are." That's all he says before he pulls his phone out and goes about checking his emails. I'm a little annoyed that he's being so short with me, but I chalk it up to him being busy, so I use the time to track my progress this week and then look up some more baby names. We can't seem to agree on a single one, so I like to make lists and send them to Ben. He then goes through them, commenting on each one and why that name isn't good. Some of his answers are actually kind of funny—like Luke for a boy reminds him of *Star Wars*, and apparently, he's traumatized from when he read *Charlotte's Web* as a kid and the poor spider died, so Charlotte was also nixed.

Twenty minutes later, we're out of the city and going down a less congested area. The longer we drive, the bigger the houses get and the farther apart they sit.

"Hey, Ben. Did you plan to stop somewhere?"

He glances up quickly and looks around. "Yep."

I wait for him to elaborate, but he gives me nothing. "Care to share where?"

"Nope." He goes back to looking at his phone, and I snatch

it from him.

"Hey, where are we going?"

He chuckles at my annoyance. "Patience. You'll see." He leans over and kisses my cheek, and I sag against him.

A few minutes later, the driver stops in front of a gorgeous two-story colonial-style home with cute country-style shutters, a large wraparound porch, a decent-sized front yard with actual green grass, and a white picket fence.

When I see a for sale sign in the front, my heart pounds in my chest. "Ben..."

He smiles and opens the door, edging out and then taking my hand to help me.

"I believe I promised you a white picket fence," he says, walking us up the U-shaped drive.

His words, confirming what I was thinking and hoping when I saw the sign, cause me to choke up with raw emotion. I'm engaged to a man I love, and we'll soon officially be a family. My hand that's not entwined with his goes to my belly—we're adding to our family. And he's gotten me my white picket fence.

Ben grabs the lockbox, types in a code, then pulls the key out, unlocking the door. We step inside, and it's completely empty, like the most beautiful blank canvas. I can instantly imagine Brody and Ben laughing with each other in the living room while they play video games, family meals at the dining room table. I glance to the left and see the massive kitchen, and thoughts of making homemade pizza with Brody—and one day our little alien—come to mind.

We walk through the house and out the back door. There's more grass—the perfect size backyard to hold a swing set and maybe even a pool—with more white fence.

We go back in, and he walks me through more of the downstairs—including the spacious master bedroom and en suite bathroom. There are five bedrooms, three bathrooms, and a large library upstairs that can double as an office.

"Brody and I came to see it the other day, when you were working late, to make sure it looked the same in person as the virtual tour," Ben says, standing in the middle of the library. "It's actually not too far from his school and only a thirty-minute drive into work. I was thinking we could make this an office, and once the baby comes, we could work from home a few days a week. I haven't put an offer on it yet because I wanted you to see it first. See if you can picture yourself living and raising a family here. So, what do you say, Sav, want to fill this home with me?"

I attempt to tell him yes, but my emotions get the best of me, and I choke out a sob, tears blurring my vision. "Yes," I finally get out. "I most definitely would love to fill this home with you."

Benjamin

SEVEN YEARS LATER

"YOU DID IT!" I WRAP MY ARMS AROUND BRODY AND PAT HIS BACK. "I'M SO damn proud of you." Today is his college graduation. He earned a business degree while spending the past four years working for me and learning the business. When he told me he wanted to follow in my footsteps, I wanted to make sure my footsteps were worthy. So over the past several years, I've worked—with the help of my wife—to make Fields Enterprises a place where people want to work and are comfortable coming to me.

When I finally met with my dad's attorney, I learned he was in debt—bad. He had depleted all of his assets, his cars were being repossessed, and his house was under foreclosure. He was always the type of man to handle shit himself, never wanting to talk. He did it with my mom when she was sick, refusing to get her help, and then again with us when he was going through whatever he was going through.

Not wanting it to continue with me, I've made it a point to make sure my door is always open, and my family and employees know they can come to me at any time.

"You know what this means, right?" Brody deadpans. "I'm one step closer to becoming the next CEO of Fields Enterprises."

I glance at my very pregnant wife as she beams with pride at Brody while holding our six-year-old son's hand—we named him Olivier, after my dad—and I chuckle. "Yeah, that's exactly what it means."

With Savannah expecting again—something we weren't sure would ever happen again since we decided not to go to a fertility clinic but instead let nature take its course, or not—I'm ready to settle down and work fewer hours. I have baseball games to coach, and with our little girl on the way—it's not confirmed, but I think she is—I imagine we'll have our hands full with her.

"I'm so proud of you," Savannah says, giving Brody a hug.

"Thanks." He roughs up Olivier's hair. "One day, you'll be walking across that stage."

Olivier dodges Brody and laughs. "I don't wanna go away. I wanna stay home with Mommy."

"Let's see if you say that in a few years," Brody tells him.

Brody didn't go away to school, but he did move out, wanting to live in the city, which to Olivier is like living on another planet.

After Paola gives Brody a hug, telling him congratulations, we head out to meet everyone for dinner to celebrate.

We arrive at the restaurant and are brought back to the private dining room where our friends and family are waiting for us since the university only allowed four tickets per graduate.

Everyone stands, congratulating Brody on a job well done while the kids run around, catching up with each other.

Savannah comes over and wraps her arms around me from the side, her head dropping against my chest. "I love that sound," she says, tightening her arms.

"What sound?" I glance down at her. "All I hear is a bunch

of people talking and kids screaming and laughing."

"Exactly. It's the sound of love...of happiness...of family." She tips her face up and presses her lips to mine. "It's a sound I'll never tire of hearing."

About the Author

Reading is like breathing in, writing is like breathing out. – Pam Allyn

Nikki Ash resides in South Florida where she is an English teacher by day and a writer by night. When she's not writing, you can find her with a book in her hand. From the Boxcar Children, to Wuthering Heights, to the latest single parent romance, she has lived and breathed every type of book. While reading and writing are her passions, her two children are her entire world. You can probably find them at a Disney park before you would find them at home on the weekends!